"You dis...

She swallowed, preparing to defend herself. Then she remembered that Jake was not her father. He did not live to find fault.

"Yes," she agreed.

"Thank God."

"What did you say?"

He laughed. "I said, thank God. If you hadn't, I'd be dead right now and you shortly after."

She'd done the right thing. For once in her life, she'd acted and she'd done the right thing.

"I should have had you cover my back, especially after seeing you shoot. But I just thought about keeping you clear of any trouble. Of course, that's crazy. If trouble finds me, it sure as hell will find you." He patted her on the shoulder. "From now on, we stay together."

Emma nodded, not trusting her voice. He did not know, couldn't know how important this was.

He stared at her, still grinning, then said, "Damn, Emma, that was some fine shooting!"

* * *

Turner's Woman
Harlequin Historical #746—March 2005

Praise for
Jenna Kernan's debut

Winter Woman
"*Winter Woman* presents a fascinating portrait
of the early days of the West and the extraordinary men
and women who traveled and settled the area....
Kernan has a knack for writing a solid western
with likable characters."
—*Romantic Times*

**DON'T MISS THESE OTHER
TITLES AVAILABLE NOW:**

#743 THE BACHELOR
Kate Bridges

#744 FALCON'S HONOR
Denise Lynn

#745 THE UNRULY CHAPERON
Elizabeth Rolls

Turner's Woman

Jenna Kernan

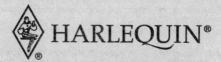

HARLEQUIN®

TORONTO • NEW YORK • LONDON
AMSTERDAM • PARIS • SYDNEY • HAMBURG
STOCKHOLM • ATHENS • TOKYO • MILAN • MADRID
PRAGUE • WARSAW • BUDAPEST • AUCKLAND

ISBN 0-373-29346-1

TURNER'S WOMAN

www.eHarlequin.com

Printed in U.S.A.

Available from Harlequin Historicals and
JENNA KERNAN

Winter Woman #671
Turner's Woman #746

Please address questions and book requests to:
Harlequin Reader Service
U.S.: 3010 Walden Ave., P.O. Box 1325, Buffalo, NY 14269
Canadian: P.O. Box 609, Fort Erie, Ont. L2A 5X3

For my husband, Jim,
for his steadfast confidence and love.

Chapter One

Rocky Mountains, 1830

The odor of coffee and chewing tobacco reached Jake Turner seconds before the jangle of metal bits in the mouths of nervous horses. He estimated there to be no more than ten greenhorns, but that made no sense. The big trading outfits never traveled with less than twenty men and he knew these riders were new-comers from the clatter of shod hooves on rock. Men who survived their first winter in these mountains knew that the ring of metal on stone was sure to draw unwanted attention, not to mention that a shoed horse left tracks impossible to miss.

Sliding off his horse, he crept forward, rifle in hand. The clearing came into view. Before him sat eight mounted men surrounded and outnumbered by a war party of twenty Mountain Crow warriors. The Indians waved their bows as their triumphant cries pierced the air. Jake's gaze swept the group and halted suddenly. He blinked, doubting his eyes.

At the back of the pack sat a woman. The outline of shapely thighs hugging her mount was clear through the pale blue skirt. He hadn't noticed her straight off, as she was dressed in a dark blue cavalry uniform and an army-issue broad felt hat. A thick honey-colored braid swept to her narrow waist. He couldn't see her face, but from the back she looked just right.

She distracted him so thoroughly that by the time he glanced at the traders it was too late. The lead man chose death over capture and reached for his rifle. It never cleared leather. The volley of arrows zipped toward the rider and a knife sank to the hilt in his chest. He slumped forward and hit the ground with a thud. The blood flowing from his mouth marked him as dead.

The man behind him got his pistol drawn.

A single gunshot split the air.

The others drew and some fired. The woman seemed to be the only one who wished to live. She lay flat on her mount as arrows streaked over her back. Jake watched the men topple like dominoes, feathered shafts sticking from their woolen jackets.

The woman screamed and fell from her horse.

Jake resisted the urge to interfere. In a moment the exchange ended. One warrior writhed in the dust, clutching his belly and twisting in agony. Beside him the traders sprawled, frozen in the unnatural postures of violent death. Jake focused on the wounded Crow and winced, knowing the suffering the man would endure before he died of his wound.

As expected, the warriors did not kill the woman right off. She was dressed as a soldier and that might complicate matters. Where had she gotten that coat?

One of the warriors shouted as he lifted a medicine shield from a trader's horse. Jake's gaze fixed in horror. He knew the pattern, had seen it many times when a guest of the horse band. It belonged to their chief Swooping Hawk—or it had belonged to him. The man had died last March. A nasty suspicion rose. Maybe these men had deserved to die, for he could think of only one way to obtain the shield of a dead chief.

Jake dragged his gaze from the massacre. Foolish men did not live long here. Before he could turn away, his attention fell again on the woman.

He could see her face now, pale and bloodless. Her gaze darted from her downed escorts to the approaching warrior.

"Damn and damn again," he muttered, then stood and called to the group, using the language now as familiar as his own.

"Hello, brothers."

Bows lifted and arrows now pointed in his direction. He slipped from cover, guiding his mounts forward. The lead warrior lifted his hand staying his men and Jake swallowed his relief. He knew this man. The arrow points dropped toward the ground.

"Do not interfere here," said White Cloud.

"Did you hunt these men?"

White Cloud nodded. "They crossed our burial ground. This man stole a medicine shield." He pointed at the dead trader at his feet, who seemed more porcupine than man, because of the glut of arrows in his chest. Of course, the warriors would want to avenge this insult to their dead chief's spirit.

Already the Indians took scalps from the corpses, the skin making a sucking sound as it clung to the skull. Jake stared at the dead men at his feet, focusing on a boy too young to shave, and could not stifle a sigh at the waste. He saw the woman sidling toward her mount, one hand on the reins. As if escape were possible.

"I think they have killed Running Fox," said White Cloud.

Jake considered the younger members of the group who had not loosened their grip on their weapons. The blood lust still flowed strong in them and Jake looked far too much like a trader. He silently cursed the woman for forcing him from cover.

She placed a foot in her stirrup and one of the warriors shouted at her. She froze.

"Best step down, miss," he said in English.

She did, releasing the saddle horn and running the few steps that separated them, then clung to his buckskin shirt. He stared down into her desperate blue eyes. His gut tightened as if she'd kicked him. He wanted to push her away and at the same time he wanted to pull her close.

"Don't let them take me," she cried.

"I'm working on it."

She didn't seem to hear him, because she repeated herself. "You have to help me."

Actually, he didn't. His world would be simpler and safer if he just rode on, leaving these fools to the fate they created. Instead, he pushed her behind him, but she refused to release her grip on his shirt, holding on as if it were her last true friend. He turned his attention to the warriors who did not look anxious to relinquish their prize.

White Cloud nodded toward her. "You know her?"

Jake shook his head.

"She dresses like a blue pony boy, but hides like a woman. I don't know if I should give her a warrior's death or make her a slave." White Cloud nudged his horse forward to consider her. "She crossed sacred ground with the others."

Jake felt the scales tip against her. "She may dress like a man but she is not. Do your women lead your warriors?"

White Cloud scowled. "Men lead, women follow."

"Then she did what was right. She followed these stupid men."

White Cloud sighed. "I have no stomach to kill this woman. Do you want her?"

In a biblical sense—yes. In the day-to-day practice of keeping a woman, he certainly did not. Better to just shoot himself in the foot and limp off. Certainly a bullet wound would be less troublesome than a woman on the trail.

He thumbed over his shoulder at his horse. "I already got one female and she's aggravation enough, but I will take her to her people."

White Cloud dismounted and stepped toward the woman. The look in the man's eyes told him that he still wanted his captive.

She crouched behind Jake, trembling.

"Hold still," he whispered.

The warrior grasped her chin and stared at the woman's

face. He released her as if scorched and stepped away. "She has ghost eyes."

Jake played on this. "Certainly she was unlucky for these men."

White Cloud nodded, his face solemn. "Perhaps I will kill her now."

As if sensing her peril, the woman's arms tightened around his waist, sending the soft mounds of her breasts against his back. He gritted his teeth as the sweet smell of her surrounded him.

"She never fired on you," Jake pointed out.

White Cloud nodded at this.

Jake made his suggestion sound like pure comment. "I don't think it is her day to die."

"Then you take her," White Cloud suggested.

"What about her horse?"

"I keep the horse."

Jake pressed his lips together, preparing to bluff and realizing as he spoke that his words were true. "I can't take her without a horse."

White Cloud pointed. "You have two horses. She can ride one."

"You're asking me to choose a woman over my supplies. No, my friend."

White Cloud looked doubtful. He glanced at the horse and then the woman.

"We'll keep everything else," he said at last.

"Of course."

"That woman clings to you like a second skin."

The words of the Crow rolled off his tongue. Jake's gift for languages served him well once again. "I already have a coat. I think I better pull her off."

"Every man should have a coat like that, especially in winter," said White Cloud. His dry humor made the corner of Jake's mouth quirk.

White Cloud glanced at the warriors who stood menacing, then to Jake. "You go now."

Jake nodded.

"Do you go to the new fort?"

"No, west. Over the mountains."

White Cloud's expression darkened. "There is nothing there but deserts and poor hunting. Better stay here."

"I'll think on it."

"Already it is snowing on the peaks," said White Cloud.

"Then, I will hurry."

"Travel well."

"And you."

He pushed the woman toward her horse and helped her mount, catching a glimpse of her shapely calf as she slipped her foot into her stirrup. Suddenly, he wanted to run up the ridge and leave her here. This woman disturbed him in a way that made her dangerous. He gritted his teeth. He had no time to turn back and take her to safety.

Fate had dropped her on his doorstep.

He grasped the horses' reins and walked with forced slowness from the clearing, then mounted up.

"Damnation," he muttered as he led them up the ridge.

They rode less than a mile when the woman recovered her nerve along with her tongue.

"Where are you taking me?"

"Hush," he said.

She looked about, lowering her head like a turtle retreating into its shell.

"Are there more Indians about?" she whispered.

He pulled up and waited as her horse stepped beside his. Their legs brushed and another wave of awareness rippled through him. She eyed him with worry. Her pink lips drew up into a bow and a flush blanketed the smooth skin of her cheeks. How many years since he'd seen a white woman?

An image of Helen flashed in his mind and his innards froze. Women were traps and if a man wanted his freedom he'd do best to avoid them. But damn, this one was well formed.

"No more talk now." He had some questions, as well, but

first he planned to get as far from White Cloud as possible. They rode through the heat of the afternoon and into the cool breeze that ushered in the evening. He picked a clearing against a series of three large boulders to rest. A dry camp, but he carried enough water for cooking.

She groaned as she slid from her horse, but said nothing as she removed the saddle and blanket, then rubbed down her chestnut gelding with a hank of dried grass. She slipped off the bridle, replacing it with a halter. Finally, she tied him to the trunk of a lodgepole pine. The woman obviously knew horses and that surprised him.

By the time she finished, he had his horse and mule hobbled and the fire struck. She folded like a rag doll before the growing flames. He glanced up and saw that dirt and tear tracks streaked her face. His heart squeezed, but he shook it off and his scowl deepened as he considered the problems her arrival signaled.

"Why are you out here?" he asked.

She startled, as if she'd forgotten his presence.

"We, I mean, I am on my way to the Rendezvous to meet my father, Henry Lancing."

Jake knew him. The man had brought sixty-odd men out here and built a fort he'd named after himself. If rumors were true, he had married a rich woman to finance his trading post. His greed surpassed his ambition and his high prices drove most trappers away. Taking his goods to the Rendezvous wouldn't change that. But Lancing was smart, placing his post at the foot of South Pass, one of two routes through the Rockies.

Jake hadn't heard anything about a daughter.

"Why weren't you following the Bighorn? The fort is on her shores."

"With the Indians pursuing, we dared not ford the river."

The Rendezvous and her father's fort lay far to the south. A detour of over a hundred miles could cost him any chance of crossing the divide this season and the mission would be halted until late spring. No delays. Proceed at all costs—that was President Jackson's directive.

"Why were you traveling with only eight men?" He crouched beside her, giving himself the option of a speedy retreat if she got hysterical.

"They killed the rest six days ago."

"Know why?"

Her gaze dropped to the fire. She did.

"Damn stupid thing that," he said.

"I told them not to cross. Then Wilcox climbed that platform. He took a drum."

Jake puzzled a moment wondering what she was talking about. Then he understood. "That wasn't a drum. That was a sacred medicine shield of their dead chief. The platform was his grave."

Her eyes widened. "There were bodies in those skins?"

"Left to return to the sky."

"Someone saw us. We couldn't outrun them."

"Shouldn't think so. Brought down the whole tribe on you."

"How did you stop them?"

"We're acquainted."

She stared at him blankly. "If you knew what would happen, why didn't you save the others?"

He scowled, not wanting to tell her that nothing in the world could have stopped that massacre. The cards were dealt the minute that man stole from their ancestors. What did she think he might have done? He scowled. "Why didn't you?"

That gave her pause. Her pretty mouth gaped a moment. "I couldn't."

He nodded. "Same reason."

"I didn't mean to sound ungrateful. You rescued me. I have the utmost respect for you."

"That might change."

"Oh no, it won't. My name is Emma Lancing."

She extended her hand. He knew better than to touch her.

Just brushing her leg made his stomach jump like a bucket full of crickets. Eventually she gave up and dropped her hand back to her knee.

She waited a moment as if she expected something. Finally she said, "And you are?"

He knew he should doff his hat, but her intrusion made him as ornery as a treed bobcat. Instead he touched the brim. "Jake Turner."

"Where are we headed, Mr. Turner—Popo Agie?"

"Just been." That much was true.

Her surprise hung between them a moment. "You aren't headed to the Rendezvous?"

Every trapper, Indian and trader in the West was headed to the Rendezvous. He might be the only man in a hundred miles heading on the opposite track.

"Come and gone."

She considered his gear. "You don't have any traps."

The woman had a head on her shoulders. A trapper would have traded his furs and restocked his stores to begin a new season of hunting. Instead of traps, his packhorses and mule were stuffed with sixty pounds of dried meat, his instruments, trade goods and ammunition.

He stared her down, refusing to respond to her inquiry.

Her eyes regarded him with caution and she held herself stiffly. "Trader?"

"That's none of your affair."

She lowered her gaze and sat in silence a moment. "Might I ask where you are headed?"

"West."

Her mouth shaped a little O and a tiny line formed between her dark eyebrows. Funny to have hair so pale and yet lashes and eyebrows the same rich color as ground coffee.

"But I have to go to Fort Lancing on the Bighorn, by South Pass. My father—well, he'll be worried."

He nodded. "I understand."

Her shoulders slumped with relief. "I'm so glad. I do apologize for inconveniencing you."

"You haven't."

She smiled and his heart squeezed, gathered in a noose. "You are a gentleman."

"I'm not that, either."

"But you are. Backtracking to deliver me to my father is very commendable."

"Woman, I'm not backtracking for you or any other. I don't believe you'll make it, but if you're fixing to try, I won't stop you. I also won't accompany you."

That comment stunned her speechless. She blinked and tears rose in her eyes. He didn't know if it was a trick or not, but he'd seen Helen do it this way. His lip compressed and he lowered his chin, preparing for the inevitable wail to follow. It never came. She only swiped at her eyes and stared.

Impaled upon her gaze, he agreed with White Cloud. Her eyes were the strangest pale blue-gray he'd ever seen. Like fog or smoke. That was it, the steel-gray smoke from the barrel of a rifle. He had been on the receiving end of an aimed rifle. Somehow he thought Emma's eyes posed the greater threat.

Chapter Two

Behind Emma Lancing lay twenty dead traders. The weight of her sorrow pressed her to the earth. Her heart hurt when she thought of those men—so young. She blinked trying to erase the images of her escorts falling—dying all about her.

She had never felt more heartsick in her twenty-three years of life. Grit blanketed her skin. Her dirty clothes clung limp and damp from perspiration and she hadn't eaten since yesterday morning. That seemed an entire lifetime ago.

Tears stung her cheeks as she stared at the coffeepot now emitting a wisp of steam. A broad callused hand reached for the handle, a scrap of buckskin shielded his palm. Her attention lifted to Jake Turner. His dress resembled that of many men she'd met who made their living in these mountains. The fringed leather shirt protecting his broad back from the elements was supple enough to reveal the powerful muscles sheathed beneath. His shoulder bag and powder horn crisscrossed his chest, falling beside his belt, which held his hunting knife and pistol, as well as several smaller dangling pouches. Leather leggings and calf-high moccasins completed his attire. Her father said trappers wore the wide-brim hat, not only to protect them from the elements, but also to distinguish themselves as white men so as not to be confused as an enemy by the Indians. This worked well with all but the Blackfoot, who hated whites and killed on sight.

Jake Turner poured the steaming liquid into a horn cup. She did not smell coffee. As he extended the beverage, she accepted it, noting bits of dried leaves and twigs floating on the surface. She thanked him, not recognizing the contents. For an instant his gaze held hers and she felt the same breathless sensation she'd experienced earlier beneath his consideration.

He'd refused to take her back. What would her father say when he discovered his new men dead and her missing? The thought made her palms damp. His rages had terrified her mother into nervous fits, sending her east thirteen years ago and leaving Emma the lone target of his domination.

She glanced about at the dark shadows as the firelight flickered over unfamiliar branches and rocks. When she left Fort Leavenworth she prayed not to have to go to her father's trading post. God played a trick, for now he granted her plea in the most terrible of ways.

"You going to drink it?" asked the man.

"Is this coffee?" she asked, praying it was not.

"Tea. Make it myself."

His deep voice caused something inside her to tremble. This man had rescued her, but refused to take her to her father. He looked very strong and could overpower her with little difficulty. What were his intentions? She wondered if he was capable of rape. Perhaps she should flee. Her gaze shifted to the darkness all around her. Rustling sounds came from the undergrowth beyond her vision.

"What was that?" she asked.

"Skunk, maybe."

That didn't sound so terrible.

"Or a wildcat."

Her breath caught. "There are wildcats about?"

"Yup. And wolves and grizzly."

She sank down to make herself less noticeable to predators. Fleeing no longer seemed prudent. She trembled. Nothing could be worse than wandering about until a mountain lion or band of savages killed her. Then she realized that was not true. There were worse possibilities—living with her father again for instance.

Think of something else. She watched the man drain his cup and pour another from the pot. How odd. Most trappers of her acquaintance lived roughly, but they all enjoyed coffee when they could get it. If he had just left the Rendezvous, he should be well supplied. Her father guzzled coffee, drinking cup after cup. She pushed the image aside and focused on the man before her as he sipped the hot tea.

"Don't you like coffee?" she asked.

"You can smell coffee brewing from half a mile. Makes it easy to find a camp. Besides, it makes me twitch."

She'd seen his steely composure while speaking to those Indians and found it difficult to imagine that anything made him twitch. He looked as solid and invulnerable as the cliffs behind him.

"Have you met my father?"

"I have. Seemed like a sensible sort, not the kind to send his daughter out with only eight men."

Emma lowered her gaze.

"We had twenty. I waited at Fort Leavenworth until he finished the outer wall. I didn't want to come." She glanced up to see his reaction to her admission and discovered not the least flicker of surprise.

"Understandable. This is no place for a white woman."

Turner's unchanged expression irked her. She straightened her shoulders preparing to face him. This man was not her father. She could stand up to him. If she didn't get to the fort soon…her stomach clenched at the possibilities.

"He'll send a search party after me."

"No doubt."

Did he plan to abduct her? That possibility turned her blood to ice.

"He'll find me." Her words made her shake with fear, knowing he would and then she would suffer. At least with her father she knew what to expect. This man was unknown to her.

He laughed.

She realized then he had no fear of her father and why should he? This man did not fall under his dominion. But she did. She must make Turner understand. "If you don't take me back, you'll answer to my father." Her threat gained no reaction other than a confident stare. Oh, how she envied him. She shook just thinking of seeing her sire again.

He smiled. "I've been considering that. Chances are about fifty-fifty I'll never live to see him."

"You're no better than the Indians, holding me captive."

"I am better. If they had you, you'd wish you were dead about now."

She swallowed hard as images of bonfires and howling natives filled her mind. With effort, she straightened. "We best head to Fort Lancing before you get into real trouble." She thought her words sounded very sensible, not revealing the earthquake of uncertainty rumbling within her.

His green eyes narrowed and he took a step in her direction. "That's twice you threatened me."

Her throat closed and she couldn't speak. A wave of panic broke. This man was a stranger, but he looked fierce. She backed down immediately.

"Won't you please take me back?"

He gave her a long sad look and shook his head. "Can't."

She judged the compassion in his eyes as a sign of weakness. Despite her resolve not to challenge him, she could not stifle her tongue.

"Won't, you mean. I demand to be taken to the fort."

He faced her, his eyes glittering dangerously. She placed her palms beside her on the earth, preparing to spring away if he set upon her.

"Listen here, you little blue coat. I saved your scalp back there. Woman or no, you're dressed like a soldier."

"But I'm not a soldier. Colonel Leavenworth gave me this coat."

"That makes little difference to the Crow. They called you Blue Pony Woman, because of those ridiculous trappings, and considered you a warrior. That entitles you to a warrior's death."

Her throat went dry and she found herself barely able to breathe the question. "A warrior's death?"

He stared her dead in the eye and answered without so much as a blink.

"Torture."

Emma knew the stories of Indian torture. They made her stomach roll. She pressed her lips tight to keep from embarrassing herself as she drew long breaths of air.

He snorted in disgust. "I saved your hide. Don't make me sorry I did."

She recognized his angry tone and could not keep the torrent of tears from her burning eyes. He stood with both hands on his hips, towering over her as she lay in the dust at his feet. She recognized the posture from her father's tirades. He always began like this. She recalled the day he discovered the gold necklace given to her by her mother before she left and shuddered. Why did he hate her so?

"Damnation, I do not need a weeping, cringing woman in my camp. I will not be turned with tears. Leaving Leavenworth was your doing, not mine. It isn't up to me to make it right."

That was true. This wasn't his fault. She huddled before him willing the tears to cease as her breathing came in ragged gasps. She was trapped in the wilderness with only this hostile stranger to protect her.

"I'm cutting for sign. Stay put." Jake swung into his saddle.

She rose to her feet to watch him go, and then sank to her knees, too heartsick to stand. What should she do?

Jake backtracked far enough to be sure they weren't followed and then a while farther. On the return trip resentment still ate at him. Spoiled brat, he knew the type, had seen enough of the officers' daughters at West Point. She'd been coddled her whole life and made to think the sun rose and set on her. Well, it most certainly did not.

Bringing her along would be the same as dragging a dead mule over the mountains. But she was a white woman. So he'd try and keep the little weeping princess alive, God help him. Likely she'd get him killed in the process. The woman jeopardized his mission.

He tugged his hat from his head and slapped it against his thigh. Duchess, his horse, took that as a direct order and broke into a trot, bringing him back to Miss Emma Lancing, before his temper adequately cooled.

He dismounted just short of camp and led Duchess along. The bay mare walked silently behind him as he approached downwind. His camp was well placed, the flame from the fire not visible from even this short distance. As he drew closer, he realized why and frowned.

Couldn't the little brat even keep a fire going? Of course not. She never had to lift a finger her entire life. There were grunts to do that work. He pictured Helen ordering her father's cadets about at West Point. Sickening.

He glanced around the clearing flecked by filtered moonlight. His eyes, accustomed to the dark, found her easily enough lying beside the glowing embers of the dying fire. He tossed several thick branches on the coals, but she did not stir.

Best get things settled right off.

He grabbed her shoulder and gave a shake.

She startled, her arm raised to protect herself from attack. Upon recognizing him she sagged and her hand fell to her side.

"You're back," she whispered.

She sounded surprised. The forlorn quality of her voice cut into his heart like an arrow point. He pressed his lips together and hardened himself against her.

"We need to parley," he said.

She struggled to a sitting position. The firelight turned her hair to copper as it danced in ringlets about her worried face. Oh, she was beautiful and she knew it. She wielded those misty eyes like daggers, cutting straight into an unsuspecting man's heart. Well, not this time. He tugged at the hem of her jacket.

"Why do you wear that?" he asked.

"I have no other."

"Why not just pin a target on your shirt?"

She blinked at him and he growled.

"I've got business. It takes me west. Crossing the Rockies before the snows will be the easy part. Beyond that there's a desert, then more mountains. I'm aiming for the Pacific. I don't know the tribes there or if they're hostile. If I make it, I'll be crossing back sometime in the spring. I don't want you along. You'll slow me down and put me at risk." Her eyes rounded at this. Long dark lashes curled like feathers. "But I won't run you off, either, because I know your papa. I have no time to tarry or take you back. You understand?"

She nodded.

"So I'm leaving it up to you. I'm heading out in the morning. If you ride along, you'll agree to follow my orders exactly, not bother me with your female curiosity and know that I'll not be delayed. If you fall behind, I will leave you behind. If you decide to turn back, you best go in the morning. Perhaps going alone is less risky than coming with me. I'll give you the horse you're riding, two days supplies and I'll draw you a map. You decide."

She tried to speak, but no words emerged.

He squinted at her. "You hear me, woman?"

Emma Lancing rose to her feet. She took a deep breath; her face seemed to mirror stunned incomprehension.

"You are letting *me* decide?"

He nodded and her mouth gaped in shock.

She shook her head in disbelief and asked again. "You want me to choose—whatever I want?"

"I just said so." Was she addled?

For a moment he almost thought he saw the shadow of a smile as she considered. Her expression sparkled with life, sending his heart thudding in his chest. Something inside him went soft and he gritted his teeth against it. The woman was a sight, prettier than new snow on a pine bough. He was just starting to realize a different kind of danger coupled with bringing her along when she spoke.

"You offer me a devil's choice—a choice between two equally bad options. I might die trying to find my father's fort or on the trail with you."

"That's about it."

"May I ask why you are heading into territory held by Mexico?"

"No."

"To my knowledge no one but Lewis and Clark has ever been overland to the Pacific and they were far to the north."

"Shows what you know. Jed Smith did it in twenty-six, but considerable south of where I'll be passing." He'd spoken at length with the man at the Rendezvous, nearly convinced him to come along, but he said the Californians would skin him for sure if he ever came back.

"If I go with you, *I* have some conditions."

He lifted his eyebrows and waited. The woman had gumption to dictate to him, when she lived or died at his mercy. Of course, manipulating men came as natural to a woman as swimming came to a beaver.

"I expect you to behave as a gentleman."

He laughed. "I surely will not."

She frowned and he thought that made her look even prettier than before. His scowl deepened.

"What I mean to say is that you will not touch me, Mr. Turner."

Understanding dawned. He scratched his chin as he considered her. She was a fine-looking woman, but the last time he tangled with one this pretty she'd nearly hamstrung him. This deal was best for them both. He doffed his hat and gave a mocking bow. "I agree not to molest your person. Anything else?"

"If I do not survive the journey, you will send word to my father of my fate."

"If I live to do so, agreed."

She stared through the darkness toward the west as if seeing something invisible to him. If he didn't know better, he'd say her expression seemed wistful. At last, she turned to him.

"You really would prefer me to head south tomorrow."

He didn't deny it.

"But I shall be riding with you, Mr. Turner, into the unknown."

Chapter Three

The next day Emma woke, rolled up her blanket and saddled her horse without a word of complaint, surprising Jake considerably. She had spent the night across the campfire wrapped in a gray wool blanket too thin for the mountains, but he'd deal with that when he got a chance. He had slept under a robe made of wolf skins, finding them warmer and lighter than buffalo.

In the gray predawn they followed the Wind River beneath the Tetons. He never got tired of staring at the sawtooth appearance of these mountains, rising from the grassland with nearly no foothills at all. They were hellish to cross, but the most beautiful mountains on God's earth.

As morning wore on, he grew accustomed to the steady clomp of her horse's shod hooves. The iron saved the animal's feet but made a terrible clatter on rock. At midday he handed her moose jerky and nothing else, as she carried her own water.

She accepted it without comment and her fingers brushed his. He felt the contact like a firebrand and yanked back his arm. Emma's eyes went wide as she clutched the jerky. He couldn't stare into those smoky depths, so he focused on the trail ahead. The woman stirred him up worse than a nest full of rattlers and she was considerably more dangerous.

He had hoped to come across a straggler, late for the Rendezvous and foist Emma on him. But his luck held and he saw no one who could relieve him of his baggage.

As the trail sloped upward through a grassy patch their horses startled several partridges from cover. He lifted his shotgun and took aim. The blast brought down one bird. The second shot, which came from behind him, brought down two.

He spun around in his saddle to stare at her. She held her shotgun with the loose confidence born of experience. He had underestimated her, assuming the weaponry she carried was more decorative than functional.

"You don't fire out here unless I say so," he admonished.

She smiled. "You fired first."

That he did.

"Where'd you learn to shoot?"

"Colonel Leavenworth. At first he thought my attempts to learn amusing, until I could outperform his men. Then he forbade me from practicing. Said it demoralized his troops."

"Damn sure demoralized me."

He slid from his mount, collected the birds from the tall yellow grass and hung them on the back of his saddle. Again he considered his decision to tie the packhorses to Emma's mount. That could be a mistake, if her horse shied. But he didn't think the girl should eat dust behind two horses and a mule all day.

He checked his animals and paused, glancing at her other firearms. She carried a standard issue Hall breech-loading rifle from Harper's Ferry. A holstered pistol hung at her waist. "You as good a shot with those?"

"Better with the rifle."

"What's your pa say about it?"

"He's never seen me shoot. I learned after he departed, but I'm certain he'd consider it unladylike."

"So is dressing like a soldier."

Her smile made his insides tighten and a shot of anticipation hit his groin. His forehead furrowed at his lack of control. Already the chit had him undressing her. Damn her for tagging along.

"As my father did not provide me with a coat, I was grateful to accept this as a parting gift from Colonel Leavenworth. I assure you, my father would heartily disapprove of my attire."

"Smart man."

Her expression turned sad and Jake fought the urge to comfort. Instead, he stepped away, resting a hand on the butt of his skinning knife. She said nothing further, so he mounted his horse.

As they left the river and turned toward Union Pass, climbing beside boulders dwarfing the horses, Jake's mind stayed fixed on the woman behind him. What made him so vulnerable to her sad eyes? Helen had tried that trick and it had nearly worked. But as Helen had never experienced an ounce of real pain in her twenty-one uneventful years, so her performance had lacked authenticity. Helen—the girl he had left behind, gladly. To think he once believed he loved her. Love that had allowed her to lead him like a bull with a ring in his nose. When she learned he planned to leave Jessup's Cut, she led him to her bed. He swallowed every lie she had spun, even when he knew she didn't come to him a virgin. When he discovered her deceit, she'd shown her true colors by turning from weeping waif to seductress in the beating of a human heart.

He would never give a woman such power again. They misused it.

His gaze returned to Emma. This woman had witnessed a massacre. He knew Helen would not have handled the situation with such courage. He thought again of the first time he saw Emma, sitting on her mount, dodging arrows.

Something big hit his back with enough force to knock him from the saddle. His horse screamed and shied. Jake rolled clear to see a mountain lion perched on his saddle, one paw gripping a dead partridge as it coiled to spring. He drew his knife and rolled to his feet, just as the cat pounced. He raised his blade. A rifle blast split the air. The lion twisted, clawing wildly, then fell to earth shaking the ground beneath his feet.

Dust settled and the cat did not move. Jake noted one bullet hole between the creature's ribs. He nudged the cat's carcass with his foot. Lifting his gaze to the woman, he found her reloading her rifle, the cork from her powder horn clenched in her white teeth. His jaw slackened in astonishment. She could not only reload on horseback, she could shoot on an instant at a moving target and hit it dead center. He gave a low whistle reassessing her. She *was* better with the rifle.

Astonishment dissolved in a haze of irritation. The cat came from downwind, of course, but he should have sensed it, heard it. He realized he'd been attacked while thinking on the damned distraction riding behind him. Inattentiveness had nearly gotten him killed. His face heated as anger mixed with shame.

He clenched his teeth trying to decide if he should shout at her or thank her. At last he settled on, "Nice shot."

She grinned, showing a beautiful smile. He felt the need to wipe it off her face.

"How are you at butchering?" he asked.

She wrinkled her nose and cringed. He smiled at that.

"Don't like the sight of blood, eh?" He laughed.

She dismounted and glided toward him with feline grace. His stomach tightened preparing for a different sort of attack.

"I have seen my share of blood these past two days. I confess no affinity for it." Her hand rested tentatively on his shoulder and he tensed preparing to draw away. "You are bleeding, Mr. Turner."

She pushed aside the thick strap of his possibles bag. His head jerked as his gaze focused on a tear in the tanned leather covering his shoulder. The lion must have punched a hole in his skin. He never even felt it. Blood welled though the gap staining his shirt. Her hand swept over his shoulders sending a ripple of sensation down his spine. Next she examined his scalp. Her probing fingers raked his hair, sending waves of delight pulsing through him.

He batted her hand away. "Leave me be, woman."

"You need bandaging," she said, her smoky eyes steady.

"What do you know about bandaging?"

"I treated the sick and wounded at Fort Leavenworth."

He couldn't think with her hovering about.

"Check the horses." He jerked his head in their direction and Emma moved away.

Jake turned to the task of skinning the cat. She was a small critter, not more than seventy pounds and skinny. The lion had smelled the dead birds and wanted them enough to attack three horses. He noted the ribs showing prominently through the tawny hide. The cat looked to be starving. As his knife sliced between sinew and skin, he found Emma's killing bullet had passed between the ribs and straight into the creature's heart. There were damn few men that could make such a shot. Begrudgingly, his respect for her grew. Twice she had showed a cool head in danger and that went a long way toward surviving in this territory.

Emma did as she was told and tended the horses. She found his mare trembling and stroked her head and neck, murmuring words of reassurance as the horse blew hot air from flaring nostrils. The painful thudding of her heart diminished as she drew comfort in the act of soothing his mare. The image of the big cat striking Jake ricocheted in her mind as she slid her hand down the horse's front leg and then over the saddle. Deep gouges raked across the leather seat. She held her breath as she measured the cuts with the tip of a finger. Feathers littered the ground and a single partridge lay beside his mount's hind feet. She scooped up the bird and retied the carcass behind his saddle. As she did so, her eye caught the moisture on the creature's hindquarters. Two parallel scratches marred the dark shaggy coat, not deep, but they could do with some liniment. Her chestnut gelding eyed the butchering nervously as she approached, the smell of blood and cat making him dance.

She lifted her hand and rubbed her mount around the base of his ears admiring his gleaming coat, marred only by the army brand. "Easy, Scout. That's my boy."

From her saddlebag, she withdrew a tin of salve and brought the liniment to his horse. The mare's skin twitched as Emma dabbed the ointment into the wounds.

Once done, she allowed the horses to graze in their bridles, despite the mess they would make of their bits. Finally, Mr. Turner finished the skinning and butchering. When he approached carrying the meat wrapped in the hide, his horse's mincing steps grew more pronounced.

He called to her. "Duchess, settle down now. You carried a bear once."

The horse stood as he prepared to tie the load behind his saddle. Then he noticed the scratches, now buried beneath black ointment. His gaze flicked to her as he carried the lion skin to his packhorse that seemed equally displeased to carry the load.

The blood coating his hands did not concern her. Instead, she focused on the steady stream that ran in a thin line from his wounded shoulder down the front fringe of his shirt.

"Will you let me tend you now?" she asked.

He frowned and the muscles at his jaw clenched, but he nodded. He rinsed his hands and grabbed a hank of grass to dry them. She motioned him to sit on a rock that stood knee-high and broad as a saddle.

"Pull off your shirt," she directed.

He hesitated, then gripped the hem of his garment dragging the soft leather over his head in one smooth tug. She froze, as the waves of awareness rippled through her. The air in her lungs seemed trapped as her breath failed. How many men had she tended at the fort—fifty? But there was no comparison. Those were boys with pale thin limbs and burned necks. They were hairless, all ribs and hollows.

This man's skin glistened golden in the sunlight. She stared at the heavy muscles of his chest and shoulders as her fingers itched to touch. A thick mat of dark hair curled over the front of his body, disappearing into the waist of his buckskin trousers. She trembled as some deep part of her responded to the raw male beauty of him.

"What ails you?" Jake began to rise. "Are you fixing to faint?"

She pressed her palm to his uninjured shoulder savoring the heat of his skin as he resumed his seat.

He watched her with concern etched on his rugged features. "You said you tended injured men."

Emma nodded, focusing on his wound instead of the shaggy raven-black hair, worn long like an Indian, brushing his shoulder. Was it soft or coarse?

"Do you have any whiskey, Mr. Turner?"

His eyebrows lifted. "Good idea."

He walked to his mule and rummaged a moment, as Emma watched the muscles of his back bunch. The two long cords descending on either side of his spine intrigued her. She pressed a hand to her own back finding only the smallest similarity between their anatomies.

She recalled the trappers of her acquaintance. Jim Bridger looked like walking rawhide and Mr. Sublette carried no extra bulk whatsoever. These men lived in the wild and their bodies showed the same trim, wiry appearance and deeply tanned skin that marked them as surely as any branding iron. They also wore full beards. A quick glance at his face confirmed that *this* trapper was accustomed to regular shaving.

She noted that the girth and power of his muscles resembled that of a lumberjack or blacksmith. He lacked the lean grace and burned skin common to men of the mountains. Neither did he stand or move like one. Trappers glided, silent as a stalking predator. This man's stiff posture seemed vaguely familiar. Suspicion knitted her forehead and rooted deep inside. His erect carriage looked distinctly military.

His strides were purposeful as he returned, echoing her misgivings. He sat before her; the blood dribbling down his chest seemed of no concern. He grasped the cork to the jug with his teeth and offered her the bottle.

She lifted the container, unable to understand the sense of

betrayal coursing through her. Her father had once been an army captain. His code of strict discipline and insistence that she obey orders unquestioningly came from that past. Of all the men in the Rockies, she did not want to be trapped with one from the military. She lifted the jug, opening the flap of skin over his wound and poured the golden fluid within.

He shot to his feet, bellowing like a wounded bull. Finally, his wild dance ceased and he focused his glare on her. Her stomach tightened as she prepared to absorb his tirade, already regretting her rash actions.

"Great God almighty, that hurts!"

"It will stop infection."

He sighed and thumped to his seat. "Give a man warning." He resumed custody of his jug, cradling it now like a lost friend and muttering. "Next time pour the whiskey into a hole where it can do some good." He took a long swallow, then stared at her. "Well?"

Was that all? Except for when the whiskey had burned him, he didn't even shout at her. He didn't tell her to use the brain God gave her or that the horses showed more common sense than she did. He didn't call her a worthless no-account.

"I'd like to use some ointment and then bandage you," she said, her voice barely a whisper.

"Get at it then. We've got miles to go."

She worked quickly now, first dabbing the clear salve into his wound, then covering it with a bit of clean muslin. Her hands shook at each contact with his broad shoulder and she bit her bottom lip until the pain brought clarity. Using her damp handkerchief she washed the drying blood from his chest, finding his skin warm, his hair coarse and the muscle beneath hard as iron. He sat still as the stone, but when she lifted her gaze she found him staring at her with an intensity that made her insides quake.

"Are you all right?" she whispered.

He shook his head. "I used to think so."

He captured the cloth and removed the drying blood from his belly. She sighed in relief, wondering if she could have finished cleaning him without bursting into flames. What was wrong with her?

"I have to bandage the wound to hold the dressing in place."

He clenched his jaw as if bracing for some pain.

"This won't hurt," she assured.

He gave her a look of skepticism, but said nothing as she wrapped the bandage over his shoulder and around the wide territory of his ribs. She could not quite reach about him without brushing his back. He twitched at the contact. At last she finished the knot and stepped away to observe her handiwork. No blood showed through the dressing and the bandage looked as if it might hold while he rode. Then she noticed the sheen of sweat covering his body. He trembled—no, that was not trembling. His body seemed to vibrate with tension. Were his injuries more serious than they appeared?

"Mr. Turner?"

"You done?"

"Yes."

He leaped to his feet as if sprung from a trap and stalked away.

She trailed behind, placing a hand on his uninjured shoulder. "Are you sure you are well?"

He shook her off and turned on her. "Don't touch me 'less you need to."

Emma recoiled and stood suddenly awkward and unsure. "What did I do?"

"I can't think with you hovering about me. I missed that cat sneaking up on me. Know why?"

His voice held irritation, but he kept his tone civil.

Unable to speak, she shook her head.

"'Cause of you! Damnation. I don't need this. I don't need a woman ogling me and stroking me, all the while telling me I can't touch her. You're a menace."

Her jaw dropped. Had she ogled him? Perhaps so. She

wanted to touch him, enjoyed it in fact. Her hand sprang to her mouth.

"Get on your horse and don't speak to me until we make camp."

She nodded and hurried away. When the tears came she was on her horse and silent. Thankfully, he never turned around to witness her shame. They traveled along a ridge. Below, the Wind River flowed like a green ribbon in the wide valley. Ahead and beyond the menacing peaks of the high Rockies lay covered in snow. She felt the cold already in her heart.

I never wanted to come here. If she had a home she'd long for it. But she had none. Instead she had a father who despised her and a hostile protector who called her a menace. *My mother—does she even remember me?* She longed for the love her mother had once given, before the illness. Her breath caught, as she realized no one in this world loved her.

Her throat burned and her sides ached. Regret churned within her belly. Why had she agreed to come along? Why had she stared at him like that? Harlot, scarlet woman. That's what Father had called Mother.

Had that driven her mad? Emma felt the darkness, lurking just beneath the surface. She didn't recognize this woman who stroked the bare skin of a complete stranger. The ideas in her mind terrified her. Emma bowed her head. How long until she went the same way? She knew she could not survive again closeted in her father's quarters under perpetual house arrest. She'd suffocate there. He would never let her go. Mother had escaped into madness.

What was her escape?

Her mother never replied to her letters. Father said she had grown much worse since leaving him. At least the sanitarium in Baltimore provided refuge from the dictator who was her husband.

A west wind brushed her face, drying her tears. She looked again to the mountains and suddenly they seemed less forbidding than the life awaiting her to the east.

* * *

Jake figured they had ridden nearly twenty-six miles today. Damn good pace considering the lion attack and all. She had not uttered a word since he had hollered at her. Guilt nipped like a dog at his heels. She'd only tended him, but it was easier to blame her than entertain the alternative. He was crazy as an elk in rut each time she touched him. He recalled the feel of her fingers dancing over his bare skin. Lordy, if he'd allowed her to wash his stomach, she would have had a surprise and no denying it. He ground his teeth wondering why fate had forced a lady on him? Why wasn't she a squaw? Indian women understood a man's needs. A squaw would crawl under your blanket at night and in the morning be gone. The perfect woman.

White women were crazy. They ordered a man to keep clear one minute and stroked him the next. He remembered her intent gaze, how it locked with his, and for one instant he felt sure she wanted him, too.

Did she know what she did to his innards when she turned those smoky eyes on him? If he had any say in it, she would never know. One touch and his skin burst into flames like tinder beneath a burning glass. It took all his willpower not to drag the woman into his arms and kiss her senseless. What would she have done if he had?

The image of Emma, hot and willing in his arms, forced another unwelcome jolt in his gut. He shook off the notion.

She'd slap your face, maybe, and she'd be right.

He stared at the mountains, knowing he had other problems. It would be another day's ride before they reached Union Pass. Men at the Rendezvous who trapped the Green River said several feet of snow covered the peaks already, but the trails were passable. An early storm could shut down his chance of making the crossing.

The only bright spot in that prospect was the possibility that he could head back and rid himself of Miss Emma Lancing. He'd like to ride on, but the horses needed rest, so he chose a spot and drew them to a halt. His gut tightened as if mule-kicked. Now he'd have to face her.

Best get it over with. He stopped by the stream and slid down, ignoring the stiffness in his legs and hips. Then he turned to the woman and froze, then took a step closer, doubting his eyes.

Her head hung in what he first thought was a posture of hopelessness. He crept forward and studied her breathing. Her hands rested on the pommel, clutching the reins. Asleep in the saddle.

Jake folded his arms across his chest and studied her. Her cheeks showed tearstains again. God, the woman spouted more water than a whale. This time she'd kept her tears quiet. That confused him. Never in his life had he seen a woman cry without an audience. He pushed aside the thought she might actually be suffering real distress and wondered instead if she feigned sleep. Now that was a trick a woman would pull. The possibility irked him.

Her chest rose and fell beneath the brass buttons emblazoned down the center of her coat. He'd like to polish the brass with the front of his shirt. His fingers itched to touch her bare skin. What secrets lay beneath the army-issue wool?

The thought brought him up short. He knew damn well what was underneath—a world of trouble, was what. He stormed to his packhorse and threw down the lion skin. Hadn't Helen's lessons been enough? White women used their bodies like currency, trading favors for wedding vows. A night of pleasure was not worth a lifetime of captivity.

He glanced at Emma who now leaned dangerously in her saddle. "Well, hell."

In three quick strides he reached her, catching her as she dropped from the horse. Her eyes flew open and she pinned him with a startled gaze.

"What happened?"

"You fell off your damn horse."

She glanced about. "I did not."

He lowered her to the ground. His reluctance to release her convinced him to do so immediately. She clung a moment, wobbling. Her body fell flush against his, sending a lightning bolt of desire firing through him. He grasped her narrow waist and stepped away again, holding her until she righted herself and then moved off. He considered her as she stretched, sending the fabric of her coat tight against her full bosom. His mouth went dry.

"Fetch some water." He turned away to gather firewood.

The task of cooking occupied him for some time. As the meat simmered in the skillet and the partridge sizzled on a spit above the coals, he proceeded to scrape the lion hide. This kept him from having to look at Emma, who seemed to have dunked her head in the stream and now combed her wet hair by firelight. A quick glance, now and again, showed that her hair turned wavy as it dried, the color going from dark to light. Her skirt clung to her legs and a possibility struck.

Had she bathed in the stream? His mind reeled with the images the thought conjured.

He turned the birds, rotating the crisp brown skin away from the coals. Emma's stomach growled so loudly, he could hear it from across the fire. She clamped a hand over her belly and her gaze shot to his. He smiled at her look of embarrassment and frowned as color flooded her cheeks, sending bands of steel around his chest so he couldn't draw a proper breath.

Damn her, again.

The tension crackled between them. He wondered how to make it stop.

"You got a plate?" he asked.

She nodded and rummaged in her bags, withdrawing a tin plate, cup and fork.

"Hungry?"

Her head bobbed again.

"You can talk you know."

"Thank you, Mr. Turner. I didn't want to disturb you."

The woman was nothing but disturbing, but he'd never tell her. Instead he sliced one partridge in two, laying the flayed bird beside a thick slice of meat from the shoulder of the lioness she'd killed. He returned her plate.

"I've never eaten mountain lion."

The corner of his mouth twitched in a half smile. "Better than the other way around."

Her fine eyebrow lifted. A moment later, understanding dawned. "I should say so."

He directed his attention to his own portion and ate.

"I have beans, flour, a slab of bacon and coffee in my pack," she said.

"Good to know." He spoke, keeping his attention firmly fastened on his meal, determining not to be distracted by her again.

He cut into his lion steak. Glancing up he found her hands folded as her lips silently offered a prayer. Reluctantly, he dragged his hat from his head. Her actions reminded him of church, home and civilization—all the things he had escaped. He scowled at her until she finished her muttering, the hunk of meat lodged in his cheek.

She cleared her throat and said, "We made good progress today, I think."

"Fair enough," he agreed and finished chewing.

Emma said nothing further as she ate. He watched her across the fire wondering what she thought about the day. When he had sat before her half-naked, he'd been certain she'd shown him desire. Now she seemed all polite veneer and quiet dignity. Had he imagined the fire burning in her eyes?

Maybe so. It damn sure burned in him strong enough to scorch his bones and cloud his thinking.

She finished her portion and he offered her another, but she refused, so he added the remaining partridge to his plate. After the meal, she gathered her utensils and wandered off into the darkness toward the stream. He wondered if he should follow, then remembered the birds she had brought down, the cat she had killed and the pistol still strapped to her belt. He returned to the pelt, ignoring the splashing. What was that sound? He squinted. Humming. She was humming, something familiar, a song he knew from his childhood, a lullaby, maybe. His knife nicked the pelt too deeply and he cursed. What the hell difference did it make, what tune she hummed? He had work to do and then he needed rest.

Emma returned and stowed her gear, then shook out her blanket and removed her coat. The white shirt beneath was not the army issue he'd worn when training at West Point. Instead, the fine fabric and lacy trim sculpted over Emma's curves. He tore his gaze away and focused on the cat skin.

"When we get over the pass, I'm going to tan this hide and make you a proper coat."

"I already have a coat."

He sighed. "That's an army jacket."

She said nothing.

"What do you think will happen if you show up in California wearing an army jacket?"

"I don't know."

"Ever been arrested?"

"No." Her level gaze met and held his. "But I've been in prison for years."

He rolled up the cleaned skin and tied it tight for carrying. "What's that suppose to mean?"

"It means for the first time in my life I am not surrounded by men, mules and manure. I can breathe here."

He scratched his neck regarding her. He felt like that out here. But women were practical. They liked men who held respectable positions in stuffy little offices scratching away with pen and ink. His teeth ground together. He'd never heard of a woman feeling trapped. She made no sense.

"Do you have family, Mr. Turner?"

It had been a long time since he made polite conversation, but he gave it a whirl.

"I have four brothers and one sister back east in Jessup's Cut, Maryland."

"Maryland? My mother is from Baltimore. Lucille Brady was her maiden name. Her father is in shipping."

"Nathan Brady?"

"Yes. You've heard of him?"

He owned half the harbor. Of course he knew him. "Heard his name."

What was the granddaughter of such a wealthy man doing out here in the wilderness? "Your mother at Fort Lancing?"

She looked as if he had struck her, recoiling slightly. Then she cleared her throat. "My mother is East, for her health, you understand."

He sensed she hid something because her fingers clutching her skirt belied the rigid smile fixed upon her lips. He didn't really want to know anything about her and had only asked to be polite, so he let the topic drop.

Emma, however, was not done. "Why do you so dislike women?"

He didn't need to answer, but found he wanted to. "That would be Helen Grant's fault. She decided to make a husband of me."

What she did to achieve her ambition turned his stomach. She'd been as ruthless as any hunter.

"She decided?" Emma's voice held disbelief.

"Even when I turned her down."

He'd believed Helen when she said she loved him. His jaw clenched as he recalled his stupidity. She had only wanted to collar him. Nearly succeeded, too. When she'd miscarried, he'd wiggled out of the trap. When she'd tried to sleep with him a second time, he'd understood the first time had been no act of passion but one of cold calculation.

Emma's gaze fixed him to the spot.

"Not the right woman or not the right time?" she asked.

"Both, I guess. Between Helen's pushing me one way and the book pulling me another, I finally just came apart."

He remembered the day he walked out. His mother, Helen and his sister all had bathed him in their tears. But he had finally seen them for what they were and refused to be swayed.

"What book?" asked Emma.

"The journal of Lewis and Clark. After that, there was no keeping me home." His pappy, a dissatisfied attorney himself, had seemed to understand. He'd correctly blamed the book. His pap had threatened to burn it, but in the end, he'd rescued his son and sent him to the University of Pennsylvania for instruction in mathematics and celestial navigation. If Jake had never read that journal, he might now be writing contracts by day and lying beside Helen at night.

"You ran away?" Emma leaned forward, looking suddenly intrigued.

"In a manner of speaking. Joined the army as a surveyor." Jake said no more. That information alone might be too revealing. But she was a woman and though naturally curious, she could not guess his business from that small revelation.

Emma's gaze narrowed and she nodded as if she had suspected this all along, which was ridiculous, of course, when she knew only what he told her.

At last her frown disappeared and the hint of a smile curled her full lips. "So you escaped. How did you do it?"

"Shook my pap's hand, told my mother I was grown and told Helen I didn't love her."

She made a sound he could not interpret, and then she said, "I admire you."

"What for?"

"Your courage. It is difficult to disappoint your family, don't you think?"

"Gets easier with distance."

She stared off into the darkness. "Perhaps so."

Chapter Four

She disturbed his rest. So, instead of waking him, the crow cawing on a rock above his head merely marked the time to rise. Jake readied the horses as dawn broke.

Emma crawled stiffly from her blanket and he cursed beneath his breath to see her hair had slipped from the single braid and now curled about her face. She looked soft, warm and inviting. He returned to packing. He noted she rose wearing her wool coat. Had the cool temperatures of the night chilled her? She wobbled toward the stream, obviously saddle sore, but she said nothing as he tightened her horse's girth. The big chestnut swung his head about and tried to take a hunk out of him. Jake sidestepped just in time and decided Emma could take care of her own damn horse.

Loaded at last, they headed up the ridge.

Morning stretched silent except for the wind and birdcalls. The harsh repeating cry of a jay brought Helen to mind. She had complained about everything up to and including the wind rearranging a wisp of hair from her bun. He eyed Emma, suspicious of her silence. He'd never met a woman like her.

Don't kid yourself. She's a woman, same as all women. Maybe just a sight tougher. Sooner or later she'll come round to the same thing—weddings and babies.

He felt the trap, hidden just before him, waiting for one misstep. Well, he'd be damned first. Jake pressed his heels into Duchess's sides increasing the distance between them.

Late in the day they headed up Union Pass. High peaks lay hidden beneath low clouds. He studied the hovering gray mass and wondered if it had snowed farther up.

At dusk, Jake battled the urge to continue. Cloud cover masked the gathering darkness, but it was near. He knew better than to face that pass late in the day. He stared skyward and cursed, for in his bones he felt the snow falling above them.

He called a halt.

The next morning he rose before dawn and cooked a stew in his only pot. There'd be no more fire until they cleared the pass. With luck, they would cross the worst in one long day. Because of the danger and unpredictability of the weather, the journey could take much longer. After cutting grass for the horses, he turned to wake Emma.

She gave a pathetic little moan as he roused her and she fought his urging to wake. Then looking about as if bewildered, she sat up without a word of protest.

"Come eat," he whispered and moved off.

She approached the fire and he offered her a tin plate laden with wildcat stew mixed with her navy beans. If she thought the meal odd for the time of day she did not say.

"We'll cross the divide today?" she asked.

He nodded, concentrating on getting the hot food into his belly as fast as possible. He glanced to the sky, noting the disappearance of clouds as the stars faded with the forthcoming dawn. When he returned his attention to the woman across the fire, he saw her plate sat upon her knees as she stared into the darkness. He wondered what she might be thinking.

"Not too late to turn back," he said. "If you've a mind to, I guess now would be a good time. The pass might only stay open another few weeks."

"Sealing me in on the western slopes?"

"Might say so."

She paused only long enough to draw a deep breath. "I've cast my lot with you, Mr. Turner. I shall move forward."

"Then I suppose you best call me Jake."

"And you may call me Emma."

She smiled and his heart rate accelerated. The woman acted on him like coffee. He scowled and remembered why he'd given up coffee. It made him nervous.

"Finish up. We got a long trail ahead."

"Tell me about it."

She ate as he cleared his throat, unaccustomed to using his voice so early in the day. "We'll be leaving the tree line and heading into scrub brush and patchy grass. Higher still the grass disappears and we're left on gravel. Slippery as ice in places. We'll cut between two peaks picking down one of the biggest rock fields I ever saw. Must have been some racket when that broke loose. The western slope is just the same in reverse, rock, grass, brush and finally pine. We want to make it to cover before full dark. It gets bitter cold on the rock face. The wind bites to the bone."

He hadn't spoken so much since he left the Rendezvous. He offered Emma more stew and she declined, so he ate the rest from the pot. He glanced up, expecting her to plague him over his table manners, but was greeted only with her cautious stare.

They headed off before the sun broke behind them. By full light they reached the scrub brush and patchy grass. The horses startled partridges from cover and he pulled his shotgun clear and fired, bringing down three birds. He gathered them up and paused to look back. To the north and south, the Rockies cut an immense jagged course across the land, stretching as far as a man could see. They were mighty and made a body feel like an ant on a rock pile. But, oh, he loved the sight of them.

"I've never seen anything so beautiful." Her words echoed his thoughts.

He didn't hide the smile. After all, she was behind him. Few men had seen such a sight and damn few women. Fact was Emma might be the first white woman to cross this way.

He mounted up and the horses scrambled over loose gravel. This time he chose a different trail than on his last journey, pausing to find a passage accessible to wagons. The route took them east of the rock field over level ground. The passage required several switchbacks, but he thought a good team of oxen might make it, though it would take many days. The sun climbed the eastern sky as they scaled the slope. Ahead, he saw what he'd feared.

Snow blanketed their path. He judged the covering to be at least a foot thick. How deep it sat higher up was any man's guess. He drew the horses to a halt.

"Damnation," he muttered.

"Oh, look. Snow!" Delight rang in Emma's voice.

He turned in his saddle to glare at her.

"No reason to sound so happy about it. We'll have to wade through that, you know."

He dismounted and threw grass before each mount. He handed Emma a hank of jerked moose, gingerly this time so as not to accidentally touch her fingers. Finally, he drew out his chronometer taking careful note of the time as the sun reached its zenith and recording the data in his journal. Later on he would make the calculations. He noted the compass reading, then sighted three peaks for his map. He scratched a few notes with his pencil before tucking his work safely away. When he glanced up he found Emma studying him in silence, a look of speculation upon her face.

By midafternoon, the horses waded through knee-deep snow. They pushed slowly along as he considered how much time it might take to cross this plain of white. Before him on the ridge, a marmot scrambled over the dirty patches and disappeared into a hole.

He drew his hat low on his forehead to reduce the glare and peered out only when necessary, keeping his eyes on the trail directly ahead. Hours passed and still they had not finished the ascent. The snow grew icy and hard enough to bear the horses' weight. Unfortunately, now they slid on the frozen slopes. If the mule went down, it might damage his equipment. He hoped he'd chosen correctly, counting on the surefootedness of the mule to keep his precious instruments safe. He cursed as his horse stumbled again and lowered his hat against the dazzling brightness of sun on ice.

"Everything is so white," called Emma.

Her words sent a sliver of apprehension through Jake.

"Even the sky seems white. Why is that?"

He spun around to see Emma sitting with her hat resting on her back. How long had she been staring into the blinding snowfield?

"Put on your hat."

She looked straight ahead, but did not seem to be looking at him. His heart slammed against his ribs as he slid from his horse, slipping on his way back to her. His suspicions proved correct as Emma did not follow him with her eyes, but continued to stare ahead at where he should be.

"I was cold. I thought the sun might warm me up."

Her red face showed sunburn. He waved his hand before her eyes. She did not move.

"Emma?" he called.

She turned her head toward him. The first flicker of fear danced across her face.

"Jake? Why can't I see you?"

"Snow-blind," he said.

She groped for him and he rested a hand upon her knee. "I'm here, Emma."

"Oh, God, Jake. I'm blind!"

"The sun is powerful up here."

"What do I do? Is it permanent? Oh, Lord, no."

He found her hand. She gripped him like a lifeline. "I'll bandage your eyes to give them a rest." His voice relayed none of the panic firing through his belly. "They should come out all right."

Often they did. He'd known this to happen. If a man was alone, he'd likely stumble off a ridge, starve to death or fall prey to wolves. Survivors mostly got their vision back, though he knew one man who never did. This information he kept inside his heart as he drew Emma down into his arms. He had carried antelope that weighed more than this woman. She clung to his chest and sobbed. This time he understood her anguish. He found himself making hushing noises that seemed to comfort her. The tears still coursed down her cheeks, but the crying ceased. Why hadn't he told her to wear her hat? It seemed such an obvious thing to do in a snowfield; he had never considered she didn't know. But how could she know? Emma was his responsibility. He would have to be more vigilant.

He wound soft tanned leather around her head and replaced her hat. Then he led her to her mount. She clung to his chest, gripping his shaggy wolf coat in both fists.

"I'm afraid to ride alone."

He dreaded riding double, not because the extra load would tax Duchess, but because he'd have to hold her.

"You'll be all right," he assured, not sounding confident at all.

"Please?"

Her entreaty tugged at his heart. He gave up without another word, leading her to Duchess and boosting her up. When he tied her horse's lead behind his saddle, the brute lashed out with his front foot. Jake decided he didn't like her horse.

Standing beside Duchess again, he paused to study Emma and knew why he didn't insist she ride alone. He wanted to hold her and welcomed the excuse.

He cursed his own weakness as he drew himself up behind her. Then he clicked his tongue to signal Duchess onward. Emma huddled against him, her cold legs molding to the muscle of his thighs. Her bottom nestled into the lee of his waist. Her back and his chest fit like hand and glove. What would it be like to sleep thus, with this woman tucked tight against him?

He shook his head as he realized she got under his skin faster than a chigger without batting an eye or sending him a coy glance. How did she do it when he warned himself against her?

It was a man's weakness. The only way to resist a beautiful woman was to stay clear of her. He couldn't even get that right. Now she trembled against him, but from fear or cold he could not tell.

He wrapped one arm about her waist and hurried Duchess along with his legs.

"Are you cold?" he asked.

Emma's teeth chattered, as she nodded. He spun in the saddle and she heard him rummaging. The world about her had gone from brilliant white to terrifying black. How had she failed to notice the snow and rock and sky gradually blending into one blanket of dazzling light?

Blind—how could she be blind?

The thought sent a fresh wave of terror through her and she resisted the urge to throw herself from the saddle and run. It made no sense, but still she knew she would do it. Is this how her mother felt? Did she have this same desperate emotion? Had the urge to run, to scream, to fly so overwhelmed that it stole her mind and drove her to madness?

The smell of musk and buffalo enveloped her as he drew a heavy cloak about them. The coarse hair of the hide tickled her nose and she turned her head.

The wind ceased to blow. Inside this dark cocoon, Jake's body warmed hers and she lay beyond the touch of the terrible mountain. He kept her safe—safe from the blinding snow and the madness within her. In his arms, she found the courage to draw another breath and then another.

The horse seemed to be heading down now.

"Have we crossed the divide?" she asked.

"A while back. We have a ways to go before we hit the tree line. That ice patch back there delayed us good and proper."

"Is it sunset?"

"Just about. Sun is creeping over the plateau below this peak. Past that I can see the Tetons. Be two more days before we cross those mountains. They're jagged as wolf's teeth, but not nearly so high as this here. I'd say this is the highest point we'll hit on this trip."

He continued to talk, his voice rumbling in her ear and against her back. The sound soothed her nerves.

"Sun is fixing to set. The clouds are changing colors. They're purple now, but in a few minutes they'll light up pink and orange. Never get tired of the sunsets. I couldn't see it in Jessup's Cut. Mostly the sun just sunk away without me taking any note except to light a lamp. Pity, really."

"I couldn't see it from the fort."

"What were you doing there?"

"Seeing to my father's comfort while he traded with the Indians on the Missouri. When he came to the Rockies to build a trading post, he left me behind." She did not tell him that it had been the best year of her life. Mud, men and manure had been preferable to her father. For the first time in her life she'd been rid of him, if only temporarily. "That's when I tended the men with fevers and injuries, while I waited for my father to send word."

"How long?"

"From June until April. When I left, Colonel Leavenworth gave me Scout and my saddle, tack and this jacket as a way of saying thank you."

"Probably glad to be rid of him," he muttered.

"What?"

He cleared his throat. "Didn't your father leave you a horse?"

He'd left her very little. She'd been embarrassed to ask for assistance from the colonel, but he'd seemed to comprehend her distress and had offered her meals in exchange for her services with the sick soldiers. "She was old and died that winter."

"Were you glad to leave?"

She hesitated. The truth or polite conversation? She drew a breath and plunged in.

"I dreaded it."

"Why come, then?"

What did he mean, why? Her father had ordered her. Did Jake think she'd had some choice, some option other than to obey her father? Then it occurred to her that he did. Here was a man who had made up his own mind and had left his family without regret. What would she give to have the courage to disobey her father?

"Where would I go that my father couldn't find me?"

"I reckon this place will do."

She laughed. "True. He can't find me here." Her thoughts grew dour. "Jake, what will you do if my vision doesn't return?"

"Oh, you only went a few hours in that snow. You'll be all right."

"How long until we know?"

"Rest your eyes until tomorrow night. Then we'll take a peek."

Two days of darkness. She gasped and huddled against him. Would he abandon her if she could not see? What else could he do? Could he drag a blind woman past Indians, through deserts and into Mexican territory?

Her experience with her father taught that men needed women who worked. Since her mother had left, Emma had sewed her father's clothing, cleaned and cooked. In return he'd provided a roof and food. It was her understanding that she was only needed for as long as she was useful because certainly he did not love her. There was nothing more useless than a blind woman. Pure terror jolted her body.

"Jake, if my vision doesn't return…"

"Don't fuss. I won't leave you, Emma."

She believed him, trusted him in a way she didn't under-

stand. Why she trusted him, she could not say. Somehow this
man was different than all others in her life.

"I don't know how to thank you."

"I guess you'd do the same."

Somehow this made her smile, lifting the edges of her
bandage. The utter darkness beyond changed her mood again.
She must wait another full day to know if she would be forever blind.

"Jake, I'm so scared."

His strong arm tightened. "I've got you."

Jake rode into the night, picking around boulders the size of
houses. The sliver of a moon rose, giving him scant light as he
left the snowfield. He followed the animal trail along a steep
ridge. For the first time he felt glad Emma could not see. This
stretch terrified his trapping team when he'd led them into the
Green River Valley. A drop of several hundred feet gaped to his
right. Still the trail lay wide enough for wagons. Duchess plodded along, surefooted as a mule. Her head bowed in an attitude
of fatigue. She'd been carrying them since sunup and they were
closer to dawn than dusk now.

Gradually, silver islands of grass appeared and with them
came the buzz of insects. He pushed on through the brush and
twisted trees, blown and stunted by winter winds he could only
imagine. The ponderosa pines came next and he breathed their
scent with relief. Not far now and they could all rest.

Emma's head lolled against him. She'd fallen asleep hours ago.
He drew his stiff shoulders together and groaned at the pain that
shot down his spine. Weary and saddle sore, that's what he was.

He rode on until he found a glacial stream running from the
ice above them. Finally, he drew up on the reins and Duchess
gave an audible groan. He patted her hindquarters.

"You are still my best girl," he whispered and then slid off
the horse, keeping one hand on Emma.

She swayed but stayed upright. He pulled her down into his
arms, letting the hide fall from his shoulders. She moaned as

he stood her up and waited until she woke enough to keep from toppling.

"Stay here with the horses."

He quickly threw the hides down and then his wolf blanket. He led her to the bed and laid her between the skins. Then he saw to the horses, giving them each an extra measure of grain. Finally, he crawled in beside Emma, dragging her warm body to his.

Just for the night, he thought, I'll just hold her for this one night.

Chapter Five

Emma shivered in the night and a strong arm pulled her close to the warmth of a solid body. Not since she was a girl had she curled in bed with another soul, but the large form behind her was not her mother. Rather, it was distinctly male. Jake. She relaxed into his embrace.

She blinked, wondering at the total darkness about her and then remembered—the blindness. Her body trembled. Fear washed through her like ice through the spring runoff and she huddled against the reassuring strength of this man.

He'd told her earlier she would see again. She latched on to those words and held fast. Her fingers curled about his forearm, judging its girth. Resting in the lee of his body, she felt protected from the terrors of the wilderness and the demons of doubt within.

She lifted the edge of the soft hide sheathing her eyes and blinked into blackness. Unwilling to let the panic take her, she reminded herself that this just might be the depth of midnight. But why were there no stars?

What if it was morning?

That brought her sitting up. The soft fur slipped from her and Jake groaned.

"Lie down," he ordered. The gravel of his voice made her doubt he was awake.

She slid down before him. Her fingers brushed his face, finding the hawkish nose, short coarse beard and closed eyelids.

"Jake, are you stirring?" she asked.

"I will be if you keep rubbing up against me."

He made no sense. "Wake up," she said.

"I am, damn it."

She spoke the question spearing her heart. "Is it morning?"

His eyes blinked open and she withdrew her hand until it rested on his soft full lower lip. His mouth moved as he spoke. She felt a tingle, like a minnow swimming in her belly.

"No."

She sighed and fell onto the wooly buffalo hide beneath her. "I'm so afraid." Her fingers now tugged at the hide sheathing her face. "I need to get this off!"

He stilled her hands, capturing her wrists in one of his own when she strained to tear at the bandages. The force of his restraint grew as she struggled, thrashing uselessly beside him.

"Let me go!"

But he did not, only held her firm, immobile as granite. Her fingers curved into claws and she attacked his face, never getting close enough to draw blood. Her mind shattered as she screamed.

"Stop it, woman. Have you lost your mind? Stop."

Lost your mind—lost your mind. The words spun into her awareness, acting like a steady breeze before fog, bringing everything into sharp focus.

What was she doing? She stilled instantly.

"Emma, can you hear me? Are you fevered?"

"No, no. I'm fine."

In slow increments he released his hold and waited, his body tense beside her. Her rapid breathing blasted between them as her heart threatened to jump from her chest. She pressed a hand over her ribs, trying to still the frantic knocking. Finally, the sound of wind rustling through the branches returned to her. The smell of pine came to her next and then the warmth of Jake, still and cautious just inches from her.

"What happened?" he asked.

"I was frightened."

"You fell asleep in the saddle. I tucked you in here with me. I never touched you. Do you understand me?"

"I wasn't afraid of that, but the blindness. Oh, Jake, I can't be blind. I've seen old women with cloudy eyes and…" She ducked her head into her hands and gasped. No—not again. Her momentary madness frightened her as much as the blindness. A blind, mad woman, that's what she'd become. Would they put her with her mother then?

Jake eased closer and laid a tentative hand on her shoulder. "Tomorrow night, wait until then. Your eyes need a rest. If you broke your arm, you wouldn't go tearing the splint off the next day, would you?"

She shook her head, then rested her hand on the reassuring bulk of his chest.

"You all right now?" The doubt in his voice, the tentative grip and stiffness of his frame told her he was braced for another attack.

Jake should know she carried the madness, but she dreaded telling him. Father said the same curse hung over her. That she must never marry, for her children might be touched, as well. He did not speak to strangers about her mother, but some of his men knew for they'd been there when it happened.

She whispered the truth. "I'm going mad."

He dismissed her fears out of hand. "Don't be silly."

"It's not silly. My mother is mad and she passed it to me."

His breathing stopped and then resumed an even rhythm, but he said nothing for a time. "Who told you this?"

"My father." She rushed on to tell him all of it. "At first she couldn't sleep. Father said the wind on the prairie drove her mad. She begged him to send her east. Then she tried to leave the fort one night. Father said she heard voices and shut her in her room. She howled and threw herself against the door for days."

"How old were you?"

"Ten."

"Jake, I'm afraid I have it, too."

"The madness?"

She nodded. "I don't hear voices, but I feel so restless. I want to leave the fort, too. It's all I think about. If I'm blind, I'll never be able to leave."

He gripped her shoulders with authority. "You already left it. You're out, remember?"

"I'm not an imbecile. I know you won't take me along if I can't see."

"It's just a bandage, Emma. Be patient."

"What about the restlessness and the urge to run away?"

He laughed. "Everybody feels like that. I felt it back in that office. I stared out at the river and wished I could jump onto one of the barges and float down to the Atlantic. One day, I did. My dad caught up with me in Baltimore before I signed on to a clipper and agreed to send me to school."

"But my father says I'm just like mother. That I'm touched, too."

"I don't know your mother. But I know you. This isn't madness. You just feel like most folks who get trapped."

"Trapped." Yes, that was right. "Not mad?"

"I don't think so."

She sagged against him letting her fear seep away like water though sand. She lay against his broad chest a long while before she realized he stroked her head as if she were a child. Her cheek rested on the soft leather of his buckskin shirt.

"I can't ever thank you enough for rescuing me."

"Those Crow are unpredictable. Might have made you a slave." That was a lie, of course. He knew they meant to kill her slowly.

"I wasn't talking about the Indians."

Jake continued stroking her hair. She sighed and nuzzled closer. He waited until her breathing told him she slept and then let his hand drop.

What in the name of God was he doing? He had only meant to protect her from her fears. She slept pressed up against him as if she were his wife and he liked it. Lord, he loved it.

This is only temporary. She's not yours and you don't want her to be. He toyed with a lock of the silk that was her hair and sighed.

Why were women such trouble and why were they so soft?

Emma spent the long day clinging to her saddle horn unable to anticipate the trail ahead. Cool air brushed her face. The sound of Scout's hooves beat a comforting rhythm as he clomped over rock and padded through thick pine needles. During the afternoon the trail leveled enough to allow a moment to release her grip on the pommel and consider last night without fear her distraction might cause her to fall off the horse.

She had slept in the same bed as a man. Did that mean she'd lain with him? In her terror, she'd clung and he had not sent her away. Instead, he had held her close and murmured comfort. She'd never before drawn comfort from a man. She had soothed wounded men, but not since she was a little girl had anyone eased her. Emma's opinion of him changed last night. He showed a hidden side of gentle strength and compassion. He had almost made her feel loved.

Ridiculous. She barely knew the man. But now she wanted to. He certainly knew something about her. That her mother was mad, for instance, and even that carefully guarded secret did not shake him. Could he be right that her feelings were not the beginnings of madness, but ordinary longings to escape the trap of her life?

How many more hours before she could remove the bandage? The neck of her horse now inclined below her pommel. They headed down. He said they'd make the foot of the Tetons by evening. She wanted to see them.

"Can you see the Tetons from here?" she asked.

"Yup. They look close, but that's a trick of the mountains. They're a ways off."

"Can you describe them to me?"

There was silence and she thought he would not oblige. Finally he spoke. "They look like jagged teeth raising straight from the plains. Rough rock already snow covered all blue and gray. Of all the mountains on the earth, I think these are the grandest. Not the highest or the meanest, but the most inspiring to the eye."

She could not keep the wistfulness from her voice. "I wish I could see them."

"I suspect they'll be waiting on you tomorrow."

Doubt bubbled, despite the confidence in his tone.

"Over to our left, there's a waterfall, can you hear it?" Jake described the falls and later a gray jay that held a grasshopper in its beak. Several ground squirrels chased each other around the trunk of a lodgepole pine, their claws scratching the bark. That afternoon she saw the world though his eyes. In his words, she found his excitement at each new discovery and recognized his ability to note things invisible to her. He read game trails, signs of beaver now long gone and changes in the clouds overhead. Somewhere late in the day, hope returned.

"If I regain my sight will you teach me to navigate?"

She waited during the pause, now understanding the silence did not mean no, but only that he took longer to consider.

"I could."

He'd given her something to anticipate. The tender feelings for him grew, seeming to swell within her like a warm breeze.

When he drew the horses to a halt, she was surprised the day had passed. His saddle creaked as he dismounted and then he stood beside her, one hand on her thigh. She felt Scout swing his head around, preparing to bite, as he always did when a man got too close. That behavior had nearly sealed his doom at Fort Leavenworth. She was the only one who could get near him, let alone ride him. Jake swatted Scout in the face with something and her horse turned his attention forward once more.

"Damn ornery brute," he muttered, then he addressed her. "Come on, I'll help you down."

She threw her leg over the horn, reached out for the man she could not see, but knew stood waiting to catch her and slipped from the saddle into his arms. He lowered her to the ground and held her a moment as she breathed the now familiar scent of herbs and buckskin that clung to him. Emma clasped her hands about his neck and tipped her head as if to look up at him, reluctant to move away.

"Thank you."

"What for?"

"For telling me all those things, for describing the world and keeping me from being alone in the dark."

"I never talked so much in my life. I'm tuckered."

She smiled and let him slide away feeling a moment's bereavement at his withdrawal. "Do you ever think what your life would be like if you hadn't jumped on that barge?"

The creak of his saddle told her he was removing the tack from Duchess. "I'd be married. I'd have children and I'd be dead inside."

She thought of her mother and how much she hated her marriage. Emma understood the trap of marriage, but she never considered it could also be so for a man.

"But men can come and go as they please. They don't have to raise the children or do the laundry. How would you be trapped?"

"I don't know how to explain it, except to say I hated clerking for my father. I hated living indoors where the only interesting things happened in the pages of a book. I needed to see something, do something for myself. If I got married I never would have seen those Tetons. Marriage is just as much a leglock for a man as a woman."

"A leg-lock?"

"It's a trap. A critter steps in the trap and the metal teeth tear into his leg. Then he either dies or he chews off his foot to escape."

She pressed a hand over her heart. "How dreadful."

"That's marriage. You're walking along and, snap, you never see it coming. Then the trap has you. You're caught."

"Then why do men propose?"

"Don't know, custom, maybe. Best for raising kids, maybe, but it's sure hell on those with wanderlust."

"Better three free feet then trapped with four?" she asked.

"Now you got it."

Another bundle of gear hit the earth beside her. He moved to her saddle and bags. She held Scout's head to prevent him from taking another shot at Jake. The task complete, Jake helped her settle to rest against a saddle.

"How long until I can take this off?"

"Full dark. That will be after supper."

She sat idle as he rustled in his bag. Next came the knocking sound of flint striking steel as he lit the fire. The smell of smoke marked his success. A familiar tearing noise reminded her of the sound of plucking a chicken. Then she remembered the quail he'd shot before the snowfield.

"I think I can pluck those birds," she said.

He pressed them into her hands. With something useful to do, she no longer felt like such a burden. That was the measure of things. One needed a purpose. Even with her father there had always been work, though he'd usually found it lacking.

Her fingers swept over the carcass and found it clean. She grasped the second bird and began ripping away the feathers.

"Sun's setting," he said.

She gave a great sigh. Just a few minutes now. He took the last plucked bird. Soon the aroma of roasting fowl reached her and her stomach gave another growl. He chuckled.

"That belly of yours might give away our position."

She smiled. After a time he pressed the stake holding the roasted quail into her hand. The meal seemed to take forever, as things do when you are anxious for them to be finished. At last he led her to the stream, where they knelt as he helped her wash the grease from her fingers. His big hands enveloped hers, warm against cold water. His familiar scent surrounded her, bringing her a comfort that came without words.

"Now I want you to keep your eyes shut until I tell you. Things will be blurry at first and it's good and dark now, so you won't see much in any case. Understand?"

She nodded and waited, holding her breath as he touched the knot imprisoning her eyes. Slowly the buckskin fell away. She pressed her lids closed and waited until nothing touched her skin but the night breeze. Panic broke in her belly and she squeezed her eyes closed tight, suddenly afraid to open them. As long as she kept them closed, there was a possibility of sight. If she opened them and could not see—what then?

"All right," he urged.

She drew a breath and opened her eyes. Darkness.

Emma blinked and turned toward Jake. His face seemed half-orange and very blurry. The fire. She turned toward the flame some twenty feet off and he grasped her chin.

"Look this way first. Can you see me, Emma?"

She blinked and his features took shape. Another blink and she read the concern etched on his face.

"Yes!" She threw herself forward landing in his arms.

He circled her in a warm embrace as she wept against the solid comfort of his chest. Lifting her chin, she stared at him. His expression changed. The joyfulness of a moment earlier dissolved into a look of wanton desire and she read every nuance. His embrace no longer comforted, it demanded and she knew he would kiss her.

His lips descended pressing hard to hers. A rush of pleasure swept through her, stealing her breath. Her breasts ached in a way she'd never experienced and she pressed herself to him. The pounding of his heart matched the frantic rhythm of her own. She opened her mouth at the steady insistence of his lips. He hesitated and then pushed her away.

Startled, she fell back onto her hands. He leaped to his feet, scowling down at her as if she were suddenly an enemy.

"Jake?"

"Bear trap," he muttered, then to her. "I only—why'd you throw yourself at me?"

"I—I didn't." Had she? Perhaps she had. She'd certainly hugged him. But the kiss. Oh my, it was her first kiss and the man she'd chosen had just finished telling her he'd rather chew off his hand than offer it in marriage.

"Don't do it again. Understand?"

She shook her head, then nodded, not knowing what was correct as she drew herself tentatively to her feet.

"Can you see me now?" he asked.

"Perfectly."

"Good."

She took a step forward and he retreated. She halted. "Thank you for taking care of me."

"You can thank me by keeping your distance and setting your blanket across the fire."

Emma bit her lip. Something between them had broken. She wanted it fixed. Last night he held her tenderly. Now he eyed her as if she were a coiled rattlesnake.

"I didn't mean to kiss you. Please don't be angry."

He pulled off his hat and dragged his fingers through his thick hair. "I know you didn't. We best get to bed. We've got the Tetons tomorrow."

He turned away and she followed him to the fire, admiring every log. A few minutes ago she would have given anything to regain her sight. Now she had her vision and all she wanted was to restore the warmth between them that had died by that little stream.

Chapter Six

Over the next week the tension between them continued to radiate like heat from a Franklin stove. Emma rode silently behind him trying to draw no notice. This was a skill she'd perfected while living with her father. At times she thought she'd grown invisible, until he'd bark an order. She spoke only in reply and stayed all questions when he paused each midday to consult a watch and compass. Often he used a metal eyepiece to study the horizon, and then scratched in his journal. He paused at rivers and streams to check the direction of their flow.

He was right about the Tetons. They were majestic. But after crossing them, Emma decided that mountains are best enjoyed from a distance.

He shot two deer and took the time to teach Emma the process of scraping and soaking the leather. At first she thought his gesture an effort at mending fences until she realized he had enlisted her help in the most strenuous, vilest job of trapping—tanning hides. Again she was valued only for the work she produced.

She cleaned the deer hides on both sides, while he prepared the lion, leaving the hair and head with the vicious upper jaw including fangs, but removing her brain. Finally, he sewed yellow glass beads into the place where the eyes once glowed, draped the head over his own and tied the cat's arms about his neck.

"Like it?" he asked.

She cringed. "It's barbaric."

"Too bad, 'cause this one is yours."

"Mine?"

"You killed it. It's your hide."

"I'm not wearing that creature on my head."

He laughed and returned to the buckskin "Some tribes believe you take a piece of the soul of the animal you kill and it becomes a part of you."

Emma could think of no animal she would rather resemble that the bravest of the beasts. She almost laughed at the ridiculousness of it. "So I have the courage of a lion now?"

"Lioness." He grinned, then extended the hideous thing.

It was the first act of kindness he'd shown her since their kiss. Had he offered her a dead lizard she would have gladly taken it. Her fingers grasped the hide, hoping this marked a new beginning, for she could not stand his rejection. She draped the skin over her shoulders, noting the satisfaction in his eyes, but refused to wear the hood up, leaving the gruesome lion head flopping on her back.

"We'll be on the Great Salt Lake by week's end," he said. "Then head across the desert."

She'd never been in a desert but found the prospect filled her with disquiet. "What is beyond the desert?"

"Don't know exactly. Mountains, eventually."

He gave her an honest answer, but this only served to remind her that the maps stopped here. She had seen her father's charts including the only two viable passes over the Rocky Mountains. Union Pass, through which she had crossed with Jake, and South Pass. Her father placed himself at the base of South Pass knowing that all trappers leaving the fertile Green River Valley would arrive on his doorstep. But west of the Salt Lake? Then there was a great blank space until the Pacific coast. What lay between? Certainly nothing inviting enough to lure trappers into the desert. What would prompt Jake to go there? She wondered if he worked for one of the fur companies. They always searched for new hunting territory. Perhaps Jake was some kind of scout. No one had ever gone from the Rockies to the Pacific on this track or at least none who tried had returned. Tomorrow, she would step off the map and into that great void. What would they find there?

That evening he returned to his journal attempting a rough sketch of the landscape before them and cursing loud and often.

"Give it to me," she said.

He hesitated. "Why?"

"Because I can render a likeness better than you."

He faltered a moment and then handed over a smaller blank journal. He didn't trust her with his main log, but did seem willing to include her. She smiled at that. Perhaps she'd made some small progress.

"Draw that range of mountains."

She lifted the pencil and began. Jake sat quietly behind her until she lowered the journal.

"Damnation. That looks just right."

She smiled at the obvious excitement in his voice. "Thank you."

"From now on, you do the drawings. I'll tell you what to sketch."

"All right." She flipped the cover closed and extended the book.

"Keep it. You'll be drawing every day, now."

"Illustrations for your novel?" she had promised not to pry and her attempt at fishing yielded no catch. She tucked the journal in her bag.

The next day, when Jake stopped to take readings, Emma pulled out her sketchbook, as she now thought of it, and drew an interesting blue flower, then she broke off the stem and pressed the specimen between the pages. By the next day, she had a sketch of a shaggy mountain goat on a crag with two babies and one of Jake with his back to her as he stood beside Duchess.

By afternoon she glimpsed the shores of the Great Salt Lake. The immensity of the water, stretching out before her, brought her to silent contemplation. A sense of awe spread through her. Suddenly, she felt like the luckiest woman alive, to see such a wonder. For the first time in her life she felt free. Wanting the experience to last, she drew out her sketchbook. Her pencil flew across the double page spread before her as he drew his horse alongside.

"Damn good."

"But it's not. It's so small. It doesn't begin to capture the color or glory of this lake."

"You're right. For that you have to be here."

She gazed at him as his glance swept the vista before them. He drew a great breath and she knew that he experienced it, too. In that instant, she understood why men faced grizzly bears and froze half the winter. It was to see the grandeur of places like this.

"It's amazing," she said.

He nodded, his gaze on the glittering surface of the lake. "The hand of God."

She wanted to touch him, to take his hand, seal their connection, but she dared not. Things were finally better between them and she would not risk that.

He glanced back at the ridgeline. "I'm gonna miss them. The desert is nothing compared to mountains. Hard traveling, no game and deadly, like hell compared to heaven."

"How long will it take to cross?" she asked, quelling the fear that tugged down deep. Jake may not trust her, but she trusted him enough to follow him into the desert.

He sighed. "Days and days. This route has never been tried. Jedediah Smith crossed considerable south along the Colorado River on the way out and then some two hundred mile south of us on the return. Lewis and Clark were all the way up in Oregon Territory. This way doesn't follow any river. It's direct, barren and untried. We'll carry enough water for several days." He turned, regarding her with a serious expression and a gripping uncertainty clenched her belly. "If we find none on the journey, we won't make it."

"But we can carry extra. You have plenty of water skins."

He smiled. "And we'll fill them all, but do you know how much we need to keep three horses, a mule and ourselves watered for a week?"

The chill danced along her spine. More than they could possibly manage. She stared out at the lake of undrinkable salt water and realized they could very likely die in the wasteland beyond.

There was no turning back now. She lifted her chin and set her jaw.

"Emma?"

She felt his gaze upon her and turned to meet his cautious stare. "If anyone can do it, Jake, it's you."

He smiled, seemingly pleased at her declaration of confidence. "Best get on. I want to leave the lake tomorrow."

They swung along the north shore following the tail of the Rockies. Emma looked at the ground, surprised at the crunching sound, which came from the horses' hooves breaking through a white crust.

"What is that, Jake?"

"Salt. Ground is loaded with it. Ruins the streams. You have to find groundwater to get clear of it and usually that's brackish."

That evening they camped beside a spring. Just as Jake warned the water tasted slightly of salt.

Jake stared down at the little up swelling of water. "If we find better, we can refill the skins. I hope this isn't the last we find, but I'll treat it like it is."

The next morning they lingered by the spring and Emma wondered what might pass before she saw this place once more. Her gut twisted as she realized that she might never set eyes on it again. She wanted to speak her doubts and hear Jake give reassurances. She glanced toward the barren west and knew he could offer few.

Jake packed the remaining gear as she held the horses. The animals drank deeply and she wondered if they sensed what lay ahead. She followed their example drinking until her belly swelled with the brackish water, as if she were a camel and she might store this life-giving liquid in her hump. A queasy feeling filled her as the water sloshed within like a wineskin.

The result of her gorging was that she had to stop and dismount three times before midday to relieve herself. On her third trip back to the horse, she found Jake taking measurements with his compass and consulting the timepiece.

She stood before him, her questions unspoken.

"All right, damn it. I'm scouting ahead for a party and that's all I'm saying."

Her eyebrow lifted. "Mapping you mean."

"Amounts to the same thing. You ready?"

She nodded, then mounted up. For some reason she'd pictured the desert as being a great flat sandy expanse, but it was not. As the lake fell behind, they followed a dry riverbed, surrounded by reddish-brown cliffs that rose thirty feet. There were plants, too, thick gray-green brush clung in stubborn patches along the dry riverbanks beside dwarfed and twisted pines. She sketched them as she rode. The white crust continued to coat the ground making her certain that nothing of any value would ever grow here.

Her hat hung so hot and heavy as the afternoon wore on, she felt tempted to draw if off, but feared the sun after her last experience.

"Do people go blind from the sun in the desert?" she asked.

Jake nodded. "They do. But mostly the heat kills them. You still sweating?"

She thought it an odd question. Of course she was. Hot droplets trickled down her back at regular intervals. "Yes."

"Headache?"

Now that he mentioned it, she did feel a dull pounding. The heat and glare made her squint. "A little."

"Drink more water."

She lifted her leather skin, startled to find it was already half-done. She had yet to see Jake touch his. Perhaps men were built differently or he was more accustomed to such hard conditions.

They did not stop for dinner and continued on into the twilight. Emma's back ached and her bottom felt raw from rocking in the saddle. Scout's head drooped and she leaned forward to give his wet shoulder a pat.

"Almost there," she whispered.

The moon rose, now glowing in its quarter and casting enough light for Jake to pick his way along. Emma shook her head as sleep stalked her. The desert held a strange silence. It took her several moments' consideration to realize she heard no owls, no insects. She listened hard for some reassurance that they were not the only living creatures in this barren place, but found none.

Jake pulled up at last and she groaned with relief. Sliding out of the saddle proved difficult and she staggered when her feet touched down. Her shoulders ached as she unfastened the girth and slid the heavy saddle into her arms, succeeding only in turning a half circle before dropping it. Next she removed the saddlebags and hobbled Scout.

There was no grass to curry the horses' lathered flanks. She stood considering what to do. Jake poured water into his hat and offered Scout a drink. The horse sucked the leather dry and then proceeded to try and eat his hat. Jake filled it again but offered it to the mule.

"I think he's still thirsty," she said.

"No doubt. But that's enough for now. I saw no trace of water today."

He'd been looking. She realized again how ill prepared she was to survive out here.

"Maybe tomorrow," she said.

The corner of his mouth quirked. "I thought you'd be crying by now."

Her eyes rounded. "Did you?"

"I've never seen a woman take such hardships without complaint. I rode right into the night and you never whined or fussed about when we were stopping."

But she had wanted to. She kept that information to herself and determined to act like a good partner, even if she was a woman. Always in the back of her mind was his warning. *If you fall behind, I'll leave you.* She was determined not to give him the chance.

He gave her another curious stare. "You're just not like any other female in my experience."

"Is that good or bad?"

"Good, I think."

She smiled and instantly was rewarded with one of his. Their eyes met and held and a wave of awareness rippled through her. He seemed to take pride in her. Impossible. She glanced away.

Emma made an effort to sort out her emotions, but gave up. They were tangled and confused. After a time, she began to wonder what occupied Jake's thoughts.

Her throat burned and her tongue felt coated with salt and dust. This was only the first day. She fingered her cheek and was surprised to find her skin as dry as dirt. Her lips seemed ready to crack. She retrieved some beeswax and mineral oil she had for burns and rubbed it over her lips, then offered it to Jake. He tried the salve and nodded his approval.

"No fire tonight. We'll eat the dried deer."

She cast down a hide to rest upon. Stars wheeled overhead. In the vast expanse of the desert night they seemed larger and closer.

"Aren't they lovely?" she asked.

He glanced up and nodded. "I'd give plenty not to see them, seems we left the clouds on the mountains. The sky is nearly always clear here."

She thought about that as she chewed the dry meat, wishing

for some of her mother's lemonade to wash it down, but settling for the brackish water from a sad little spring. The tingling
of doubt surfaced again.

"How long can we live without water?" she asked.

He rested against his saddle on a skin beside hers. "I know
a man who had a similar problem once." Jake launched into a
tall tale about a man named Hugh Glass and how he survived
a grizzly attack and days and days in the wilderness before stag-
gering into camp.

"He did show me his scars," said Jake. "They were dreadful. I don't know how he survived." Jake sank to a reclining position and clasped his hands behind his head. "Best settle in. I
plan an early start, before it gets too hot." He drew out a fur.
"You'll need this."

Emma knew she would not. It was still so hot that it was hard
to breathe.

"The temperature falls quick out here. Soon it will be cold.
Just keep it close by."

"Thank you."

She lay only a foot from him and stared up at the heavens.
It wasn't until sometime later she realized he'd never answered
her question about how long a man could live without water.
Instead, he told her a grand tale until she forgot all about her
worries. She smiled in the darkness and inched closer. What a
remarkable man.

Chapter Seven

Their water ran out on the fifth day. Jake considered the expanse of sage stretching to the bluish haze that might be a plateau or the foothills of some mountain range. Either way the distance would take them at least two more days. Without water, they'd never make it.

At midday, the sun beat down on them with savagery that seemed to have no end. He heard a groan, then a thud and turned to see his packhorse on his side.

"Great God Almighty." He slid from Duchess and rounded on the horse, but no amount of slapping with the reins or cursing would make the beast rise.

He rubbed his chin, then glanced at Emma's puffy sunburned face and cracked lips. Dried blood filled the fissures. How long before she went the way of his horse? He'd been in a similar spot in twenty-eight, south on the Colorado. They'd eaten the packhorses and mules as they'd died. He'd hoped never to have to eat horse flesh again. Where was the damn spring?

He stated the obvious. "He's done."

"If we had a little water for him, I'm sure he'd go on."

He told her the hard truth. "We don't. We drank the last this morning."

Her eyes went wide. He knew the instant she comprehended their dire straits for her gaze danced frantically about. Whether she searched for rescue or escape he was not certain. She found neither.

"What shall we do?" she whispered, sounding like a frightened child.

He knew it hurt to speak. His throat burned and his tongue felt too big for his mouth. The headache behind his eyes grew fiercer as death stalked him. Dying of thirst was one of the most miserable ways to go.

"I'm going to put that horse out of his misery and we'll eat his flesh."

"Oh, no! Please don't kill him. He faithfully carried your things all this way."

He tugged on his hat in frustration. Women—when they weren't twisting a man to their will, they were fawning over some dumb animal. Loved their damn cats more than people.

Piece by piece he unpacked the horse, moving the necessary supplies to his other packhorse and the mule, then abandoned the rest. Even with the load removed the horse did not rise, preferring to roll to his side and lower his head to the sand. Jake turned and found Emma staring at him with sad eyes.

"Must you?" she asked.

"You promised to follow orders. Here's one. Take the mule and the horses over to that ledge." He pointed to the outcropping of red stone providing the only close shade. The spot would stay sheltered except for the long hours of the morning. "Unpack everything and stow it under the cliff. Leave Duchess saddled. Understand?"

She opened her mouth as if to argue, then stopped herself and nodded. He watched her draw the animals away and tie them to a thorny bush. He turned to the horse drawing his butcher knife from its sheath and steeling himself to what must be done. This death would be more merciful than leaving the poor creature behind. An animal alone and vulnerable drew buzzards faster than a turd draws flies. Scavengers wouldn't wait until the horse died. No, they'd take his eyes first and then pick at any soft flesh they could rip into with their sharp beaks.

He positioned the cooking pot, laid a gentle hand on the horse's shoulder and sliced cleanly through the great vessel at the neck. Blood poured into the container and spilled into the thirsty sand. The horse shook his head and kicked weakly. His head dropped to the sand and his eyes rolled back as his ribs sagged. His last breath fanned the desert.

"Forgive me," Jake whispered, stroking the still neck.

He glanced toward the cliff and saw Emma standing as a silent witness to his brutality, then he stripped meat from the great hindquarters and brought it to her with the life-giving fluid.

She said nothing as he lit a fire of sage and roasted the meat. He offered the pot.

"Drink some."

She drew up her shoulders and quivered. "I can't."

"Might make the difference between living and dying."

Emma gave a tortured swallow and shook her head. "I'm sorry I'm so weak."

He sighed and lifted the iron bucket to his lips closing his eyes in an unsuccessful effort to ignore the taste and feel as the warm, viscous fluid passed down his parched throat. He lowered the kettle and glared at Emma, daring her to object. She looked away.

The thin strips of meat cooked quickly. He scowled as precious drops of fluid fell into the fire, hissing into steam. Better to eat the flesh raw and save every ounce of moisture. He glanced at Emma and knew she would not.

He offered her a rare piece. Her nose wrinkled, but she accepted it.

"Don't think about it," he suggested.

She gave him a look of desperation. Her hand trembled.

"He's dead. He can't feel anything. If you don't eat every bit of that, you'll be dead, too. Now do what I'm telling you."

She hesitated.

"That's an order."

Her lips parted and she took a tiny bite. He turned to his own portion, tearing into the dry, leathery meat with his teeth. Judging from the consistency, he was astonished his horse had lasted as long as it did.

He glanced at Duchess, the other packhorse and his mule and gritted his teeth. They all needed water. He knew the animals would not live even one more day without it. Horses, mule and then Emma. She wouldn't last long on foot. The grief accompanying that thought rocked him to the core. Up until that second, he believed the most important thing was to complete his mission and get the necessary information to Washington. When had that changed?

He didn't know—but it had. Emma's life hung in the balance. He must find water.

A glance at the sky told him that he had a few more hours of daylight. Without gear, he could travel faster, scout ahead and find a spring. His gaze rested on her big horse. Here the extra muscle and bulk was a liability. The animal was near done.

Emma gagged on the meat, but managed to swallow. She would have to stay behind and wait.

"I'm going ahead to find water."

Her eyes rounded as she set aside her portion. "Alone?"

He nodded and she sprang to her feet. "But I didn't fall behind. I can keep up."

Suddenly he understood. The first day he had met her, he had laid down the law. She was to follow his orders, not ask questions and keep up or be left behind. Emma stood trembling before him, her fingers reaching to grasp at his shirt in desperation. He had seen the same expression the day he had rescued her from the Crow.

"Please. Don't leave me. If I can't go, then kill me, too. Don't abandon me to this hell on earth."

He gripped her shoulders. "Emma, I'm coming back."

"No. I didn't fall behind."

She was past hearing. He shook her and she blinked.

"I'm scouting for water. Do you understand?"

No tears this time. Was she capable of tears or was her body so depleted of water she had none? The thought cut at his heart. He must hurry.

Emma's fingers dropped from his buckskin and she sank to the ground. "I understand."

He knew in that instant that she didn't believe him. She accepted that he would abandon her.

"I'm coming back."

Her head hung forward in an attitude of defeat. She did not move or speak.

For several moments he stood speechless. Without hope, how long would she last? That thought scared him into action. She did not believe his words. He went to his bags, still hanging behind his saddle. He drew out his chronometer, sextant and finally his journal with the green leather cover. He set these precious offerings at her feet and waited. Slowly her gaze moved to the fruits of his efforts. Her hand reached and she fingered the oak box of the chronometer.

"Wind this in the morning. Protect the horse and mule. Don't leave this spot or I won't be able to find you when I come back with water."

He waited. Her fingers touched his journal. She pressed the book to her bosom and hugged tight. Then her gaze lifted to meet his.

"You're coming back." It was a statement and the certainty shone in her eyes.

"Yes. Tomorrow, I hope, before dark."

She nodded.

"Rest and eat as much of the meat as you can. Stay in the shade."

"And guard the animals."

"That's right." He strung a hide over a section of ledge hoping to afford her a measure of shade come morning. When he turned back, she stood clutching his journal.

"Tomorrow, by dark," she whispered.

He stood before her wanting to tell her something, wanting to assure her that he'd return. But he knew he might fail. He swallowed his doubt. He had no room for it.

He lifted a hand to stroke her burned face. "See you tomorrow."

Her eyes fluttered closed and she smiled. Her lips cracked. He felt the tear as if it were his own. No time to waste. He needed to ride. Turning, he strode away ignoring the invisible bond that pulled him to her.

He gave her one final glance, then mounted up. She looked thin and burned and about done. He pressed his heels into the horse's sides and headed out into the open desert.

First he made for the bluff to the south, climbing steadily for the next hour. From the top, he gained a view of the wasteland beyond and gleaned little hope. The rock and sand stretched out endlessly in all directions. Heat rising from the desert made the ground seem liquid, dancing before his weary eyes. He knew the shortest distance out was to the west and, although nothing before him gave solace, he continued on that path throughout the afternoon and into the evening.

That night he did not stop. The drop in temperature and the half moon made traveling a comparative pleasure. Also to rest reduced his chances. Duchess carried less weight than the packhorse and she was younger, only four. But he knew she could not last much longer. None of them could. If the horse died, how would he get back to her?

He dreaded the coming of the day, knowing that when the sun rose, the temperatures would soar and she would suffer. By tomorrow he'd be too far to return to Emma by sunset of the second evening. The journal gave her hope. Hope alone would not sustain her. She needed water.

Where was the damn spring?

Streaks of color crept across the eastern sky, stalking him like a hunter. Dawn broke, painting the desert pink. As morning wore on, the harsh rays blinded him.

Duchess sensed it first. Her ears perked and she whinnied. He stopped and listened. There came the sound of running water. He allowed Duchess her head and she made straight for the spring.

Please God, let it be drinkable.

Water bubbled out of a fissure in the rocky ground and pooled into a greenish hollow no bigger than a washtub. There was nothing nearby to indicate it existed. For a heart-stopping moment he feared it did not.

He pulled Duchess up, despite her near frantic effort to reach water as he slid down and knelt beside the pool. Warm water filled his hand. He lifted it to his lips and drank.

His eyes fell shut in a silent prayer. *Thank you, sweet Lord.*

Duchess nudged him and he stepped aside to allow his horse access as he fell to his stomach on the scorching rock. The sound of his horse slurping drowned out his own. He gulped and gulped until his belly filled with the life-giving fluid.

He dragged down the water skins, filling all three to bursting. His horse finished. The spring now lay half-full. He watched the water trickle from the rock, slowly refilling the pool and realized a large party would easily exhaust such a small spring. He must find a better source for wagon trains.

He wished he had his gear to record the location of his discovery. Emma had it. She'd watch over his precious belongings until he reached her. The sun lay past its zenith as he tied the water on his horse and mounted up. He did not sleep last night and he would not sleep this night, either. Now that Duchess was watered, they could set a faster pace. If he hurried, he might reach her by sunup. But he had promised to return by dark. He glanced skyward and knew he would never make it.

Grasping the reins, he steered his horse the way they had come. As he journeyed east, he dwelled on Emma's unrelenting suffering. As day ground into night, he knew he missed his promised rendezvous. What would she think? Possibilities filled his mind. She must know he was delayed. That was all. The horse's hooves fell in steady rhythm, but too slowly.

Stars pierced the night sky, shining with cold indifference as he struggled to reach her.

Please, Emma, please be all right.

Chapter Eight

⤟⤟⤞⤞

Emma watched Jake disappear in the strange waves of shimmering heat rising from the dry ground, then she sank to the sand still clutching the journal. The wretched horse meat revived her somewhat, though the pounding in her head did not abate and she continued to believe her skull might slit open at any moment.

Her mind dwelled on water. All the things she ever drank in her lifetime seemed to return to haunt her. Her most fixed memory was of dumping out a full mug of coffee because it had grown cold. How she mourned that folly now, as if her repentance might somehow bring the fluid back to her.

She lifted the last piece of horse flesh vowing that if she survived this ordeal, she would never eat such a vile meal again and never, ever throw away a cup of unfinished coffee. Her horse and the mule stood in silent desperation, resting first a front foot and then a hind one as the afternoon dragged toward evening. She occasionally peeked out from behind the curtain of leather he had rigged for her. It was possible that he might find water quite quickly. Certainly—it might be only just past that ridge before them.

Evening came and she kept the fire burning to help him find her. During the night she opened the pages of his journal and began to read, drawing comfort from the strong steady strokes of his pen.

She continued through the pages. Each day he recorded their latitude and longitude. He noted game sighted, the course of waterways and their direction. Through some geometric maneuvering he'd even calculated the breadth of the rivers.

The journal was an impersonal, succinct record. She reached the day of her arrival into his life and frowned in disappointment to see their meeting handled in the same analytical accounting.

Encountered a party of Mountain Crow warriors engaging a group of traders who had desecrated a gravesite. The Crow quickly dispatched them losing but one man. One of the traders' party survived, a Miss Emma Lancing, daughter of Henry Lancing. At this point I intervened and secured Miss Lancing's release. Departed with same following the Yellowstone River WSW having no time to backtrack and return her to her people on the Bighorn if I have hopes of clearing Union Pass before the snows.

Her heart sank. The words carried none of the emotion of the day and no indication about how he felt about her joining him. The pounding in her head made reading arduous. She set aside the proof he would return and lay upon the wooly sheepskin he had left.

A thought struck her. He meant to return. It did not mean he would succeed. What if he did not find water in time? He was not invincible, after all. This little hollow in the rock might be her final resting place.

This brought her out from beneath the ledge. Standing made her head throb ruthlessly and she knew her strength was spent. Tomorrow, he'd be here by sunset tomorrow. She crawled beneath the ledge and closed her pulsing eyes. Swallowing did no good. Never had her mouth felt so dry. *Keep still; rest so when he returns he'll find you alive.*

She strained her ears to hear the fall of Duchess's hooves, but heard nothing but the desperate pulsing of her own heart.

The night passed in torture. Emma dozed and dreamed of drinking only to rouse to find herself trapped in miserable heat and desperate unrelenting thirst. At last the morning came. This day, she welcomed the light, even knowing the sun brought more heat. It also brought Jake to her. She reached for his precious clock and carefully wound the knob.

An unfamiliar cry brought her crawling from her den. Dozens of huge black buzzards circled, marking the place where the horse carcass lay bloating in the sun. Scout and the mule flicked their ears nervously and glanced at the buzzards. Before long the bravest landed.

Emma's stomach knotted as she watched the vile birds rip at the poor beast's eyes and mouth. More landed and more. The birds tore away flesh and screeched and flapped as they warred over the bloody bits. Soon the carcass lay open and the vital organs strewn.

As the birds continued their rancid meal, Emma rocked herself slowly back and forth, watching. This would be her end, as well? Would they wait until she died?

She saw the answer when one of the birds landed on the mule who lashed out sending the creature flapping skyward. Emma set her teeth together. How long until they came for her?

As evening approached, Emma could no longer sit upright. She leaned against the rocks waiting. Beside her lay her pistol. If he did not come by sunup, she would use it to kill herself. It was the only way to ensure the dreadful birds did not take her alive.

Jake saw them at sunrise. Vultures wheeled about marking the place where he'd left her. He urged Duchess to greater speed, breaking into a trot. How far?

Three miles. The birds smelled death. He could not staunch the panic seizing his stomach. They were after the carcass. But which carcass? He'd been gone nearly two days.

He erupted into a cold sweat. Dread settled like a heavy mantle as he pushed toward his journey's end. In his lifetime Jake had faced wolf packs, bears, Indians and Mexican raiders. None gripped his heart with the freezing, paralyzing terror that came when imagining those buzzards landing on his Emma.

His Emma—when had she become his?

The day you saved her life. Now hurry or you will have saved her only for the buzzards.

The echoing report of her pistol stopped him. Why did she discharge her gun? There were too many birds to kill with a pistol; a shotgun would have been better. Pistols were only good at close range, like for killing a man. His stomach dropped.

Had she given up hope?

He kicked Duchess into a full gallop, tearing across the blistering sand and rock like the hounds of hell. The birds rose into the air and he noted their numbers. There must be three dozen.

"Emma!"

He couldn't hear her. Just a moment longer and he'd cleared the rock. He threw himself off the horse. Emma lay sprawled on her side clutching the pistol. On the ground before her lay the black-feathered carcass of the buzzard that had ventured too close.

Her horse and his mule stood anxious, eyeing the birds now flying above them in a dark curtain.

Jake rushed to Emma, drawing her into his arms. Her cheeks glowed pink and sand clung to her face. He brushed it away and her eyes fluttered.

"Jake?" The word croaked in a tortured whisper.

Relief and panic assaulted him in equal measure. She lived, but barely.

He lifted the water skin to her lips. She grasped it and drank. When at last she lowered the skin she smiled, her cracked lips open. He didn't understand it. She'd been a burden, still was, but he could not bear to see her suffer, couldn't abide the thought that some harm might befall her. Suddenly he realized that she was more than a burden, she was a liability, because he placed her above his duty.

"You came," she whispered.

"I said I would."

She nodded. "I know. But I didn't think you'd return in time."

The horse and mule now smelled the water and began to shriek. He filled his hat and watered them until they'd finished two skins, leaving him only a half-full one. Thirst is a funny thing. If a man goes without food, it will take his body weeks to recover from the ordeal. But with water it is not that way. Very quickly the horses perked up and Emma was on her feet. He breathed a sigh of relief and then remembered how far they had to go to reach water and how soon they would be thirsty again.

"The spring is a full day's ride from here." Farther really, but a full day and half the night seemed too much for her just now.

"Then we'd best be away." She gathered up his equipment and extended his journal. "I think this kept me alive."

He accepted the volume, staring a moment at the green leather cover. This record might make the difference. His words and his measurements could give the United States a viable route that linked east and west. With the mapping of an overland trail there would be no stopping America's advances. At last he lifted his gaze to meet hers.

"You didn't believe me when I said I'd come for you."

She smiled. "When I held your journal, I believed you would return if you could."

"I'll always come," he assured her, reaching out with one hand.

And then she was in his arms and he held her tight. Emma was safe. That seemed suddenly paramount. Oh no, the mission came first. He hardened his resolve against the feel of her, soft and warm against him. He knew this trail and would not tread it again. The information he obtained meant more than his own life. But not, he realized with a painful lump in his throat, more than hers.

He pushed her away and she went, gazing up at him with

smoky eyes. She was his weakness, his Achilles' heel. These emotions she stirred put them both at risk. He scowled at her.

"We best ride."

Her confused expression pressed at his heart as he packed their gear. The two headed out, leading the mule and forsaking the denuded carcass of his packhorse to the vultures. Heat rose making the desert swim before his tired eyes. He'd rest tonight, as soon as they found the spring.

Through the hot afternoon, he stewed in his own juices. He stopped once to pass Emma the last of the water. She drank sparingly, as if not trusting they would find more.

Evening came and he found himself nodding off in his saddle. He shook his head again and again, but sleep seemed determined to take him.

"Emma," he called.

She appeared beside him.

"I can't stay awake any longer and the spring is still a few hours ahead."

"Perhaps I can find it."

Finding that spring would be like finding a flea on a dog. Locating the water would be difficult for him in the dark. For her, it would be nigh on impossible.

"You have to keep me awake. If I nod off, I might miss it."

"Why don't we rest awhile?"

"No. I need to get you and the horses to water tonight."

"We could talk. That might help."

He nodded, scratching the beard that felt like a fur pelt tied to his face. "You start."

She hesitated for a moment, and then began. "What is your favorite color?"

He scowled. "Blue. Yours?"

"I like blue, as well. Favorite cake?"

"Oatmeal, you?"

"Lemon."

As the moon rose over the desert, he discovered that Emma

did not like carrots cooked, but tolerated them raw. His eyelids seemed heavy as iron skillets.

"Emma, you understand that if I fall asleep and miss the spring the horses will die first, then us, so for God's sake stop talking about vegetables and tell me something interesting."

He heard her intake of breath, then a pause. Finally she spoke. "I think my father drove my mother mad and now he's doing the same to me."

His head turned and he glanced at her. "What?"

"He is so cruel."

Jake eyed her warily. Something changed in her voice. She sounded on the point of tears. But he knew this man. He was greedy, yes, but seemed to look after his men. Though he was apparently cold and demanding, his traders accepted his leadership unquestioningly.

"What do you mean, cruel?" Images of Lancing striking Emma rose in Jake's mind. The picture disturbed him more than he cared to admit. "Does he beat you?"

"The injuries he inflicted were never so obvious. He constantly berated my mother until she wept. She could do nothing right. She begged to go East, but he refused. She lost weight and couldn't sleep. Then she took to her bed. Father said it was the prairie winds, but I know better."

Jake considered this, as impressions of the public and private lives of the man crashed against one another like boulders in the spring runoff.

"Now she's in a hospital and Father says her mind is gone, that she has gotten worse. He says the doctors have no hope." She turned to him, her eyes blazing with fury. "I don't want to go back."

"What do you mean?"

"He started on me when she left. Now I'm the prisoner."

The denial sprang quick as he struggled against believing her accusations. "He's trying to keep you safe from Indians and unscrupulous men and such."

"He called me names I cannot repeat. Said no man would have me, because I carried the madness like her. I used to believe him. But I shot a mountain lion and survived the desert. Look at me, my mind didn't snap. I'm not weak. I'm stronger than I ever dreamed possible."

He smiled at the pride echoing in her voice. Then he considered her words more carefully and suspicion nibbled. "If you don't aim to go back, what are your plans?"

"I don't know, but I won't go back, not ever. I'd like to visit my mother." She shook herself as if rousing from some trance. "What about you, Jake? Will you go East?"

He didn't think this an idle question. It was the kind of pointed question Helen asked when she steered him to places she wanted him to go. Perhaps she thought to stay with him. What other options were there for her? His stomach knotted as he cast a glance her way. He had nothing but respect for Emma Lancing, so much that he nearly forgot that a wedding ring was every woman's plan in life.

"That's none of your affair."

Her head dropped and he knew he'd hurt her feelings. He set his jaw, refusing to allow the guilt to gnaw at him. Damn her for trying to manipulate him. Despite his resolve he found his next words coming softer than customary.

"I love the West. I plan to make it my home."

She nodded her agreement and his scowl deepened. "I know why. I've never felt so free as when I'm out here."

He glanced at the stars cast across the heavens. He understood about freedom. But it came at great cost. Life in this wilderness was uncertain. Perhaps that was why he never felt more alive. Her soft voice interrupted his reverie.

"Will you settle here, perhaps buy land?" she asked.

His hackles went up. He'd be damned if he'd stick his neck in the yoke to drag a plow for this woman or any other or closet himself in an office, measuring his life in the blue scrawl of his ink while she filled his house with howling babies.

"You mean do I plan to take a wife and raise a litter of kids."

The smile dropped from her features and her eyes rounded. He had not meant to snap at her like a mud turtle.

Emma's gaze turned speculative as her eyebrows lifted. She considered him in silence a moment as he scowled at her like a hound with a thorn in his paw.

"Helen again?"

The woman had a knack for hitting the nail directly on the head.

"What did she do exactly that had made you so prickly?" she asked.

He wouldn't tell her.

"Don't see how's that your affair."

"It isn't. but I'd still like to know."

He considered her for a minute, gazing across barren ground cast in moonlight. Emma had just told him something deeply personal about her family. He found the urge to do the same.

"Helen took up with the Kitson boy for a time. Then he joined the army and left Jessup's Cut. Next thing I knew I was courting her. She started talking about marriage right off. I told her I wanted to sail the Pacific or see the West. Next thing I know she's kissing me and…" Jake rubbed the back of his neck thinking of how Helen pressed his hand to her full breast and lifted her skirts. It all happened so fast. Thinking back on it he wondered how she knew so much about how such things were done. She wasn't even wearing bloomers. "Well, afterward, she said I had to marry her after what we done. I didn't want to. She told me she was going to have a baby, so I agreed."

He glanced at Emma to see if she was shocked. She stared at him with a gaze that showed no disapproval.

"Go on," she said.

"Something happened and the baby came early, before we even told our folks. But now our secret was out. I overheard my mother talking to Pa. She said the baby was nearly full grown. You understand? It wasn't mine."

Emma's eyes rounded. "Why did she tell you that you were the father?"

"She got in trouble with the Kitson boy and tried to pass his child off on me."

Emma's gasp cut the night. He stared at her in wonder.

"How could she do such a thing?"

"Desperation, maybe. Worse part was I told her I found out her game and wouldn't marry her. First she cried and then—" Jake swallowed the bile that rose in his throat "—she tried to take me to her bed again."

Shock echoed in her voice. "No."

"She did. But I didn't fall for that same trap twice. I left that night on a barge and made it to Baltimore. Helen went to my folks and told them the baby had been mime and how I refused to marry her. My pa came after me. When I told him my side, he believed me over her. He gave her folks money and they left town. Then he sent me to school in Pennsylvania."

"Wicked woman. You are lucky your father believed you. Mine would not have even given me time to explain."

"Anyway, I'm not anxious to settle down."

"Very good, Mr. Turner. I heartily agree."

She agreed with him? He never expected a woman to approve of his wanderlust. Women were constant and practical and settled. They weren't supposed to go gallivanting about the West, dodging Indians and mountain lions. And she enjoyed it. If that didn't beat all. Emma should be sniveling and clinging to him like a frightened child. Instead she seemed to have blossomed in this harsh landscape, like a cactus rose.

Chapter Nine

Why had she told him? Emma never spoke about her family to anyone. The topic cut too close to her heart.

She threw her bedroll beside the fire and plunked upon the coiled blanket. They'd reached the spring. She should be joyful. Instead she brewed like a pot of tea. The horses, poor creatures, drank and drank as if they'd never have their fill. So did she, for that matter.

Jake shook out a deer hide and fell forward onto his belly. Seconds later he gave a soft snore.

When she finally told the truth, Jake assumed that she exaggerated, that her father acted in her best interest. She knew better. After Mother left, Emma took her place, doing his bidding and receiving his derision. But she was stronger than her mother. She had lasted thirteen years.

She could marry to escape him. But would she? Her mother and father had shown her the misery of a bad marriage. As a wife she'd be powerless, depending solely on her husband. Through marriage she would only switch one master for another. Her father told her repeatedly that no man would want her, when the truth was she wanted no man.

When she asked Jake if he planned to stay in the West he cast her a look of suspicion. A chill rolled down her spine as she recalled his admissions about Helen. He had good reason to be gun-shy of women. Now she understood why he raised his guard against her as if she meant to hog-tie him in marriage. He had nothing to fear on that account. She'd sooner swallow her tongue than say a wedding vow.

The night perched at the brink of morning, relinquishing its grip by slow degrees. His shadowy outline became more distinct by the minute as he slept.

He was just like her father, or he would be if she were ever stupid enough to give him total control over her. She sniffed. That day would never come. One overbearing male in her life was quite enough.

At last she lay upon her skin to rest until he roused her. They left the spring and headed away from the sixty-mile desert. That's what he called it, for the distance they traveled from the river to the spring. He paused at noon to take more measurements. In all this time, he had never trapped a single animal, only shooting what they needed for food. Scouting he said, but for what and for whom? At first she thought one of the larger trapping outfits sponsored him to find new prospects as the beaver east of the Rockies dwindled. But now she wondered. Trappers did not care about latitudes.

That night he found no shelter, so they camped on the prairie grass, with the horses and mule staked on leads nearby. A shower of sparks from the fire lifted toward the heavens, briefly sending up a glowing spray of orange beneath a million stars. Far off, a coyote called, but there was no answering cry and only the insects broke the night's stillness.

"This is a lonesome place," said Emma.

His familiar voice calmed her soul. "Not much water, grass is spotty. No elk or moose or buffalo, so no wolves or grizzly. Hell, I haven't even seen a jackrabbit."

She wiggled closer to him. He did not send her away and she stopped before her leg touched his.

"We need some game. Dried meat is nearly finished."

She admired his stillness against the night. After a long silence he rose and retrieved his stargazing instrument. She scowled at the thing.

In the morning she saw a scrawny rabbit and soon after a lone coyote loped along a ridge. When he sighted them, he disappeared behind the knoll. Soon after, Jake stopped and made his calculations. Emma could no longer contain her resentment, when he returned carrying his chronometer mounted in a padded box.

"When are you going to tell me why you are out here?"

"That's none of your affair."

She blinked, her expression unchanged. "So you have said, but when we reach a Mexican settlement, I would think they might have some questions."

"I'll handle that." He shoved his journal in his saddlebag with more force than necessary.

"Of course, but did it occur to you that they might question me, as well?"

His posture went rigid and his gaze turned cold. She tried to control herself, but her heart leaped as if she needed to run. She kept her seat as he strode the three paces that separated them, swallowing her fear before continuing.

"And if they do, did it further occur to you that my story and yours might not be in complete alignment?"

He stared up at her as she watched his nostrils flare. He was angry, no doubt about it. Surely he'd shout at her now. What if he ordered her away? A gripping panic seized her and suddenly she could not catch her breath.

"All right. We'll talk when we make camp."

Emma's breath came back in a rush. Had she won? She had—he'd agreed to tell her something. She blinked at him as he mounted, still amazed that she had stood her ground and won. It wasn't until much later, she realized she was smiling.

Jake shot a small antelope late in the afternoon and busied himself with skinning and trimming the creature. Emma's pleasure faded as she considered all the possibilities that might bring a man alone into the wilderness. Whatever he was about, it was dangerous.

They camped against a wall of sheer rock. Emma unpacked the horses and mule while Jake prepared the fire and set the two flanks of the antelope to roast on a spit. Throughout the preparation and the meal, Jake cast her glances as if she had grown a second head. At last he finished his enormous portion and eased back, then he rubbed his hands together as he regarded her with a twinkling bright gaze. She held her breath in anticipation waiting.

"I thought by not involving you, I might protect you, also I'm under orders to maintain secrecy. But you are involved, willing or not, and your ignorance puts us at risk."

"Ignorance of what?"

"I'm a spy."

The air rushed from her lungs. He could not have surprised her more thoroughly if he had told her he had been raised by wolves.

"A what?"

"Well, I suppose I am not officially a spy until we enter Mexican territory, after we cross the Sierra Nevada. Until then, I'm just a cartographer and surveyor."

"I knew you made maps."

"Trouble is the Spanish cannot know. They must think I am a hunter, like Jed Smith. They were mighty ticklish at him popping up in their territory last year. Until then, they felt secure in their knowledge that the overland route was impossible."

"For whom are you spying?" She found herself leaning so far forward her face grew hot from the nearness to the fire.

"The president."

"President of what?" She stared in confusion and then a thought dawned. Oh, no—not *the* president. "Not of the United States!"

He nodded and her mouth went dry. Who was this stranger

before her? This man, she thought she knew, but did not. She didn't know anything.

"I'm to categorize flora and fauna, as well, though that's your job now. I can't render creatures."

Emma thought of all the sketches of badgers, prairie dogs, marmots and antelope she had created since he'd handed over that journal to her. Her eyes widened and her voice escaped in a squeak. "I'm a spy, too."

His laugh did not reassure her. "No, but traveling with one is nearly the same. If they discover my purpose, they'll hang me."

Her stomach dropped several inches as this thought landed in her belly like a blacksmith's anvil.

"Oh, no."

His easy smile did not seem the expression of a man facing the noose.

"Why did you tell me?"

"You've earned it." Jake drew out his journal and held it between his two large hands, making a human binder for his precious pages. "The information in this log will open the West. Jackson wants California. I mean to give it to him."

The world seemed to be tilting badly beneath her. Emma rocked back, bracing herself against the solid stone behind her. Jake was not a hunter or trapper or even a scout. She knew he'd been charting a course. The truth had been obvious, even to her inexperienced eyes. But never had she for one instant thought that this man, whom she had believed to be a trapper of some sort, was an agent of the President of the United States.

Considering him with emerging awe, she wondered why she had not. He could read, map, cipher, scout and spoke more dialects than she could count on both hands. The man was supremely suited to this exact mission, as if he'd been born for it.

"Stop looking at me as if I sprouted wings."

She realized then, that her mouth hung open. With effort, she drew herself together and attempted to put her thoughts to words.

"But you have. I don't know you."

He chuckled at that. "How does anyone know anyone? I thought I knew your father. Now, I wonder."

She considered this. Public lives, private lives—secrets and truths.

"Why tell me now?"

"You've nearly got it figured, anyway, and I trust you."

His words brought a strange aching pride to her. No one ever trusted her with anything more important than fetching water. "I'm honored."

"Don't be. I've put you in danger. If I could think of a single way to keep you clear of this entire business, I'd jump on it like a grizzly on a newborn elk."

She lowered her head. "I wasn't part of the plan."

"Nope."

Emma lifted her gaze to meet his as comprehension dawned. He could have left her with the Crow, should have, in fact. Her life was not as important as this task he undertook. Her presence jeopardized his mission. Suddenly she understood the surliness, the resentment. He didn't hate her. He protected her, adopted her and took her along even when doing so slowed him down. What would her father have done in a similar situation? The answer came immediately, sending a shiver of certainty down her spine. He would have left her behind.

But not Jake.

He could have left her in the mountains or in the desert. Instead, he'd done his best for her.

"I'm sorry."

His smile never touched the sorrow in his eyes. "Don't know why—wasn't your doing to cross that burial ground. Never thought to admit it, but I've enjoyed your company. But we're near Mexican Territory now. I've been puzzling over what to do next. I had a story figured. I'm not sure the Spanish will believe it now."

"What were you going to tell them?" She drew up her knees

and rested her chin on her palm as she studied him. He impressed her the first time she'd laid eyes on him. But now—the man risked his life for his country. He went alone into the wilderness to blaze a trail for others. How she admired him.

"I'm the lone survivor of an attack by the Mojave Indians. The rest of my party was killed. I lost everything, but my horse and mule. With certain death behind me and possible death ahead, I chose the desert. I recalled that Jed Smith made it across, so I figured I'd try."

"Sounds convincing. But now you have me."

"Yeah. Trappers don't travel with women. Another thing you should know. I'm following Jed Smith's footsteps, after a fashion. We're on a different path, but it leads to the same place. You, on the other hand, are going where no other of your gender has ever been. To my knowledge, no white woman ever crossed the divide. Certainly none has ever crossed that desert."

He let that sink in. A glowing pride kindled by his words rose within her. Despite the weeks of deprivation, she felt stronger than ever in her life. What she did now held importance beyond herself.

"Trouble is this mission is so secret that if we do make it home, no one must ever know. There will be no parade waiting for us, like for Lewis and Clark. You understand, Emma? You'll have to live your life without telling a soul of what you accomplished."

Her first thought was that no one would ever believe her. Her second? Neither one of them would survive, so it would not matter. But what if they did? Could she keep her silence? Her answer came with certainty.

"If I live through this, I most assuredly can hold my tongue."

His eyes held doubt. "Women are not known for that particular quality."

"Nor are men known for sacrificing duty for compassion. But here I sit as living proof that a man can live counter to his nature."

"You're a most unusual woman, Emma. You know that?"

She waved a hand at him, brushing away the compliment like bread crumbs from her table. "How will you explain your equipment?"

"Most trappers carry a spyglass."

"The Spanish would recognize the instruments of mapmaking."

"I'll stow some in a dry spot, but the rest—I need some of my equipment to finish the map."

Emma nodded. "Is there anything else that might give you away?"

"Other than you?"

She recognized the teasing tone, but his words were true. They cut into her heart. "I do not want to put you at risk. Perhaps you can stow me, as well."

His eyebrows shot up and she recognized that this was one possibility he had not considered. She waited in silence as a mantle of cold dread fell over her shoulders. How the thought of abandonment terrorized her. But she would not beg to be dragged along. She could do this small thing to help him succeed. A quick shake of his head decided the matter.

Her insides went liquid from the tiny gesture. She was glad she was not standing, for certainly her knees would have buckled.

"We'll stay together, but everything that could be associated with the army will be destroyed."

Her coat. She fingered the dark wool, buttons flashing in the firelight as comprehension dawned. Any hint of a military operation would be the kiss of death.

"Of course."

"Everything."

"I understand. You can search all my gear. I'll burn it all."

"Not just your gear, Emma."

She stared at him, wondering why his mouth now looked so grim. He glanced over her shoulder at the horses and a lightning bolt of understanding struck. Tears sprang to her eyes.

"Not Scout," she cried. She stumbled the distance toward her trusted friend. She'd rescued him from slaughter at Fort Leavenworth and secured the commander's permission to care for him. She was the only one who could manage him which was why he'd been deemed expendable, unworthy even to carry gear. In all the bitterness and despair that was her life, Scout gave her a place to pour her heart's sorrow. The troubles that she'd never told a soul were whispered into his cavernous ears. Those ears pricked as if aware she had something important to say. She turned to Jake who stood beside the creature's hindquarters. Her hand rested on the soft velvet of his powerful neck. "Please, not Scout."

Jake ran a hand over the horse's flank pausing at the deep scar on his rump. "He's branded."

"We could brand him again, to cover it."

He shook his head. "Too risky. A sharp eye would notice a double brand."

Emma's gaze fixed on the dark scar tissue forming the bold block letters, U.S. There would be no explaining away a horse branded by the United States cavalry and no alternative other than to turn back and keep her horse. She swallowed the lump that occluded her throat.

Jake rested a hand on her shoulder. She curled against him, blinking away the hot splash of tears. One strong arm cradled her shoulders, but he did not draw her in. She felt a new tension in him now. He seemed reluctant to comfort her. If she were to help him, she must be stronger than this. She bit her lip and drew several rapid breaths in a supreme effort to gather her emotions before stepping away. She nodded her head in acceptance. He would shoot her horse.

Jake lifted his hat and scratched his head, considering. "Maybe I'll just drive him off."

Relief washed through her.

"Once we get out of this useless territory, we'll go through your kit. As for right now, I want to get to and over those mountains."

"You talk as if you can see them." Emma gazed west into the darkness.

"I feel like I can. You'll see them, too, tomorrow."

He was right, as usual. By late morning the blue outline came into view, creeping up the horizon as they journeyed west. The following day, she made out the snowcaps and uncertainty gnawed at her. At last, she could stand it no longer.

"There's snow already," she said, trying to sound very rational.

"High up the ice never melts away. You're looking at last year's snowfall. It's packed down so tight you could drive a team of oxen over the ice. The new snow is what's treacherous. When it comes, it falls fast and furious. A man could get trapped up there under maybe twenty feet of snow. Just buried alive."

She could not suppress the shudder that rocked her shoulders.

He laughed. "We're still down here in the desert. No need to put on your coat just yet."

When he stopped at noon to make his recordings, she held the horses without resentment. As she watched him, she felt pride to be of some small help as he went about his work. When he returned to her, cupping the green leather cover of his journal in his confident hand, she beamed at him. His mouth quirked, but his eyes showed a wary watchfulness that reminded her of a lone wolf.

Jake found water more easily now and by the fifth day they sat at the foot of the mountains. Even as they made their way up the easy slope of the foothills, Emma kept her gaze focused on the peaks that now towered above her.

When Jake stopped to take measurements, she drew down her journal and diligently recorded the landscape about them. She sketched the stark relief of the jagged vista, taking no romantic liberties of rearranging the view to better suit her ideas of composition. Now she rendered all she saw with the utmost accuracy.

When Jake completed his readings, she was not quite done. He paused to watch her work. When she finished, she handed him the sketch.

"Damn near perfect. This record might be as useful as the maps." He traced the outline of her sketch of the ridgeline with his index finger and cast a glance up at the mountains. "My maps don't show topography." He flipped through her work and nodded. "Excellent." He returned the pad. "Keep up the good work."

She glowed inside like a coal banked in ash. His Spartan praise pleased her enormously. Her life had been filled with few moments when her value was noted.

The pleasure stirred by his words carried her as they traveled from the foothills to the first pass. She wondered how he knew which trail to take? The animal paths crisscrossed all about them and, by his own admission, he had never been west of the desert, but he moved as if he knew every inch of the way.

When the deer trails vanished he followed the narrow path of mountain goats. Emma watched the creatures loping up the rock as they drew close. They climbed the increasing grade throughout the cold, dry afternoon until they reached the snow line.

The horses' hooves bit into the grainy ice. The crunching reminded her of the sound made when she ground dried bread into crumbs. At first the granular snow thinly covered the ground, leaving large bare patches, particularly in the deep valleys. Emma frowned as she noted the large rocks and gravel filling the gaps.

Jake followed the direction of her gaze.

"Avalanches," he said. "In the spring, the ice beneath the snow breaks loose and sends the entire mess down the mountain like a giant sled, ripping anything not anchored tight as it goes. I've seen one. Sounded like thunder and looked like a rolling wave of white."

Emma cast her eyes to the left and right, now feeling the menace of the snow resting above them and congratulating herself on making the crossing in the fall and not springtime until she realized that when she next saw this pass, it would *be* spring.

The flutter in her belly accompanied an outbreak of cold

sweat on her face. *You have to cross over them first, before you worry about returning.*

By twilight, ice covered the world. Even without the sun, the surface glowed a ghastly blue-white as they crunched along over snow of which she was quite happy not to know the depth. As the hour to stop came and went, Emma wondered if they would travel all night. Her joints grew stiff and her bones ached with the biting cold.

She drew out her lion skin and draped it over the wool coat. The hide cut the wind considerably. As they went, she blew on her hands when she could no longer feel the reins. Jake's horse plodded on, her neck bent wearily. They crossed a ridge, avoiding the peak and then beginning their descent. She smiled in relief. That had not been so bad. It was some time later that she realized they were headed up once more.

He rested at daybreak. Emma slid from her saddle as a weariness too great to name gripped her with the cold. Numb with fatigue, she fumbled with the girth and then dragged her saddle from Scout. Her horse nudged her in a motion designed to extort a treat.

She rubbed his muzzle. "Sorry, boy. No carrot today."

If anyone deserved a carrot, it was her horse. If she was weary from riding, how tired must he feel? With sorrow, she realized he was as hungry as she, likely more; she at least had dried jerky.

Jake brought his hat. She peered inside surprised to see water. Her water skin froze hours ago and she could not imagine how he kept his liquid.

"Oh, thank you."

Scout stuck his nose in the hat, sucking the fluid. Once empty, Jake added grain and waited while her horse munched.

"He's trying to eat my hat again." Jake pulled it away.

"I'm about ready to do the same."

He offered her a kind of dried biscuit and more jerky.

The bread required considerable gnawing. When she finished, her jaw ached from the effort. He handed her a horn cup full of water.

"How did you manage this?"

"Kept a flask against my belly."

She paused, the cup hovering at her lips, not understanding why her heart should choose this moment to race, sending blood pounding like hoof beats in her ears. The image of a flask, pressed warm and tight against his flat stomach made her own stomach flip and flop like a pancake on a hot griddle.

"What's wrong?" he asked.

It was then that she realized she stood frozen, like the ice about her, the cup still perched on her lips. She turned her wrist and noted the water's warmth as it slid down her throat. She handed back the cup, wondering if he noticed her rapid breathing.

He did.

"Are you ill?"

"Yes, no—oh, I don't know. I'm…exhausted." What a twit.

"We'll rest here a bit and leave by noon."

That would be only a few hours. The air felt very cold, but she recognized the temperature was much milder than it had been during the night. They would have less trouble keeping warm now.

"I only have one buffalo robe. We'll share it."

Suddenly she imagined herself tucked safe and tight against the warmth of his stomach, just like the water flask. Ridiculous to be jealous of the silly vessel, but she was. They had not rested together since the Rockies, in fact he avoided touching her since their kiss. Now necessity forced him to her once more and she was glad.

He shook out the heavy robe and she added her blanket. Over this he draped his wolf-hide cloak. He climbed in without removing a stitch of clothing.

"Should I take off my boots?"

"Leave everything on. It will keep you warmer."

She slid in beside him, disappointed at the cool feel of their

bed. Overcome by cold and exhaustion, Emma inched closer
to the heat she craved.

He didn't send her away. Instead he rolled them to their sides
and pulled her flush against him. Her back lay against his chest
and her bottom, oh my, her backside was now pressed inti-
mately to his nether regions. The warmth of his thighs found
her first, seeping through the folds of her skirt and petticoats.
Gradually she stopped shivering and her breathing slowed.
Who would have believed that on this frozen mountain, she
would find such warmth? Safe in the harbor of his embrace she
gave a sigh.

"Don't get used to it," he said.

She tensed. Did he think she was throwing herself at him
again? Perhaps she was. Her mind was divided. If she did not
want to give a man dominion over her person, why did she long
to sleep in Jake's arms?

Chapter Ten

Jake knew he should make her a proper coat of buffalo. But with the desert and the amount of snow on the mountains, he felt the pressure of time. Also, he had seen no buffalo since he had left the eastern side of the Rockies.

He hadn't realized how cold she'd grown until they stopped and he discovered her blue lips. Why hadn't she said something?

He never knew a woman to be so strong. Helen once had a splinter in her finger and you would have thought she was dying. The wails only got worse when he tried to dig it out.

Jake lowered his chin to the top of Emma's head. She never said a word.

If he left her to that ridiculous woolen blanket, she would freeze to death. It was easier to just drag her under his buffalo robe and warm her with his body. Her teeth clattered a long while, but at last she quieted, the trembling ceased and she fell into slumber. Tired as he was, he found sleep eluded him. He knew his body was exhausted, so why then did he feel this gnawing tension tugging at his gut. He sighed, drawing in a breath of cold air, laced with the scent he now recognized as Emma's, sweet and light as meadow flowers.

The reason for his tension lay beneath his nose. Why did she have to be stoic and understanding and so damn brave?

It was enough to drive a man crazy. He stared at the inside of his own eyelids for quite a while, enumerating the reasons he needed to keep clear of her while his traitorous body pressed her close. This would be so much easier if she only had some irritating habits like sucking her teeth or drumming her fingernails.

The trouble was that he found everything about her appealing. Just the shape and feel of her body was enough to bring a lesser man to heel. But Emma wielded weapons more dangerous, like a gentle heart and a brave spirit. She seemed to have embraced his mission to the point that she had offered to stay behind to help him succeed.

What other woman would offer to stay alone in the wilderness for any reason? He could not fathom her. She contradicted all his hard-won understanding about her gender.

Just think about what would happen if you did take up with her, he told himself. How long before she'd demand he settle down? That little band of gold gave a woman ideas that you were bought and paid for.

Perhaps if he just bedded her once, he could get her out of his system. She sighed in her sleep and snuggled close. He groaned. The stupidity of his idea hit him in the groin. Once would never be enough. He wanted her. He admitted it, but that did not mean he wanted to marry her.

To offer less than marriage would be to insult an honorable woman. He had too much respect for Emma to do anything that would shame her. Besides, she might not even want to take up with him. Perhaps he should ask her what she planned to do if they made it east, just to see what she said. He remembered the day she asked him the same question and he snapped at her like a mud turtle.

She scooted down and the swell of her breast brushed his arm. His breathing stopped and he tensed, resisting the urge to measure the size and shape of her with his hand. Instead, he groaned and rolled away, putting his back to her. But she followed him even in her sleep, slipping her small arms about his waist and pressing her bosom to his back. It was in this position that sleep finally relieved him.

When the sun came to its zenith, he awakened to discover his body fully aroused before he even opened his eyes. His little miss now curled about him like ivy, one leg thrown over his and her slender arm threaded beneath his own to drape familiarly across his belly.

His pulse pounded in his groin and the sunlight burned his eyes. He patted her wrist and she gave a groan, nestling farther into her burrow. Jake knew he must get up immediately or drag her underneath him. He threw off the buffalo robe welcoming the blast of cold air. He grabbed the water skin he'd slept on like a pillow to keep it from freezing.

Moving away from Emma proved more difficult than he'd admit. Like two magnets, pulling together, she seemed to draw him with invisible force. The farther he walked the weaker the hold, until he felt truly free at last. Glancing back, he saw the robe frosted with ice like the top of a cake, the fragile layer broken and missing on his side.

He fed and watered the horses. Scout flattened his ears at Jake's approach, but called a temporary truce when he saw the oats in his hat. Jake considered the animal as he munched his breakfast. He meant to shoot the horse when they reached the valley. By that time, much of the provisions he'd packed would be depleted and he could move Emma to his remaining packhorse. It was a shame to waste such a magnificent animal, but not worth the risk to have the beast arrive in Monterey with the U.S. brand on his flank. He'd been about to tell Emma when he glanced at her.

Damn women and their tactics. His resolve melted with her tears and he folded like a house of cards. He should have told her what would happen and why, and then dealt with the wailing. Now he didn't know if he should let the gelding loose then track it and shoot it without her knowing or trade it to Indians and pray they kept well east until after he was away in the springtime.

The horse finished his meal and his ears flattened again, indicating the truce ended.

"I ought to put a bullet between your eyes right now."

The horse blew hot air as if daring him to try.

He saddled Duchess and readied the packhorse and mule. He knew from experience that her mount would not let him anywhere near with a saddle. Not fancying a kick, he waited for Emma.

She staggered to her feet a short time later. He gave her privacy as she disappeared behind a boulder for a few minutes.

When she emerged, her eyes were completely open, if bloodshot, and she smiled as if the few stolen hours were a full night's rest.

"Good morning."

He nodded, not mentioning that it was well into the afternoon and wondering if she knew that her bangs lifted up like the comb of a rooster. Somehow made her look more endearing. A tiny tug pulled at his heart as he savored seeing her rise warm and rumpled from his bed. It was a sight only a husband knew.

That thought brought him up short. She hadn't collared him yet. He rolled the bedding as if the hides were responsible for his upset and then looped the wolf skin over his shoulders once more, changing it from blanket to cloak with one piece of rawhide. She wore the lion cape and he paused to pull the hood up over her head. She cast a dubious glance at the fangs now nestled in her hair and sighed, emitting a wisp of white steam.

"Suits you," he said, thinking the honey color of her hair echoed the tawny yellow of the hide. She said nothing, only set her lips together in a tight line as he looped the arms of the fur around her neck. The golden trade beads caught the light and he smiled at his scowling partner. Diana, goddess of the hunt, was angry.

When Emma was mounted, he helped drape the buffalo robe over her shoulders, determined that she stay warm this final day in the mountains. By evening they would reach the edge of the snowfield, descending into the thick pines. Tonight he planned to give himself no excuse for sleeping double. The experience was too hard on him.

As they rode along he pictured the line of oxen lumbering up the steep slopes and down the rocky inclines. An unforgiving trip, dangerous and difficult, he decided—but possible.

They crossed along a ridge that gave a glimpse of the valley still far below them. He paused at the sight. The vista took his breath away. Behind him, Emma gasped and said, "Oh, my."

Across the valley stood half of a magnificent gray granite mountain cleaved in two by some ancient forces too great to fathom, leaving a steep escarpment. He was thankful they didn't have to descend from that side, then admitted to himself that this lip of the canyon looked equally challenging, with no obvious path to the valley floor. His attention fell next to a waterfall, cascading hundreds of feet in a thin ribbon of silver. Another smaller falls broke in two places on its drop.

Emma pulled up beside him. "Look how beautiful."

His gaze lifted from the valley to the mountains beyond. None were snowcapped, instead ridges of granite poked naked from the pines covering the lower reaches. He pondered their route.

"I have to draw this," Emma said, already sliding from her saddle.

"Don't forget the mountains beyond. I have to pick a course. Once in the valley, I won't have this perspective."

He dismounted and made compass readings of various peaks recording their locations in his journal. Emma took the opportunity to sketch the trail ahead as it sloped sharply downward. He glanced at the sky. Darkness loomed. They'd never make the valley by nightfall. Best to finish the drawings and measurements and then return the way they came. Tomorrow he would begin again following animal trails to the river he saw far below his feet. When Emma spoke, it startled him.

"How's this?" Emma turned the page to him.

He glanced from the drawing comparing it to its source, and nodded at the accuracy of detail. "Damn good."

"Imagine what I could do with my watercolors." She gave a melancholy sigh as she considered the sketch. "Will we head down now?"

"Too dangerous in the dark. We'll backtrack to the meadow."

In a few minutes he chose a spot and left Emma to unpack the horses while he scouted the area. He found little game and no sign of Indians. Finally, he shot a groundhog and brought his meager offering to Emma.

She seemed delighted to have it.

"I'm so tired of dried meat!"

A hearty fire awaited him, a neat pile of wood lay stacked nearby and his buffalo robe beyond. He frowned, noting she made only one bed. He glanced at her and raised an eyebrow.

"The buffalo robes are so much more comfortable on the ground and warmer than my blanket. Is it a terrible inconvenience?"

He gritted his teeth wondering if she had the faintest inkling of what she put him through each time she cuddled against him beneath the robes. He looked at the hopeful innocence of her expression and decided she did not.

"It is an inconvenience." His determination wavered as Emma's expression turned forlorn. "Damn it, this is the last time, understand? And I'm killing the next buffalo I see. You need your own bedding. This isn't proper."

She raised her hands in supplication. "But nothing unseemly has occurred. You've been the perfect gentleman."

He stepped forward menacingly. "That won't be the case if you keep crawling into my bed like my squaw. There's a limit to my restraint."

Her eyes went wide at this and she swallowed hard. Good, let her feel uncertain for a change.

"After tonight, if you come to my bed, it will not be for sleep. Understand?"

She stepped away and nodded vigorously. He busied himself with skinning and dressing the groundhog. She did not speak, trying unsuccessfully to become invisible again. He'd seen her do this before. Whenever he grew angry, she backed down and disappeared, staying small and silent. He'd never seen anybody do that. He remembered what she'd said about her father's bullying and grew regretful. She'd been cold last night. Tonight would likely be cold again. It wasn't really her fault she didn't have the proper gear for a trip she never expected to make. He rubbed his beard and considered her, sitting with her eyes downcast, her mouth grim as she worked silently upon her sketch by firelight.

He checked the meat and found it cooked.

"Emma, what do you do when your father hollers at you?"

Her chin trembled and she fixed her gaze on him. He stayed relaxed and still as she regained control of herself.

"Usually I try to escape to my bedroom or the stables and stay clear of him until his temper cools."

"But that's not possible here."

She shook her head. "No."

"Did you ever stand up to him?"

Her gaze fell to the fire and he knew the answer before she spoke. "I've wanted to. I've imagined it, but I never found the courage. He's so intimidating."

Jake thought back and decided her father did have a certain menacing bearing and critical expression. "Any of his men ever face him down?"

"Not to my knowledge."

"What about your mom?"

She hesitated and he noted the catch in her voice. "Once. He turned his temper on me. She stepped in. He hit her across the face and told her never to interfere again."

Jake's insides tightened with anger he had no means of dispersing. "What happened then?"

"He turned on me and she stepped in again. He slapped her

so hard her ear bled. After that she stopped speaking for a while."

"Your father should be horsewhipped." Her look of hopelessness nearly undid him. It took all his strength not to gather this woman in his arms. The urge to protect her blazed to life like nothing he'd ever experienced. He was lost in the power of his hatred and that worried him.

He forced his attention to the groundhog, slicing away the meat with his knife. They ate in silence as sparks lifted into the night sky, winking out like fireflies. After the meal, there was nothing to do but go to bed. He told her to go first as he had some mathematical equations to complete. The truth was that he could not stand this tension between them and hoped if she fell asleep first, it might be easier for him to find his own rest.

He opened his journal and concentrated on calculating the longitude as her skirts rustled on the grass. She left the circle of fire, fading into the night. He listened carefully until she returned cast in the orange light of the flames. Their gazes met and his insides tensed. Her glance fell away and she sank to the ground, slipping beneath his buffalo robe.

Never had he shared a bed with a woman and not made love to her. Having Emma beside him and denying himself the bliss he knew they would surely share made his body stiffen in preparation for what could not be. Considering the pleasure he could bring her drove him into the night. He walked back to the ridge. Darkness now marked the valley below and above him the stars winked. Somewhere to the left an owl screeched. He lay on the granite and located the constellations. Polaris marked the Big Dipper, pointing the way to the Little Dipper. There was Orion's belt and the Great Bear. When his body grew cold as the rock beneath him, he surrendered. Surely she must be asleep by now. He stalked silently to camp and found the logs he'd stacked on the fire had collapsed upon themselves. He added more and then climbed beneath the robe.

He hesitated wondering what was wrong. He listened and

realized immediately. Emma was not asleep. Oh, she lay quiet and still, her breathing coming in even strokes, but it was not the same as when she slept. He was as familiar with the light sigh she made while dreaming as he was with his own face. Damn her, he'd given her plenty of time.

Should he speak to her? Ask her what troubled her mind to keep her awake? Then he considered that it might be the same thing that nagged at him. That thought brought his teeth clamping together like the steel of a sprung trap. He'd not ask her a thing. Not when the answer might make him do something he'd regret tomorrow and likely for the rest of his life. This was the last time, damn her, that she'd share his bed.

He settled in, resting his head on the water skin. Above him pine boughs waved in the light breeze making the stars appear to blink on and off. If she could stand it, he could. How long he lay rigid, beside her he did not know. At last her breathing slowed to sleep. He let go a huge sigh and tumbled after her.

He woke feeling more exhausted than when he crossed the desert. He needed sleep. Something had to change. What were the chances of finding a buffalo today, he wondered as he rolled the skins. No matter, he'd give her this robe. Better to freeze than lay warm next to a woman his body hungered for more strongly than food.

The strain between them continued to dog him as he broke camp and headed out. The day went badly. Rain fell hard all morning. Two of the trails he chose were impassable and they had to backtrack. He began to wonder if there was any way into the valley, when a deer path on the southern rim appeared promising. By midafternoon the rain stopped and shortly afterward they reached the river.

In the valley lay a large open meadow with a narrow snaking river threading through the center. Wildflowers bloomed in orange and yellow beside the pines that ringed the clearing. The falls seen from the rim now overwhelmed them. Water cascaded down the gray cliffs to join the river sending rainbow mist into the air. Looming over all was the great granite half dome, standing guard like the captain of the valley.

"I've never seen such a perfect place. If I were a man, I'd build a cabin here and never leave this valley."

He stared at her in stunned silence. If she were a man? What rubbish was this? He lifted the water skin, preparing to drink.

"But you are not. So what will you do?"

She stared up at the waterfall. "Take a bath."

He choked on the water. She smiled as he sputtered.

"Stay here," she said.

"No. I haven't scouted this valley yet."

"All we've seen so far is deer and elk."

"You follow me. If it is safe, you'll have your bath."

She rested a hand on her hip and scowled. "With you watching?"

"Is that an invitation?"

Her face reddened. "Most certainly not!"

He thought her objection was too fast and too final. He stared at her and her ears pinkened. The little miss was considering it.

"First we scout the valley."

The size of the area made the job impossible, so he only traveled up the hollow to her waterfall. The way was rocky, but passable. There was no sign of Indians or grizzly. Once satisfied, he pulled up beside an eddy large enough for bathing. "You can use this one and I'll move upstream and do the same."

"How do I know you won't spy on me?"

He laughed. "Since I am a spy, I guess you don't."

He did not wait for her answer, but pressed his heel to Duchess's ribs and continued along with the packhorse and mule.

The sound of her scream brought him up short. He spun in his saddle and stared back, his rifle already drawn. Emma stood in the pool, her skirts up to her knees. His gaze latched on to a slim white calf before she dropped her skirts. He shook his head and sheathed his rifle.

She shrugged apologetically. "The water is like ice."

"Where do you think it comes from?" he asked, letting her work out the equation.

Understanding dawned. "The ice in the mountains above us."

"Right." He turned to go. He needed to be close enough to hear her scream, but far enough to not hear her splashing. Up ahead he found the place and slid from the saddle. He laid his buckskin carefully on the rocks, deciding he needed to find some clay with which to clean them. He turned his attention next to his beard, trimming it with his knife and then retrieving his shaving soap and razor. The blade took some time to sharpen, but he brought it around. He used the same soap to wash his torso and privates. Damn, but she was right about the water. Just like bathing in a glacier.

A soft bit of buckskin drew the cold water from his skin, as he shivered. Once dry he stretched out naked on a rock to sun himself like a snake, knowing how long women took with their ablutions. He closed his eyes enjoying the warmth of the stone beneath him and the sunshine dancing on his closed eyelids.

Chapter Eleven

Emma kept her eye on Jake until he disappeared beyond the large boulders littering the stream. Last night he had confirmed her suspicion. He felt the same attraction she battled daily, struggling against the urge to touch and be touched. It made no sense. He was every bit as overbearing as her father. Why in the world should she be attracted to such a man?

The mule moved behind the rocks following his master and she deemed it safe to remove her damp clothing. She paused to sit on a rock and soaked her toes in the ice water finding the frigid temperatures refreshing on her aching feet. Lingering like this would be heaven, but there was no telling when he would return. So she stripped out of her clothing, hanging her damp skirt on a bush to dry and dropping the rest in a heap on the rock. How she longed to wash them, but then she would have nothing to wear, although she could wash her drawers and two petticoats. They would not be noticed. Well, of course they would, drying on a rock. Would he think that improper, as well?

Last night, cold and fatigue had driven her to set only one bed. But when he had told her there was a limit to his patience she'd understood that deep within her, in a place she did not understand, she craved him more than warmth. If she was completely honest with herself, she would admit that she wanted to lay

wrapped in his arms, warmed by his embrace. She even wanted
him to kiss her again. Despite the certainty that she did not want
to marry, he stirred places she could not seem to contain.

If she succumbed again to such weakness, he'd told her
what to expect. The prospect terrified and intrigued. What
would it be like to be loved by such a man? Her shoulders shivered and she tried to blame the frigid water. Then shook her
head in defeat. How long could she resist him?

Think of something else. She decided to wash her shirt, and
drawers and in short order they lay out on the warm rocks and
draped over bushes to dry. She did not have enough resolve to
plunge into the water and instead sat on the flat rock, while she
wetted, soaped and rinsed her body in sections leaving her hair
for last. One invigorating dunk and she scrubbed the soap into
her hair. Three more and the soap rinsed away. By the time she
was finished she shivered all over.

She drew on her damp shirt and one petticoat. Her hair, now
in a tangle, took a good deal of time to comb. When she finished, her arms ached. Finally, she slipped into her skirt and
nearly dry shirt, feeling slightly odd without her drawers.

Satisfied at last, she glanced up the trail and saw no sign of
Jake. She allowed herself a moment to sit in the sunshine of a
warm afternoon. The light breeze made short work of drying
her thin chemise and bloomers. She donned the clean wardrobe
with a sigh of pleasure. Then she replaced the shirt. Her hair
took longer to dry, so she left it unbound.

Still Jake had not returned. The roar of the falls drowned out
all other sound, so she could not hear him. She called his name
and waited. She packed up her dry clothing. Niggling concern
at last pointed her feet up the path beside the stream, leading
Scout around rocks and beneath pine boughs.

Emma found his horse and mule first and left Scout with
them. She called again and then broke cover to step out onto
the bank of the stream. Before her the water rushed and bubbled. A flash of panic flooded through her as she considered

that Jake might have been swept away, but he would have landed in her pool, surely.

Then she saw a flash of white and found him lying naked as a newborn on a rock in the sunshine. She gasped. Had he fainted or was he injured? She rushed to him, marking only vaguely the long, lean legs and flat stomach. Her gaze raked him, searching for some injury and instead fixed on his sex, which lay nestled in dark curly hair.

She skidded to a halt and he came awake, rolling to his feet and gripping his pistol. The barrel pointed at her abdomen. She gaped at him as recognition dawned in his eyes. He lowered the gun and turned away, snatching up his breeches. A muffled curse reached her as he dragged on the buckskin.

Then he rounded on her. "What the hell are you doing sneaking up on me?"

"I—I thought you were injured."

"Do I look injured?" He extended his hands to the side presenting his wide chest for her inspection.

Her mouth went dry and no words emerged. She shook her head. Finally she croaked, "You were laying down."

"Well, that's how I sleep. Lord knows I didn't get much last night. First you steal half my bed and now you creep up on me while I'm resting.

"I'm sorry." Her cheeks burned.

"Next time toss a pebble at me. I could have shot you."

She stood mired in mortification, wishing only for the rock beneath her feet to split open and admit her into some deep fissure. How could she have charged down here and then gaped at him? As long as she lived, she would never rid herself of the image of him upon that rock.

Then she noticed something. He looked different, more handsome if possible. The beard!

"You shaved!"

He stroked his strong jaw, sending a flock of butterflies fluttering through her belly. "We're in Mexican territory now. Mexicans don't wear beards."

"I see." But she didn't. She could not get past the dazzling beauty of him and realized that her job only grew more difficult. If not for his overbearing ways, she could almost fall in love with him. He was handsome, strong, smart and very resourceful. Also, she admired him greatly for making such a journey for his country. Well, it didn't matter, in any case. He wanted no part of her.

But that was not entirely true. He'd admitted he wanted to bed her. Another lightning bolt of awareness sped up her spine as he stepped closer. He wanted her, but not to marry. And she did not want him for a husband.

A flickering of an idea danced across her mind. An affair. She'd heard of women taking lovers. But they were married. A single woman risked a baby she could not explain. Of that much she was certain.

"Your hair looks pretty down." He stepped closer, reaching out.

Here was her chance to kiss him or move away. Indecision pinned her to the spot. He leaned forward lifting a strand of hair and bringing it to his lips. He inhaled.

"Lavender?" he asked.

She nodded.

He did not remove his hand, instead, threading his fingers through her hair until her head tipped in a position to accept his kiss.

Fear of beginning what she could not finish tipped the balance in her mind toward escape. He leaned forward, the green of his eyes seeming more brilliant than sunshine through leaves. She drew a breath.

"Please release me." Her words were the merest whisper. She was not certain she heard them herself. But his hand slid away and he stepped back. His expression was etched with confusion.

"I'm sorry." Her voice came a little stronger now. "I don't— that is, I think this would be a mistake."

His gaze pierced her. His expression reminded her of an eagle's and suddenly she felt like a fleeing rabbit. She stumbled away.

"You're right," he said. "Seeing you with your hair like that, it just did something to my insides. I had no right."

He turned to gather his shirt and tugged on his moccasins. She left him and waited by the horses, taking the opportunity to braid her hair in a tight cord. He arrived a moment later and they returned to the valley. A silent tension pulled at her throughout the early evening, as he found a snug hollow, against a rock face beside a stream to camp. Nearby, a grove of pines provided cover. It was from this spot that Emma shot an antelope. Jake seemed pleased with her again.

"A head shot. That means we can use the entire skin. We'll need several hides for clothing. But this will do for supper."

She scraped the hide, while he readied their meal. After they ate, he showed her how to prepare a mixture of brains and ash to preserve and soften the hair. He spread the concoction over the hide and rolled it up inside like the filling of a sponge cake. The process was thoroughly disgusting, but she bore it because the work took her mind off the embarrassment of their earlier encounter. She wanted his kiss, but she did not want the obligation of being his woman. Here in the wilderness, she had only just tasted freedom and she liked it. She did not know what she might do upon their return, or even if they would return. She only knew that coming and going, doing as she pleased was a cherished gift, not to be squandered by falling prey to some baser need that she did not fully understand. She recognized this lusting as the threat it was. At all costs, she would maintain her autonomy.

"Takes about three days to work. Tomorrow, we'll scout the valley and hunt."

"That sounds wonderful." She determined to find and kill a buffalo and by so doing, seize her independence.

That night she curled as close to the fire as she dared, dressed in her lion skin and wrapped in her blanket. Jake gave her a buckskin, as well, which she used as ground cover, to keep the moisture from seeping into her clothing. If she was cold, she considered it a small price to pay.

As she stared at the fire, she wondered if Jake expected her to come to him? The question bit at her as she burrowed beneath the lion skin. He'd have a long wait. Once she killed a buffalo, they would see who had the warmer bed.

Her eyelids drooped and she surrendered to her resolve to slumber. In the deep of the night she heard the wolves call. Their echoing cries brought her shivering awake. She clutched the blanket and stared past the dull glow of the dying embers into the blackness of the cloudy night. The urge to crawl to Jake's side came again, stronger this time, with the need for protection from the night's predators. She held herself apart, stubbornly refusing to move in his direction. She trembled in the rough wool of her blanket cradling her holstered pistol to her bosom. Freedom required sacrifice.

She slept fitfully. At long last birdcall signaled the dawn and she crawled out of bed, stretching. Jake fried the antelope's liver for breakfast as Emma saddled Scout and packed the horse and mule. They spent the morning riding in a wide loop around the valley at the base of the eastern cliffs. There seemed no way down other than the route Jake found on the southern edge. He took readings at noon showing Emma how to use the compass. Later, he let Emma ride point and navigate their return to camp.

"I love this valley," she said.

"This is still mountain country, high up. Inhospitable come winter, but my, it's a sight now."

"I'd put a cabin right over there." She pointed to a spot beside the stream on the low ground.

His smile disappeared. "I just told you. Come winter this valley will be snow up to here." He lifted his hand over his head. "And come spring the rising water would sweep your cabin into the river. Why are women always chattering about building cabins, anyway?"

It was the first time she'd mentioned it. The first time she'd ever found a place in which she longed to linger. She didn't understand his quicksilver moods. Men always complained that women were moody. But here they were enjoying the day one minute and now he looked positively peeved.

"I like it here."

"Well I'm not building you a cabin, if that's what you're asking." He scowled at her as if she would challenge him. A menacing smile twisted his lips. "Actually, I should build you one and leave you to it. See how you like it when you can't open your cabin door because of the snow."

"Make the door open in and I shall be able to open it regardless of the weather." Drat the man. He acted like a child.

He shook his head in disgust. "Women," he muttered, drawing Duchess to a walk.

"Men," she echoed. This brought his head around and he gave her an irritated scowl.

"What's that?"

"I was just saying I like this valley. I didn't ask you to build me a cabin or stay here with me. I don't want you to stay with me."

"Why not?" Now his expression held a touch of indignation. So he didn't want to stay here, but he also didn't want her not to want him to.

"I'm not linking up with a man."

"Looks like you already have."

"Not permanently. When I can get a chance, I most certainly plan to get clear of you."

Now he stopped his horse. "That's ridiculous. First, you have no place to go and, second, all women want a permanent arrangement with a man."

He was as irritating as sand in her boot. "Says who?"

"I do. Women want houses and children and husbands, but not in that order."

"All women?" she asked.

"Of course."

"And what do men want?"

"Peace and quiet."

"Well Mr. Turner, I am sad to say you are misinformed. This woman, for example, most certainly does not want marriage. In fact, I am heartily opposed to an institution that makes a woman no better than a slave—worse, in fact, for she has no hope of emancipation, save death."

"What are you on about?"

"Marriage. A way for a man to get a woman to pick up after him, clean his clothes, feed him and raise his children, while he enjoys his peace and quiet. A situation to be avoided at all costs."

He looked at her as if she were mad. But now she felt sane and strong and angry. He'd started this one, but she was more than ready to finish it. The blood coursed through her making her ears pound. She felt ready to strike him; he upset her so.

"That's ridiculous. All women want—"

"Not this one! This one watched her mother's marriage most closely and I will never, ever marry."

He straightened in his saddle as if unsure how to proceed against her vehemence.

"You just haven't met the right man. Sooner or later you'll want to hog-tie some beau."

"I perceive it rather the other way around and plan to avoid the noose."

"So you don't plan to marry."

"Now you begin to hear me."

"Ever."

"Correct."

"What about children?"

"What about them?"

"Don't you want children?"

She hesitated only long enough to make a face. "No."

"That's unnatural."

"Do you want them?"

"I'm a man," he said.

"I realize that. Answer the question."

"Maybe a son." He considered her. "What will you do then?"

"I only know what I won't do. I won't marry and I won't return to my father. The rest is uncertain."

"Most things are."

Chapter Twelve

Jake didn't understand it. He didn't understand her. He thought last night would be easier, with Emma sleeping on the other side of the fire. But now he missed her.

He pictured her by the waterfall and shook his head in dismay, admitting he would rather face a grizzly than Emma with her hair down. The sight made all his high ideals dissolve like lard in a hot skillet. All he could think of was kissing her and she seemed agreeable. Then *she'd* rejected him. He couldn't believe it. Never had a woman declined his advances. Most women threw themselves at him. But not his little Emma. Oh, no. She didn't want a man or marriage. Ridiculous. If he could only figure out why she'd said those outlandish things, he could understand her game.

And he was certain she played some game. Maybe it was hard to get, making him chase her. Well, he wouldn't, because if he caught her, he would love her and then everything would be ruined. So why was it all he could think about?

He spotted the herd of elk grazing by the meadow and slid from his mount. Behind him Emma did the same, without him uttering a word. He secured the horses and crept to the edge of the pines. A moment later, Emma lay on her belly beside him, taking aim.

This didn't look like the same woman who had gripped her tattered blanket against the cries of wolves. Last night she had trembled, her eyes flashing as she searched the menacing darkness. He'd been smug with confidence that she would come to him. But she hadn't.

She'd stuck it out in her thin wool blanket and in the morning told him she didn't want him. Well, he didn't want her, either.

But he did. Damn those traders for crossing sacred ground.

"Which one you aiming at?" he whispered.

"On the left, with the rack."

"Fine. On three, then." He counted down and squeezed the trigger, his shot coming with Emma's. His elk reared up and then fell hard on his side. Her target looked about a moment then sunk to his knees as blood poured from his nose. The herd sprang to motion at the gunshots and dashed away.

He stood. "Good shot! We'll be restocked inside a week."

"So soon?"

He was unprepared for the sorrow reflected in her eyes.

"I need to make you buckskin trappings. That will take some time."

Even her smile was sad.

"Time to destroy my army gear?" she asked.

He nodded.

"Even my saddle?"

"Eventually."

After skinning and butchering the elk, he guided them to camp and set about the process of smoking the thin strips of meat for travel. Finally, the fire did its work and he sat back.

"Lay out your gear so I can go over it," he said.

He proceeded to take the sheath for her knife, the holster for her pistol, jacket, boots, belt buckle, saddle blanket, cooking kit and hat.

"I need my hat," she protested.

"I'll make you one." He considered her long, dirty skirt.

"What about that?" he asked.

"What about it?"

"It's the same color as a soldier's trousers."

She lifted her chin, her gaze turning defiant. "I'll have you know I purchased this fabric in a mercantile in St. Louis."

"What's beneath the skirt?"

Her shoulders stiffened. "That is none of your affair."

He lowered his chin. "It is if there is anything army issue under there?"

"Do you think they branded me like a horse?"

He smiled. "A bit of that lion did rub off on you."

She faltered at the compliment.

"All right then," he said. "I'll take your say-so."

She inched toward her horse and her eyes misted. His ribs seemed to constrict his breathing as he watched her with her damn horse. He stifled a curse.

"Scout?"

"Soon."

The afternoon was spent smoking meat and preparing the hides. In the days that followed, they hunted together. The valley teemed with game: elk, deer, antelope and moose. He never saw the wolves, but the evidence of their scavenging on his kills was clear enough. Denuded trees told him there were grizzly about, but so far he'd avoided them.

Emma learned to use his compass to navigate and at night he even taught her how to use his sextant to measure the angle of Polaris. She learned to fashion moccasins and smoke the buckskin to make it water resistant. Gradually the green hides changed from bone-white to golden-brown and were ready for fixing. She knew how to sew and had a simple shirt finished in no time. He made himself a new pair of breeches and shirt, happy to discard the old. On the fifth day, they found a small herd of buffalo. He shot a mother and yearling calf, sure that would be enough to make a sleeping robe and a new coat for Emma.

He replaced her saddle blanket with a thick sheepskin.

She said Scout would prefer that to the coarse woolen one he wore each day. Next he created new leather reins for her bridle.

They were nearly ready.

Emma looked fine dressed in her new buckskin shirt. He'd given her trade beads and showed her how to thread them through the fringe. They flashed in the sun, red and blue.

He burned her army coat and buried the buttons, then turned to assess her transformation. Emma stood before him dressed in an ankle-length elk-skin skirt and matching fringed shirt. The strap of her new pouch and the cord of her powder horn crisscrossed between her full breasts. He admired the fringed holster he'd created for her pistol and the little pouches for her other necessaries hanging from her new belt.

"You look like a mountain man's woman."

She scowled.

"I'm not your woman."

He scratched his chin. "Suit yourself."

Jake turned to the clean tanned hide of elk. He'd prepared this skin with great care, scraping the leather very thin. He crushed ash from the fire and mixed it with a powder made from ground elk's hooves and then added water to make a kind of rough ink. He dipped the nib of his pen into the brew and began to copy at one end. Emma sat beside him sewing her buffalo coat. He was working on the Great Salt Lake, when she glanced up.

"What's that?" she asked.

"I'm copying my map."

She leaned forward to study the work as he flipped to the page in his journal recording the desert.

"It's very good. But why do you need it?"

"In case the Spanish find the journal."

Her eyes grew cautious and she sat in silence for a time. At last she could no longer contain her uneasiness. "That will be easier to find than the journal."

"Not when I'm finished with it." He focused on the work and Emma returned to lacing the great coat, but she came back to stand beside the skin several times throughout the afternoon. Once he finished he trimmed the hide and doubled the thickness, then used his awl to punch holes for the tethers.

"A bag?" she asked.

He held the leather as he would carry it.

"Very clever. You can't see the map unless you deconstruct the bag."

"That's the idea."

The next day he made a paper copy and stored it in the hollow stock of his gun. When he locked the secret compartment he found Emma's gaze upon him once more.

"What about your journal?"

"I'll hide that in my saddle."

"The sextant and clock?"

"I have to bury the chronometer, but I can store the sextant in the stock, as well."

Emma's eyes held all the apprehension she did not voice.

"Well?" he asked at last.

"What if they find it?"

Emma dawdled over packing. "I was thinking about Scout. Wouldn't this be a wonderful place to leave him?"

He shook his head. "Without other horses, he'd be easy prey for wolves. Plus, this valley is buried in snow most of the winter. He'd starve to death. Better to wait until we are out of these mountains. We'll trade him to the first Indians we see."

She gazed out at the yellow grass as if struggling to picture this place blanketed in snow.

"I'm worried about him."

And so she should be.

"Why's that?" He kept his tone casual.

"He won't let anyone ride him but me. Who would buy him?"

Jake smiled at this. "Oh, come now."

"Truly. He threw the sergeant at arms and the smithy and even the bronc buster. That's why they gelded him, but it made no difference. If anything, it made him worse."

"I'd feel the same way about it myself," he muttered.

"What?" she said.

He turned to face her. "He won't throw me."

Her expression carried doubt. "I think you should trust me on this."

"I can handle him."

He held his hand out for the reins. She tried to speak again, but he raised his hand.

"Let me take him for a ride."

Her eyes widened. "He doesn't like men and no woman but me has ever dared to mount up."

He extended his hand. She hesitated and then laid the reins in his palm. She pushed the lion head off her own and moved away. He turned his attention to Scout and smiled. He knew how women exaggerated such things.

As he placed one foot in the stirrup, Scout's head swung about. He whacked him with his hat and the gelding's head veered forward once more. Show him who is boss, he thought, gathering the reins tight, so the horse could not lower his head and buck. Then he transferred his weight to the stirrup. He got one foot halfway over the saddle before Scout erupted into wild crow hopping. Jake grabbed the saddle horn, but lost one rein in the process. That was all the leeway the big animal needed. His head dropped and his hind feet lashed the air. Twisting and bucking, Scout careened toward the rock. Jake leaned away to keep from colliding with the stone face, thus losing his center. One more buck and he sailed up and over the horse's neck. He landed heavily on his side, lifting a cloud of dust.

Scout trotted toward his mistress who gathered his reins.

"Damn," he muttered.

"If it makes you feel any better, you lasted longer than any of the others."

Jake rubbed his bruised shoulder. "It doesn't."

"You see the problem?"

He thought the gelding might make good eating, once he fattened up a bit, but he kept his opinion to himself.

"That is one ill-mannered creature."

She stroked Scout's muzzle and whispered into his ears. Jake scratched his head. He could swear the animal understood what she was saying.

Recovering his hat, but not his dignity, he headed over to where she stood between him and the brute. The picture she made standing before the huge chestnut as if her skirts might protect the creature from his retribution, made him laugh.

"I'm not going to shoot him."

She sighed, obviously relieved.

"Yet," he added.

Her look told him she was uncertain if he jested and in truth, he did not know himself. Now he had two good reasons to dispose of the animal, their safety and his pride.

"Come on," he said. "We're burning daylight."

As they climbed the western slope, he felt a tug of regret. The valley held a certain majesty and made a natural place to rest a train of wagons. The plentiful game, water and lumber made it ideal, but Jake's reluctance was not practical. It was sentimental. Here the waterfalls fell from the sky down granite cliffs high enough to brush the clouds. Here he and Emma hunted and talked and tanned leather. He wondered if he'd ever capture such a time of peace again?

The journey from the foothills took three more hard days travel. Jake picked the route and carefully noted it in his journal. At last the craggy hills dissolved into rolling lowlands. Duchess halted and tried to eat, but he steered her along the rock until he found a stream. Here he drew up.

The time of meeting grew near. He needed to dispose of Scout and her army saddle.

After the camp was set up and a fire prepared, they sat together enjoying the last of the turkey Emma had bagged the day before. Jake waited until she finished before beginning the matter at hand.

"We might see Indians tomorrow and soon we will be on land owned by the Spanish missionaries."

Emma's expression turned solemn. "We're close, then."

"Three or four days at most."

"Will you try to go unnoticed?" Her tone sounded hopeful.

"If I am caught sneaking around there will be no doubt as to my purpose. Better to approach the government officials and petition for assistance. We have to get our stories aligned exactly in case we are questioned separately."

She stared a long moment into the fire. "Funny, but for a time there, I nearly forgot why you came. The journey began to seem like a grand adventure."

"It is that. I need your help now. We must be together."

Did she understand his orders? He vowed to let nothing prevent him from completing this journey save death. Now Emma sat before him as obstacle or ally. Only she could tell.

"I'll do whatever you need."

Serious doubts rose up in his mind. She was a woman and thus a natural liar, but she must be constant, unwavering and convincing.

"Emma, I want you to tell me a lie, a whopper. I want you to make me believe you. Can you do that?"

Her eyes lifted to the night sky as she considered. Then her gaze pinned him again and she nodded. "Have I told you about my little sister, Elizabeth?"

He shook his head.

"She was born with twisted limbs. It was very sad. My father would not claim her. He refused to admit such a thing could come from his loins. He blamed Mother." Her eyes filled with tears, which hovered on the ledge of her lower lids. "He told her never to show their child in public. He wished her dead and my mother damned. Poor little lamb, it wasn't her fault."

The tears fell and Jake resisted the impulse to wrap his arms about her.

She dabbed at her eyes. "She never reached her first birthday. I suppose it was a mercy when God took her. I still mention her in my prayers each night."

Emma sat in silence as Jake considered the crippled child.

"What part was a lie?" he asked.

"All of it."

His eyes went wide. Admiration mixed with horror. She gave no indication of a lie. She sat still and straight, even crying on cue. The woman terrified him.

Emma smiled. "My mother had a stillborn child, but she was perfect. She named her Rachel."

"My God, that was good. How did you make yourself cry?"

"It's a sad story."

He shook his head in amazement.

"All right, now we need to get our stories aligned. You know much about the Bible?"

"I've read it and I attended services before coming west."

"Good. You're a missionary's wife."

She choked. "I'm married? I don't know if I can convince anyone that I am, that I've—been familiar with a man."

He scowled. "You just convinced me that you had a crippled sister."

She said nothing.

"I was trail boss for the wagon train. The Mojave killed your husband and the others. Being the boss gives me good reason to have the compass, sextant and telescope. Only my journal and the chronometer must be hidden from them."

"What was his name?"

"Whose name?"

"My husband's."

"Oh." He scratched his bare cheek, considering. "You pick."

"John Martin."

Jake's eyes narrowed. She'd chosen so quickly. "Who's John Martin?"

Her gaze dropped to the fire. "No one."

He slapped his knee. "See, now I know you're lying. You couldn't look at me. Always look them in the eye when you're lying."

Her gaze lifted and there was a dangerous glitter there.

"He asked me to marry him. But my father refused to allow the match."

He sat as if belly punched. Emma had been in love. He shook himself as if he were wet. Why should he care? He had no claim on her, nor did he want any. But he did care. The information festered like a thorn in his foot.

"Who was he?"

"An army captain. Father spoke with Colonel Leavenworth and he was transferred."

He could not keep the pleasure inside him from quirking his mouth. "You sound happy about it."

"I'm not, but I see now I did not love him, though I did admire him. I only wish to let you know why I am unwed at twenty-three."

"I thought you said you didn't want to marry?" He'd caught her in another lie.

"That's true. But there was a time when I wished to leave my father so badly that marriage seemed very appealing. Now I understand I would just be changing one bad circumstance for another."

He frowned. They were supposed to be discussing their alibi, not her old flames.

"Can we get back to the matters at hand?"

"Certainly."

He didn't like her stiff posture or the stubborn lift of her chin.

"So your husband was John Martin. He hired me to lead five wagons through the Rockies. You wanted to minister to the Nez Perce, but we stumbled into a war with the Mojave."

"The Nez Perce live too far northeast to ever war with the Mojave."

He sighed. "The Spanish won't know that. They've never been farther east than we're sitting."

She nodded. "I see."

He went on spinning the tale and had to admit that Emma noticed all weak points and filled in missing details. She gave names to all the other missionaries and even their horses. He thought that was extreme, but his memory was good and he cataloged all the details she insisted upon. He described the attack and how each man died. She wondered how long she'd been married and where and when? They camped for two days on the western slope of the Sierra Nevada and worked the story forward and backward until they matched as neatly as a pair of carriage horses.

On the morning of the third day, they headed west once more. On a ridge above a rocky meadow they came upon wild mustangs.

He turned to Emma and found her already weeping.

"I know. I have to let him go," she said.

She slid off Scout and hugged him. Scout's ears were alert as he called to the horses below. Jake first noted the stallion guarding his thirteen mares. The big dapple gray would never let another male near his harem. But what about a gelding? He didn't know. The alternative was to kill the beast and let the buzzards destroy the brand. But, he could not bring himself to shoot her horse.

She removed the saddle and then slipped the bridle from Scout's head. Her tears seemed to scald him. She laid her cheek upon the beast's forehead. Jake's chest tightened as he considered having to cut Duchess loose.

It was a hard thing.

She stepped away and Scout stood waiting. Emma lifted her arm and pushed his head toward the herd. Her hand fell away and Scout continued to stand before his mistress. Jake removed his hat and slapped the horse's rump. Scout exploded into a gallop, heading down the hill.

Jake moved beside Emma as he watched the big stallion charge forward to stop the intruder. This could be bloody. Scout would either beat the big horse, submit as a member of the herd or be run off.

The stallion reared up and kicked at Scout, who dodged him and continued toward the mares. The dapple gray cut him off, biting at his haunches. Scout kicked, but continued forward. The mares ran in the other direction over the hill and disappeared. Scout followed with the stallion in pursuit.

When they'd gone, Jake found his arm around Emma. She clung to his shirt, the fringe of his buckskin woven into her fingers.

"Will he be all right?" she asked.

He didn't think so, but kept his tongue. "Oh, yes. He's free now. Isn't that what you want for yourself?"

"But that stallion was chasing him."

"Being free isn't as easy as having someone care for you. There is more risk."

"Maybe we should follow them."

He let his arm slide away. Time for some hard truths. "They headed south. We're going west. Scout's on his own. If he follows us, I'll shoot him."

Her eyes widened. "You wouldn't."

"He puts us in danger."

She said nothing further.

He took the time to bury her saddle before loading most of the gear from the packhorse onto the mule and dividing the rest between the two remaining horses. Then he threw the sheepskin over the packhorse's withers as a temporary saddle. When he finished he found Emma still staring after Scout. She looked as if she'd lost her last friend and he considered that perhaps she had.

"You said you raised him up?" he asked.

She nodded, still staring south. "The boys at the fort in Leavenworth used to throw rocks at him because he had swollen knees. I used to wrap his legs with cold bandages. I took him to the stream and made him soak up to his belly. When his knees healed, the sergeant tried to take him back, but by then he'd only answer to me."

He scowled after the horse, hoping to have seen the last of him. When he turned to her he found she considered him.

"You hate him, too, don't you?"

"No. I don't. But I know where those wild horses come from—the Spanish. Maybe this herd is up against the mountains and they won't find them. But when they round up in the spring, someone might catch him. If they do and that horse comes to the attention of the authorities, there'll be trouble."

"We will be gone in the spring."

There was nothing to be done now in any case. "Maybe so." He pointed toward her new mount. "Come on, I'll help you up."

He held his fingers laced together like a stirrup and she placed her moccasin within. He'd done the best he could with her wardrobe. She now had Indian footwear, a wide-brimmed leather hat, her stained blue skirt and petticoats and a buckskin shirt. He thought the elk suited her. With her golden hair, the buckskin looked just right. Of course, he didn't tell her that. But he wasn't beyond noticing her calf as she swung up onto the sheepskin. She shifted her bottom and something grabbed him in the gut and twisted.

She glanced at the dirt that marked the grave of her buried saddle. She gave a long sigh, but said nothing.

"Takes some getting used to," he said.

The rest of the afternoon he felt guilty for not giving her his saddle. She never mentioned it, so why did he feel obligated? He didn't know, except perhaps that she was still his responsibility.

If not for him, she'd be dead or worse than dead by now. If not for him, she'd be riding her horse upon her saddle right now.

That evening he sighted smoke coming from somewhere ahead. He judged it to be five miles off. He pulled up and made camp in a grove of cottonwoods. All about them lay open grassland. Perfect for grazing cáttle or horses, but damn poor cover.

"No fire tonight," he said.

"I think there is enough wood," she said.

"I spotted a line of smoke ahead of us. I don't want whoever it is to know we're here just yet. Unload the gear and lay out the skins. I'm going to scout. I'll be back after dark." He dismounted only long enough to relieve Duchess of the extra gear, then started off. Then he pulled up, turning to her. She stood, clasping the reins of the mule and his packhorse. "Keep your rifle handy. When I come back I'll whistle like this." He imitated the cry of a hawk.

"I understand." She took a step closer but the reins held her up. Her serious gaze pinned him. "Be careful."

She looked as if she wanted to say more, but did not. He wheeled away, loping over the rolling hills. When he got close, he slid from the saddle and hobbled his horse. Crawling on his belly to the top of the knoll he saw he was outnumbered six to one.

Chapter Thirteen

Emma sat alert with the rifle ready upon her lap. She chose not to cock her weapon, knowing that the act took only an instant. Alone in the darkness, sound became the center of her world. The rustle of the wind through the tall grass and cottonwood leaves dominated. Occasionally, a crackling of dried leaves drew her attention as a small animal scurried through the underbrush.

The moon was in its quarter, giving just enough light to see about her, but not enough to pierce the darkness of the glade in which she waited. She wondered how Scout fared with his new companions. She knew this was best, still it hurt that he did not follow her or even glance back before disappearing. Granted, he was being chased at the time. Was he lost in the dark, as well?

If the herd rejected him, the wolves would take him. She hunched, wondering how far they were from her? Soon afterward, coyotes began their chorus and she shuddered at the bone-chilling song. If they set on her all together, what would she do? The swish of her horse's tail and the nervous sidestepping of hooves told her the animals shared her concern.

Where was the man?

Hours had passed since he'd ridden toward that blasted

smoke. Then another chilling thought struck her. What if he
didn't return?

He might be captured even now. She gripped the gun in a
hold tight enough to wring a chicken's neck. What if they tortured him?

She leaped up. The mule cast her a nervous glance, the
whites of his eyes clear in the moonlight. Jake told her to stay
put. Even if she defied him, could she find her way in the darkness? She turned a full circle unsure of which way he went.
What should she do?

Her pulse pounded in her ears, momentarily drowning out
all the sounds about her. The impulse to fire the gun came from
nowhere and she staunched the rash thought as ludicrous. Panic
would gain her nothing.

"Settle down, Emma, and think."

She forced herself down to the log, wishing she could light
a fire. Perhaps he couldn't find her in the darkness. One grove
of cottonwood looked much like another. He might just have
stopped to wait for daylight. He'd be along then.

If he wasn't, she meant to find him. Over time her breathing slowed and the cold sweat dried on her forehead. Her bottom went numb from sitting. She occupied her mind trying to
determine how many coyotes called and she came up with
seven, judging by the direction of their cries.

At last she heard hoofbeats and then the whistle of a hawk.
Duchess halted. His saddle gave a familiar creak as he dismounted.
Relief came in a long sigh as she stood stiffly to greet him.

"Emma?" he called.

She stepped out of the grove, staring at the shadowy figure.

"I'm here. Are you all right?"

She fought a battle against rushing forward and hugging
him. How she longed to touch him and assure herself all was
safe. She shifted the rifle to her right hand, pointing the barrel
to the ground as she stepped forward and settled for resting a
hand on his shoulder and giving a squeeze.

"I'm fine," he said.

"You were gone so long."

She could make out his face now, beneath the brim of his hat. His features looked drawn and his eyes blinked wearily.

"They were ten miles off. I misjudged the distance on the plain."

"Ten miles! You've ridden twenty miles?"

Even his nod was tired.

She took charge, sliding the rifle beneath her arm as she grasped Duchess's reins and his elbow. She tied the horse to a branch and steered him to the bedding laid out and ready for him. He fell in with a groan.

"Indians, six families. They have no horses, but do have metal knives and are clothed in cowhide. Appear to be living on antelope, mostly. We'll make contact tomorrow."

She realized, if not for her, he would have camped closer to them. Instead he had to ride many extra miles. No matter how she tried to be helpful, she still burdened him and cost him time and effort.

"I'm sorry I didn't come along."

He opened one eye. "I told you to stay put. Damn difficult finding this grove in the darkness, though."

"I'm glad you did. I was so worried."

He grunted. "Hate to leave you stranded. I'll always come back if I'm able."

He misunderstood her. Of course she was afraid to be left alone in the wilderness, but his safety concerned her more.

"I was worried about *you,* not me."

He smiled and patted her hand. "You want to rest here beside me awhile?"

"What about what you said, about the limits to your patience?"

He gave a rough laugh. "Emma, I'm too tired to be impatient tonight."

She smiled. "Let me just see to your horse."

"Obliged."

His breathing changed before she even had time to stand. She removed the bridle from Duchess and hobbled her. The animal did not seem eager to graze. Likely, she'd eaten as Jake scouted the Indians. His horse breathed deeply at the saddle's removal and moved beside the packhorse, taking advantage of his swishing tail to keep the flies off her face.

Emma gathered her buffalo hide and lay beside Jake. His arm snaked out and he clasped her waist, reeling her in like a fish until she pressed snug against his side. The comfort of lying in his arms was one of the great pleasures of her life. Too bad he set such conditions about her bed and his. But this night, he seemed to need her as much as she needed him. She cuddled against him and he held her tight. In a moment she was warm and safe. The coyotes' cry lost its menace and she tumbled asleep beside him.

She woke at dawn to the birdcalls and tried to rise, but Jake groaned and refused to release her, so she closed her eyes and soon slept again. The next time she woke the birds flitted through the brush. Beyond the trees, wispy clouds played across a bright blue sky.

Her attempts to slip away met with initial resistance, but then he gave up and she rose from the hides. After washing in the stream, she readied a meal of cold biscuits and leftover jackrabbit. Jake staggered up from the nest of furs and disappeared into a grove of cottonwoods. He returned to retrieve his razor and soap, then shaved by the stream.

She smiled as he appeared again, ignoring the red in his eyes.

"How'd you sleep?" he asked, not quite able to keep the smile from quirking his lips.

"I dreamed I was wrestling a bear and could not extract myself from his arms."

He laughed at that.

"Sometimes the bear wins."

She nodded. "Apparently. How did *you* sleep?"

His gentle smile sent lightning bolts of awareness through her insides.

"I dreamed I held a little kitten and for once she let me pet her."

Emma stood, suddenly outraged. "I did not!"

"Only a little."

She eased back down. "You shall ruin my reputation."

He nodded and grabbed the leg of the hare, biting deep into the meat with glistening white teeth. Why did that make her stomach flutter so?

She turned away, heading to the river to fill the water skins. Jake stayed behind to brew his tea over a tiny fire the smoke of which she could not even see from the bank. When she returned, she found him slicing into his saddle with his butcher knife.

"What are you doing?"

He did not glance up. "Hiding my journal. Start packing the mule."

She rolled their bedding as he separated the leather folds of the worn saddle. She finished her work and sat close by to watch his. Inside the saddle, where there should be padding was a compartment just the size of his journal. Her forehead furrowed.

"You had this all planned."

He glanced up and gave her a quick smile. "Of course."

He lowered his precious journal into the safety of the chamber and drew the pieces together, stitching through the existing holes with a fine bit of catgut. When he finished, she could barely tell the difference between his work and the saddle maker's.

"The new gut looks different," she said.

He smiled and lifted a dollop of mud and mixed it with grease. This he rubbed into his stitches until they blended flawlessly.

They set off shortly afterward and headed in the direction he had scouted, Jake riding upon his journal. She felt vulnerable crossing open grassland. There was no hiding place except the cottonwood that grew along stream banks.

Jake told her to wait with the mule while he made contact. She did as he asked, but after a time she hobbled her horse and the mule and crept up to the top of the hill where she could peer through the yellow grass at the grouping of huts beside the river.

Their homes seemed little more than tumbledown shacks made of sticks and bundles of grass. Two men stood beside Jake. They were engaged in a wild form of sign language. She could not understand a bit of it. From inside the huts women and children peeked out from behind hides at the stranger in their midst. Her eye caught movement by the river. Creeping up the bank came two men with grass tied to their heads. A knife blade gleamed between a man's clenched teeth. Her heart leaped in her chest, sending blood surging through her.

She swung the rifle forward and took aim. She did not know if they were members of the tribe or enemies, but it amounted to the same.

Should she call to Jake, fire a warning shot or take aim to kill?

She drew a breath and shouted. "Jake! Attackers."

Standing now, she pointed at the approaching force.

She squeezed the trigger, sending a puff of smoke before the closest man. The gunshot rang in the air and more warriors emerged from the grass at a run. The men beside Jake drew their knives and charged the intruders. Jake drew his pistol and fired at the lead man. More and more men sprang from the riverbank. Emma reloaded and fired through a man's thigh. He screamed and spun, disappearing in the tall grass.

Why had she left her shotgun with the horse? Too far for the revolver, she thought as she poured gunpowder into the muzzle of her rifle for a second time. The men beside Jake grappled with an enemy warrior who leaped onto his chest, slicing his throat.

Emma straightened, horrified as blood sprayed from the wound like a fountain. Men ran from the huts to fight and the women sprang toward the river. Jake raced toward Duchess and swept up into the saddle in one graceful bound. He fired his rifle over his shoulder at the pursuing warriors, killing the closest man. An Indian lifted a knife, aiming at Jake's unprotected back. Emma took aim and fired. The man's wrist exploded into blood and bone. The others paused, and Duchess galloped up the hill.

"Grab my hand," he said as he leaned toward her.

She glanced down the hill and saw the men charging after him, then the hand reaching for her. Oh, my God, he means me to swing up behind him. In that instant of understanding, she realized it was her only chance.

She gripped her rifle and thrust out her hand. His fingers clasped her wrist, biting into flesh. She jumped as he tugged. For an instant the world fell away beneath her. She glimpsed the grass speeding by and then her seat landed hard on the lip of his saddle. Her breath left her at the jarring impact. She gripped his waist as Jake tore down the hill. At the bottom he sprang from the saddle.

"Stay here," he called.

He neatly sliced the hobbles on the mule and horse. Grasping the reins of the mule in one hand and his rifle in the other, he vaulted onto the packhorse from behind landing on the horse's bare back. He dug his heels into the animal's flanks and it sprang into a gallop.

"Ride," he called.

She dug her heels into Duchess's sides, galloping behind him. When she dared a glance, she saw warriors drawing their bows, arrows notched and ready.

Chapter Fourteen

Arrows streaked across the blue sky. Emma kicked Duchess' sides, slapping the leather reins against her neck as the shafts fell all about them like sleet. She braced for the impact that never came. Across the prairie they raced, not pausing until reaching the cover of the cottonwoods far down the valley.

The horses' sides heaved like bellows as Jake glanced to her. Emma pulled up beside him.

"We lost them," she said.

His gaze flicked to her. She felt her stomach drop. His expression was not angry exactly, but tense.

"You disobeyed me."

She swallowed, preparing to defend herself from this next attack. Then remembered that he was not her father. Jake did not live to find fault. He did not see every act of free will as a direct attack on his authority.

"Yes," she agreed.

"Thank God."

She was prepared to explain, excuse and pacify. Instead her mouth gaped. Her recovery came slowly. She cocked her head.

"What did you say?"

He laughed. "I said, thank God. If you hadn't, I'd be dead right now and you shortly after."

She'd done the right thing. For once in her life, she'd acted and she'd done the right thing. A smile broke upon her lips.

"I should have had you cover my back, especially after seeing you shoot. But, I just thought about keeping you clear of any trouble. Of course, that's crazy. If trouble finds me, it sure as hell will find you." He patted her on the shoulder. "From now on, we stay together."

Emma nodded, not trusting her voice. He did not know, couldn't know how important this was.

He stared at her, still grinning then said, "Damn, Emma, that was some shooting!"

He called her Emma often now. She liked the easy familiarity he brought to it. She hated to hear her father call her name. From him, it sounded like condemnation, a call to chastisement.

"Best get the horses watered and then be off."

She followed him to the stream and held the reins loose allowing the horses to drink. She decided to use his name in the same intimate way.

"I've never seen anyone leap onto a horse like you did today, Jake." She waited to see if he noticed her use of his name but he gave no indication.

"The Sioux do it better than I do."

"You do it very well," she assured, recalling the astonishing sight.

"If I live to be a hundred, I don't think I'll ever forget you flying up behind me. Your foot went clean up to here." He held his hand chin high. "You looked like a circus acrobat."

His grin showed approval. She basked in the warm glow of his smile. Nothing ever felt better, unless it was his kiss.

"I didn't think myself capable of such a feat."

"Amazing what a body can do when pressed by circumstances."

She nodded her agreement. "When I realized what you meant me to do, I knew I couldn't but then I saw those Indians and I just—just—"

"Trusted me."

Emma blinked at him. That was true. She did trust him. When had that come about? She had been determined not to place faith in any man and here she'd gone and done just that.

Her body trembled now, the strain of the encounter making her legs turn to jelly. Wobbling dangerously, she tipped into Duchess's shoulder.

Jake righted her. "What's wrong? Are you hurt?"

"I think the terror of it just hit me. Perhaps I rode too fast for it to catch me until now."

She folded to the bank and he squatted on his haunches beside her, allowing their mounts to graze.

"I've seen men go like this. They make it through the battle, doing everything they must. Then the thing is over and they start to shake. I guess some kind of dam gives way."

She nodded. That was just right. She couldn't feel or even think when the Indians attacked.

"Who where they?" she asked.

"Damned if I know."

Her mind flashed images of the encounter. Oh, Lord, she shot a man—no, two.

"Jake," she whispered, and he inched closer. "I hit two."

"I know."

"I've never shot a man before."

He held her hand and squeezed until she looked into the calm reassurance of his eyes. "You did what you had to and saved my life. I'm grateful. In the army, we say, you did your duty. There is no shame in it."

"I feel sick inside."

He cocked his head. "Now listen here, those Indians meant to skin me and you both."

She took solace in his words, let them seep into the darkness that filled her. Gradually, she noticed the warmth of his hand, the constancy of his gaze and the unwavering understanding in his eyes.

He had been there. He understood.

"You got over it?" she asked.

"It comes with time."

She nodded, returning to the here and now. "We best be off."

They followed the stream back to the river until it joined another and then another. Here at the convergence of three waterways, Jake paused.

"We'll camp here."

"It's early yet," Emma noted.

"I have some work to do."

He spent the next hour searching the woods by the rivers.

"What are we looking for?" she asked.

"A hiding place for my chronometer. I need a place I'll easily find again and one that will stay dry."

He discovered what he sought at the base of a large cedar tree. There, some animal had dug out a hole below the roots. He enlarged the opening until only his legs remained above ground.

When he emerged he was covered with sandy soil, but his grin quite dazzled her.

"Abandoned. Might have been a badger, judging from the smell."

He wrapped the outer box of his chronometer with oiled buckskin and then lowered it into a crate. This he dragged into the den. He did not rest until he replaced the dirt he excavated from the opening. Then he stood and brushed off his clothing.

"That should hold her."

Emma stood stroking the packhorse's neck and Jake cocked his head.

"Have you given him a name yet?"

To do so felt like a betrayal to Scout. She knew that was silly and Jake seemed anxious for her to have him named, though never cared to find one for himself. Had he? She never heard him call the packhorse by name.

"What do you call him?" she asked.

"Most of the names I call him can't be repeated."

* * *

Twice now she'd pulled his fanny out of the fire. Both times she acted on her own without consulting him. Jake should be angry that she consistently disobeyed orders. But she was not in the military. What would he have done in a similar circumstance?

No reason to fault the woman for using the brain God gave her and, if he was honest, he would admit that if she'd been a man, he'd have insisted she cover his back instead of leaving her to mind the horses.

From now on, he'd give her the respect she'd earned. She deserved that much.

She rode behind the mule now, because, without a saddle, he could find no way to secure the mule to her horse. He called her forward and she moved in beside Duchess.

"I got some information from those fellows before the shooting started," he began.

Her eyebrow lifted and he noticed how tan her face had grown, despite the wide-brimmed hat he'd made from elk and antelope.

"Based on what I can figure, I believe we will find either missionaries or Christian Indians within a day or two."

"Good."

He smiled. "No more arrows or ice, but a different kind of danger. You remember the story?"

"I could repeat it in my sleep."

"You don't talk in your sleep," he said, and waited for her reaction, which came immediately when her cheeks turned a wonderful bright pink.

"What will you tell them when questioned about our relationship on the trail?"

"Who would ask about that?"

Her look was incredulous. "The priests."

Certainly they would. Men of the cloth thought a white collar gave them leave to poke into all manner of private doings.

"We best decide now," he said.

She nodded. "If you reveal that we shared the same bed, you will compromise me. No man would have me after that."

"I would never do that."

"But I want you to."

"What?"

"If the Spanish think I'm your woman they will leave me be and that might be best. I see no point in appearing receptive to marriage, when it would complicate matters."

"What if they just think you're a…" He considered what word to use that would not offend and decided there was none. "A woman of low moral character?"

Her gaze snapped to his. "Do you think so?"

"No, but they might."

"That would be a nuisance. Perhaps the truth?"

He shook his head. "I never touched you. We never shared the same bed. Not in that way. In any case, I never did touch you." Though he wanted to every night. How he managed to control himself was beyond him. The woman grew harder to resist each day. Right now, for example. Her cheeks pink from the sun and a light spattering of freckles across her nose, she was beautiful.

Her expression turned serious. "I'll do what you think is best."

He had no right to make this decision. He'd underestimated her and marginalized her. Despite that, she let him choose.

"That mean you trust me?"

"Yes. I do. Plus you have more experience than I in these matters. If you want to present us as a couple, I'll do so. I'll even pretend I'm your wife, up to a point. If you want me to be a married woman who is grieving her husband, I'm certain I can be convincing."

"Grieving widow, as we discussed. I'd have to be a cad to molest a widow and it might deter other men." Though some men liked widows. They had experience and knew how to take precautions. Much safer than dallying with a virgin which was the fire he was playing with.

"All right then. We have lived together, singly these two

months. You have been the perfect gentleman and I have conducted myself as a lady."

"From this moment."

"Done."

They rode side by side for the remainder of the day. Near nightfall he picked up a path that looked well worn, like a cattle trail. At sunset they came across the first cows. Jake cut a yearling away from the herd and shot it easily through the heart. He skinned the beast and staked the hide on a pole.

"Why are you doing that?" Emma asked.

"Cattle here are only valued for their hides and tallow. Any traveler is welcome to take a cow or two as long as he leaves the hide for the owner."

"But that's stealing."

"Not here it isn't. Here it's custom, according to Jed Smith. Cows breed and feed on open range. There are more of them than the ranchero could possibly use. We take what we can eat and leave the rest for the wolves."

Emma looked at the carcass. "That's wasteful."

"You wouldn't think so if you were a wolf."

The simple turning of her lips warmed his insides and he realized he enjoyed bringing that smile.

"Been a while since I've had beef," he said.

Soon the fire crackled merrily. Emma added more cottonwood to the flames. By the time the stars appeared, they chewed on steaks that overflowed their plates.

Emma finished her portion and tried the ribs.

"I can't believe how good this tastes," she said, slicing into the thick, pink meat. "I hope to never eat jerky again."

"With luck you'll be eating jerky come spring."

Her eyes widened. "Yes, of course."

"You still plan on coming with me, don't you?"

"I do. Why would you ask?"

"Because you told me you won't go back to your father. So I just wondered if you might be thinking of staying out here."

"I hadn't considered it." Her gaze turned to the fire.

He cursed himself, because now she was considering it, weighing what opportunities she might find in California. She was a beautiful woman and supposedly a widow. Even without dowry or land, she was a catch. A wealthy man could easily overlook those shortcomings for a fetching bride.

Why did he care? He wanted to be rid of her, didn't he?

He ground his teeth together and watched the fat drip from the ribs into the fire. Two months ago he would have jumped at any chance to unload her. But now? He'd grown accustomed to her company. She didn't badger him with endless talk or make annoying demands. For the first time in his life he'd found a woman he respected and liked.

And she was as pretty as any woman he'd ever met. Too damn pretty for her own good. She'd draw men like a horse draws flies. He'd have to act as her keeper.

He frowned.

She didn't need a guardian, unless it was to protect her from him. *He* was the threat, because he wanted her, but not for a wife. He never planned to take a wife.

Would Emma agree to be his mistress? He glanced her way and found her deep in thought. He'd never know unless he asked. He could seduce her. He knew for a fact that she responded to him. But that thought made him feel dirty. He didn't want to trick her into this.

But maybe she wanted to. After all, she said she didn't want to marry. Perhaps she'd agree to ride with him and be his. If she really didn't want to lose her freedom, she might be receptive to an arrangement. Then they could both avoid wedding vows and part when it suited them.

He gathered his nerve and cleared his throat. She directed her smoky eyes at him. He knew she waited for him to speak, but the intensity of her regard and the topic of import combined to make him speechless. A cold sweat broke out on his forehead.

"Jake, are you ill?"

"Maybe so, but I have something to ask you."

"Yes?"

Best go slow, scout the area first then slip in if the coast was clear.

"You told me once you don't plan to marry."

"That's correct."

"Ever?"

"I don't think so, but I suppose anything is possible."

Early signs looked good, so he inched closer to the issue.

"You think you'll ever be with a man?"

He waited for her to slap his face. She straightened and shock registered in her expression. Time to pull back.

"Because I just wondered if a woman who chooses to live single ever wants a man? I know men who never married but they take a woman now and then."

"I don't know how to answer that."

"I just wondered if men are the only ones who feel the occasional need for companionship."

"I think you and I have rather a different definition for companionship. For me it means company. For you, well, not keeping company."

"Keeping company is one way to describe it."

Her eyebrows knit. "I've never had such a discussion, but since you raised the question, I have one for you. Have you fallen prey to such urges?"

"Prey?" He laughed. "A time or two."

"Two?"

"Emma, a man doesn't kiss and tell. I've been with a woman, more than one. But that's all I'm saying."

She nodded as if he'd confirmed her low opinion of him. "Indians?"

"Some."

Her eyebrow lifted at that. "Married?"

"Never." Though the first woman he'd ever bedded had been a widow and a client of his father's. His pappy had settled her estate and he'd settled the itch she could not scratch. She'd taught him a great deal about women, including some very important lessons on how to enjoy lovemaking without risk of a baby.

Her voice dropped to a whisper. "What about a virgin?"

His throat suddenly went bone-dry and swallowing brought no relief. That was one area where the widow had been of no use. He could not seem to tear his gaze away from the intent stare Emma focused upon him. He shook his head. "No."

Chapter Fifteen

Emma could not believe this conversation. Men simply did not ask women about their urges, as he put it. As far as she knew, women were not allowed to have such things. Though it would explain the longing that took her even now. She did want to sit close to him. She dreamed of his kisses and imagined sleeping beside him every night.

He had experience. Was he offering to initiate her into the ways between a man and woman?

That thought made her skin tingle. Did she have urges?

Yes.

Admitting them was another matter. Somehow she could not resist asking him about his encounters. He'd had more already than she would have in a lifetime. That was another difference between them.

"If I were to admit to sleeping with widowers and warriors, I'd be run out of town on a rail. But a man can do such things, even boast of them." He made to answer but she stopped him with a hand. "I've heard the men in their barracks. They brag of conquests and seductions as if they would receive their stripes for such debauchery."

"Well they do earn them. It's how a boy becomes a man."

She snorted. Women marked such things in the changes of

their bodies and the blood, which she'd dealt with only last week, rinsing out her rags at night by the river. Jake knew so little about living closely with a woman he'd thought she only washed her handkerchiefs. For a man of such experience, he obviously had gaps in his education.

"A woman does not need a man to verify her womanhood."

"Then she misses the pleasure of it."

"Pleasure!" She laughed. "Have you ever witnessed a birth?" She regarded him sharply.

He shook his head.

"Ever changed a diaper?"

He grimaced.

"I have. Your pleasures come at great cost."

His gaze was unblinking. "Babies can be avoided."

She stilled. Did he jest? He looked very serious. Were such things possible? Excitement dimpled her skin. She believed that a baby came of all interaction between a man and woman. That was what mother had told her when she was young. "Careful of your skirts, Em. If a man gets under them, he'll put a baby in your belly. Wait until after you marry or you'll shame us."

Jake sat still and expectant, staring at her like a hungry wolf. Soon they'd be back in civilization. They would again be under the rules of society and the church.

But tonight she was still free.

"How?"

Jake wanted her. His body was rigid with it. But the caution of the wilderness coursed strong in him. Despite what she said, he doubted very much he could make love to her and then get clear.

It never worked out that way. No strings attached, that's what the widow had told him, but she'd blown like a northeastern wind when he'd broken it off. Helen traded her body for marriage. He'd met squaws who performed the same service for a knife blade. Invisible strings were there, always.

Emma looked at him with a mixture of longing and fear. His

breathing changed, coming rough and fast, as if his body was already anticipating the pleasure, wanting it more than anything, until the need blotted out all reason.

He leaned forward and she lifted her chin to accept his kiss. Her mouth pressed to his and her arms flew about his neck, trapping him to her. He dragged her across his lap, raining kisses down her throat as she made small moaning sounds that fired his blood. He tugged at her belt and managed to pull the wide band of leather away. His hands slid over her hip, leaving the leather of her skirts to venture over the soft, flat skin of her belly. The heat of her startled him. He traveled over the ridges of her ribs and paused at the sloping mound of her breasts. She writhed, more than anxious for his touch. He gave it to her, blanketing the soft flesh with his hands.

She arched against him at the pressure he gave. Her nipples pebbled beneath his palms and he dipped to take another kiss. This was no light brushing of lips. He held her to him, demanding entrance to her mouth. Her lips parted and his tongue slid within, claiming her.

His body beat in a rising wave of desire. He cautioned himself to turn back and cursed as he knew it was already too late.

Emma lay across his lap, clinging and writhing. He'd never wanted a woman this much, needed to claim her as his. He would be the first and the last.

That thought and the implications of his feelings brought some semblance of cognition.

"Emma, are you sure you want this? Tell me. Tell me now."

She shook her head and gripped the front of his buckskin, drawing him forward.

"Teach me," she whispered.

She wanted him and he was lost. The truth of it worked like a drug, moving through his body, filling him and readying him to make her his.

He drew her upright, pulled away her buckskin shirt. In the firelight he saw the beauty of her form and his breath caught.

He gazed on perfect orbs with budding nipples, a slender torso and the dimple of her navel. He clasped her waist and followed it to the toggle at the side, working the bit of bone through the slit with clumsy fingers.

She stood before him and released the hooks and buttons of three petticoats, then slid from her moccasins.

He reached for the ribbon laces of her pantaloons and dragged them forward releasing the bow. The waist gaped, revealing the dark thatch of curls at the juncture of her thighs. She dropped the last curtain that separated them and let it fall. He sat back in wonder at the perfect picture of feminine beauty she presented.

"Do I please you?" she asked. The nervous tension in her voice, the doubt made her seem more vulnerable.

A virgin—beautiful, lush and nervous.

"I've never seen anything so lovely."

He reached for her, but she evaded. "I'd like to see you. I've never seen a man, all of him, I mean."

"You saw me at the river."

She blushed. "That was different. You were…resting."

"I was asleep and you were spying."

Her blush deepened as he stood and tugged off his moccasins. He carefully laid aside the pistol, powder horn and knife and then drew off his shirt. Then he stood, barefooted, wearing only his breeches. His gaze met hers. She stood still as stone. Her attention seemed fastened upon his chest. His pulse pounded, sending blood to all the appropriate regions as her gaze dipped to his skin breeches, made tight by his arousal.

He gripped the waist and released the attachment, then slid them down and off his body, letting the garment fall upon her discarded skirts. He watched her eyes travel over him, relishing her gaze nearly as much as her touch. When her attention reached his sex, her eyes went wide as she stepped away. It was why he had hesitated to let her see him. He feared she would recoil.

"Don't be afraid." He extended his hand. "You have to trust me, Emma."

Their fingers touched. The strength of her grip startled him. He needed to go slow.

"Come lie with me." He led her to the pile of furs, thinking this the perfect place, the perfect time for Emma to know the touch of a man. He thanked the fates that he would be the one.

He sank to the furs, letting the soft wolf skins caress him as he guided her down beside him. He closed his eyes, held her tightly to his chest and touched heaven as he felt her arms encircle his waist. All the weeks and months of wanting fell away. She was his. He lowered his head and kissed her with all the passion in his soul.

His lips demanded. His tongue sought access. Emma parted her lips and felt his tongue glide over her own. He delved within as she trembled against him.

His fingers caressed her throat. One hand continued to travel down her shoulder and back as the other moved to cup the swell of her breast. Her nipple contracted into a hard point, as she pressed herself more firmly into his hand and sighed.

She drew him as close as the power in her arms allowed, molding to him like hot wax. His hands strayed to the gentle sway of her hips and slid behind to cup her pear-shaped bottom.

Her gaze never left his. She saw the pleasure her body gave him reflected in his eyes. She relished the gentle touch of his hand as it brushed her hip. For the first time she enjoyed the aching want, knowing at last, it could be fulfilled. Her body trembled with need. Her eyes beckoned.

"I've never felt like this before."

He smiled. "You are the most beautiful woman in the world," he whispered as he drew her close once more.

"Prettier than your other women?"

"They do not even match your shadow."

Slowly, he caressed her from shoulder to thigh.

She drew her bottom lip through her teeth as she considered

his physical readiness. His size frightened her, but the desire to feel his male shaft sparked within her.

"I want to touch you," she whispered.

"You're already touching me."

She cast her glance down and heard his sharp intake of breath. Her face heated. She had shocked him with her boldness.

Reaching, he captured her hand and pressed it firmly against his erection. As her trembling fingers encircled him, he groaned.

"You don't know the power you have. You could unman me with the simplest caress."

He rolled her to her back into the plush furs and parted her thighs with a knee. His hand stroked her breasts. A sheen of sweat broke over her skin and she saw his body shimmered with moisture, as well. He caressed her as his mouth descended to kiss her breast. She writhed beneath him in sweet torment. She pressed herself hard against his suckling mouth, wanting more. His hand descended lower, traveling across her belly. She trembled as sweet sensation rippled from his feathery touch. Her body braced as his seeking fingers traveled through the curls between her legs. The sharp, stabbing pleasure caused her to cry out. He fondled her, parting the folds of flesh. She felt moisture issue from her and wiggled to escape.

"Let me touch you."

The longing in his voice stirred her soul. She could deny him nothing. She relaxed and he stroked her, gliding over her slippery flesh. The pleasure intensified with each caress adding to the growing ache within her. She bucked and clawed at his shoulders needing him, desperate for their joining. She felt him move between her legs. His hands grasped her hips. He called to her.

"Emma, look at me."

Drugged by his ministrations, she opened her heavy-lidded eyes.

Why had he stopped? She whimpered, longing for the pleasure of his touch. She rocked her hips invitingly and felt his male flesh press against her. Her eyes opened wide as she stared into the intensity of his gaze. His jaw tensed and she understood he would take her. Her eyes widened, but she nodded her consent.

He held her hips firmly and with one liquid thrust claimed her as his own. She cried out as the thin veil of maidenhood tore away. The pain was sharp and transient, replaced by the insistent, throbbing need to move. Still gazing into his clear eyes, she began to rock her hips, in a movement as old as woman.

Emma watched a look of agony move across his features. He closed his eyes, wrapping his arms about her. Fiercely, he pinioned her beneath him. His hand descended to caress as he moved in fluid strokes, designed to drive her mad. The pleasure grew to sweet agony.

"Help me. Oh, Lord, I can't bear it."

His thumb flicked over her and the throbbing delight broke loose. She arched as shimmering sensation flowed outward from his touch. Her cries faded and she fell to the furs. As the echoes of delight receded, she opened her eyes and found him frozen, an expression of intense pain etched in the lines of his face. She reached for him but he stopped her with his voice.

"Don't move. Keep still, Emma."

He lowered his forehead to her as she lay motionless, but for her heart beating in wild terror.

She felt his shaft throbbing deep within her body. She longed to rock against him, but he forbade her. Something was wrong.

"What is it?" she whispered.

"Shhh," he breathed.

Then in a frantic withdrawal, he jerked away, gripping himself as if his male flesh were an attacking snake. He fell forward on to her and she felt a warm gush of fluid at the same moment he cried out her name.

She held her breath as her heartbeat drummed in her ears, still afraid to move.

"God, that was close," he moaned. "I've never—I almost. Dear God."

She listened to his mumblings, but could make no sense of them. "What happened?"

He lifted his heavy torso from her and smiled. His fingers brushed the hair from her face.

"Are you all right, Emma? Did I hurt you too much?"

In her concern for him, she quite forgot to think about herself.

"I'm, yes, I'm well." Her face heated as images and memories of the sensations collided with her reaction to him. "I never felt anything like that. I thought I'd die for a moment."

He smiled. "Coupling can be dramatic."

No wonder the soldiers were always after her to slip away to some secluded spot. She'd never gone. Now she was very glad—happy that the first time was with this man.

"Is it always like that?"

He gave a tired smile and chuckled, making her feel dumb as a fence post.

"No. That was special."

She wondered suddenly how she compared to his other women, but could not bring herself to ask.

"Did you enjoy it?" she asked.

He laughed at that. "Couldn't you tell I did? You nearly made me lose control."

She gazed at him in bewilderment, not understanding what occurred. "I think I lost control."

He nodded. "You definitely did. That's good for a woman. But not so good for a man."

"Does it hurt?"

He rolled to his side, drawing her along. She felt the rumble in his chest as he laughed softly. "No, it doesn't hurt. But if I lose control, my seed comes. You understand?"

She shook her head. How could she be so ignorant? She didn't understand a word of what he was telling her. Her mother had never spoken to her of such things. Emma had still been a child when she'd left. One finger beneath her chin brought her back to meet his gaze.

"Emma, look at me. If I lose control while inside you, then my seed is released. You could have a baby."

She sat upright, understanding falling like a bucket of ice water. The warm lethargy and the lovely contentment dissolved as the implications of her actions slammed into her like a fist. When the passion came, she'd forgotten all about consequences in her mad rush to experience his touch. How could she?

Her hands covered her mouth. "I completely forgot."

"Easy to do when involved with a man."

"If you hadn't, we could." She fell to the furs. "Will it be all right?"

"Yes, Emma." He drew her close. "There's no danger."

But there was. He was a danger, because now she knew she could not trust herself. In moments of passion, reason and judgment both deserted her.

Chapter Sixteen

Emma chose to sleep in her buffalo robe across the fire after their lovemaking. Jake let her go, glad not to have her there beside him to remind him of his weakness. He tossed, restless, through the night and then waited for the dawn.

He'd never been so close to making such a colossal mistake. She took away all his long-learned control.

My God, he'd almost lost his seed within her like some green boy, instead of a man of experience. She trusted him and he'd nearly failed her. He saw the look of shock and knew she understood how close they'd come to disaster. Never, not once since his very first time had a woman so overwhelmed him. But that first time was marked by inexperience. He could not place the blame in that account again.

Emma held power over him, whether she knew it or not. That made her dangerous. If she had moved, twitched even, he knew he would have been all done. How had he gotten to such a frenzy?

Because he wanted her first time to be wonderful. He wanted her to know the pleasures a man could bring his mate, so she would want to be his woman. More than that, he wanted to possess her, claim her as his own. The truth rocked him.

He stilled as another thought flashed through his brain like lightning. She was not his. He had not claimed her, but only took from her what was not his to take, the gift she should have brought to her husband and in the process proved his lack of restraint. Seeing his actions as purely selfish, he bowed his head in shame. He wanted her and so, took her, damn the consequences.

Playing with fire—the danger of his actions haunted him. He glanced across the dying coals to where she rested. She beckoned even as she lay curled in her bed. His body ached to touch her again. How he longed to fuse their bodies and souls until they came together. That nearly happened. If it had, there would be no recourse—he would have to marry her.

They still needed to talk. He dreaded the conversation. He must make her understand that this could not happen again, even as his body stiffened with desire at the thought of loving her.

Now he wished they were not here alone in this world of grass. He needed to be away from her, if only for a few hours to clear his thinking.

The excuse of finding breakfast brought him up and to his saddle. She woke as he prepared to ride.

"I'll be back."

She blinked at him. He thought she looked pale and tired. The circles beneath her eyes spoke of a restless night. He felt much the same. Turning Duchess, he left the forlorn sight behind.

Guilt pierced with sharp claws, but he shook them off, reminding himself that she'd been willing and he was a man. It was bound to happen. Alone with a beautiful woman for months, what could he expect? He was not a saint.

Although he had avoided other beautiful women, even ones set on seduction. What made Emma different?

He didn't know, but she was. She sat apart from any woman in his experience. He glanced about the open plain feeling as lost as a greenhorn without a compass.

Wild turkeys gobbled from the thicket by the river and he drew his shotgun bringing down a fat tom. Dismounting, he retrieved the bird.

Soon he would be too busy with the Spanish to worry about the mess he'd created with Emma.

A thought stopped him. Women were emotional creatures. His actions might have changed her willingness to help him with his mission. Also, such a relationship made women think they had ownership of a man. She didn't and it was best she understood that right off.

He grasped the limp turkey and wheeled toward Emma.

Emma readied the bedding for travel, busying her hands and trying to ignore the stiffness between her legs. She waited until Jake was well gone before heading to the river to wash. Striping all her garments from the waist down she stood in her buckskin shirt, thinking the cold water might soothe her.

When she glanced down she froze as she took in the dried blood streaking her thighs. It was too early for her monthly flow. She remembered the quick stab of pain when he entered her. Had he torn something inside?

She checked and found no fresh blood. Whatever the source, the flow seemed to have ceased. She squatted and washed away the signs of their meeting, wishing she could so easily remove the memories from her mind.

She deserved what she got. Hadn't she welcomed him? When he'd given her a chance to retreat, she'd rejected it. The desire to feel him inside had overtaken all her caution and good sense.

Was it worth it? She sighed. His lovemaking had been wonderful. Even as her muscles ached, she knew she would do it again if given the opportunity. That frightened her.

He'd asked her to trust him and she had. But he'd come within a hairbreadth of losing his seed within her. A sharp pang of fear pierced her and she lay her hands over her flat stomach. Never trust a man. Must she write it out or have it branded on her forehead?

She could not allow him to touch her. That was when her mind went fuzzy. His nearness turned her will to corn mush.

The intelligent thing to do was to pretend it had not happened and keep her distance from him. He was like liquor, a pleasure at the time, but a mighty headache the next morning.

Yes, that would help. Just think of him that way. She returned to camp and laid the wood for a fire, but did not know if she should light it, so she waited. Before long she heard Duchess's hooves falling on the hard-packed ground.

He carried a fine fat turkey.

"Shall I strike the fire?" she asked.

He nodded and she hit the flint with steel until a spark landed in the dry birch fungus cradled in her palm. Then she transferred the ember to the dry grass tinder and blew. First she coaxed a wisp of smoke and then a flame.

Jake plucked most of the feathers and singed away the rest. Then he dressed and staked the bird for roasting. With the task complete, uneasy silence fell between them. She thought he made an effort to keep things just the way they had been, but they were not. Last night had changed them and pretending to the contrary did not make it less true.

She waited in vain, for he made no mention of their encounter. Finally she raised it.

"I have considered my foray into lovemaking and decided it was a mistake."

His head snapped up and his eyes narrowed. "Do you? Why's that?"

"Not that I didn't enjoy the experience. Parts of it were… quite marvelous." His mouth quirked at that. "But now I realize the danger. I am not anxious to bear a child, especially here in the wilderness." His expression turned hard and his eyes glittered dangerously. Still she pressed on. "I am not finding fault. I was as much to blame in the matter as you, more perhaps, because it is a woman's job to deny such advances. In any case, I think it best if we continued on as we were—singly."

At that Jake leaned against a downed log and his mouth gaped.

"Don't you have anything to say?" she asked.

"You don't expect me to marry you?"

"I'd rather you didn't."

He raked a hand through his hair, giving it a tug. The sharp sting of pain convinced him he wasn't dreaming. What was happening? He was going to lay down the law, not the other way around. She'd stolen his thunder. Now he found himself annoyed that she didn't want to be his woman. He'd never been on the receiving end of a rejection and found he did not like it one bit. Perhaps he misunderstood.

"You do not want to share my bedroll again?"

"Now you understand."

A pang of regret vibrated inside him. "Did I hurt you, Emma?"

She lowered her gaze and he felt like the blackest heart in the West. Of course he'd hurt her. That was the way with virgins.

"There is always some pain for a woman the first time and some blood."

Her head snapped up. Had she found blood on her thighs as he'd found her virgin's blood smeared across his belly like a brand of shame?

"The next time you lie with a man, there will be none of that."

"Thank you, but I shall not do that again."

He did not understand the ache her words caused him. He should be happy, relieved. She did not want him shackled. She wanted nothing to do with him.

"What about my mission?" he asked.

She met his gaze. "None of that has changed. I consider it our mission and will play my part to my best. I think I should be rather more convincing as a widow now that I have some small experience."

Small indeed and one she regretted. He blamed himself for his eagerness to take what was not his.

"I'm sorry, Emma."

She held his gaze a moment and then glanced away and nodded as if unable to speak.

The tension between them that had been so unbearable before the coupling, now dissolved into uneasy silence steeped with regret.

He found the turkey barely palatable and his appetite vanished. Still he forced the food down, knowing they had a hard day's ride.

When they finished, he kicked dirt on the coals and tied the bedding onto the mule. For his mind, they could not reach the Spanish settlements soon enough.

But it was three more days and nights before they saw their first Mexicans.

The men rode over the ridge, reining in their horses. Jake could not make out much beneath the oversize sombreros. One man wore a brightly striped serape, the other a short cowhide jacket. They leaned together in obvious conversation as Jake made slow progress in their direction.

At some signal they rode at a full gallop, their horses eating up the ground between them. Jake halted, his stomach tightening. He extracted his sextant from his pouch and then drew his rifle.

"What are you doing?" asked Emma. "They aren't attacking."

"I have to hide this."

He pressed the release button at the front of the stock and twisted the metal covering the butt end, opening the hidden chamber. Then he wrapped the sextant in a bit of leather and slid it into the hole. In an instant he had the lid closed and locked down.

It had begun.

The two rancheros turned out to be neophytes, Christianized Indians. The men spoke Spanish and flanked Jake and Emma as they escorted them toward San Jose Mission. As they rode he gathered information on the rivers and mountains to the north and south. Neither had crossed the Sierra Nevada but their knowledge of the coast was useful.

Jake gazed out at the herd of cattle. Not since he'd left the buffalo on the Great Plains had he seen such numbers.

"How many head, brother?" he asked in fluent Spanish.

"Over twenty thousand on our count last spring."

They rode on through the dust raised by the milling herd. The cows ambled out of the way as the horses cut through the center like a hot knife through tallow. Behind them, the gap closed as the cows continued to munch the rich grass that remained green even though it was nearly November.

"We also raise wheat, barley, lentils, oats, corn and have the finest muskmelons in California."

The men rambled on about the mission and its riches. Jake collected each word. By the time they reached the wheatfields he knew the layout including church, store, workrooms and living quarters. The Christianized Indian laborers lived in grass huts nearby.

They drew near the mission, sighting the adobe church. Several brothers in gray habits gathered in the yard to greet them.

Before the group stood a florid-cheeked man with sparse gray hair that nearly matched his robes. His smile welcomed and he stepped forward as they dismounted.

"Roberto, Angel, you have brought us guests."

"Yes, Padre Duran. These are Americans."

The missionary's mouth gaped in surprise and Jake noticed his teeth were stained. Another jittery coffee drinker, he supposed.

"Americans, surely not." He extended his hand to Jake. "I am Padre Narciso Duran."

"Jake Turner. I'm happy to meet you, Padre. We are sorely in need of your hospitality." He shook the man's hand, reserving any show of strength, in favor of warmth. "This is Señora Emma Martin. Unfortunately she does not speak Spanish."

Emma smiled at the priest and offered her hand. Duran clasped hers warmly and nodded. "Welcome, my child. Come in out of the sun. Angel, see to their belongings."

They were ushered into a courtyard. Father Duran led them to a room buzzing with activity as many neophytes came and went carrying trays of food. Jake spied the first bread he had seen since his departure from St. Louis, two years earlier.

Emma's eyes widened at the bounty presented. Figs and fresh peaches, grapes, sliced roast beef, cool sliced melon and cooked pumpkin lay before them.

Duran bowed his head and gave thanks then smiled broadly. "Eat, my friends."

Jake tried to eat sparingly, but found himself devouring an entire loaf with sweet butter. He sliced a peach and sticky juice ran down his fingers.

Father Duran was the perfect host, waiting until after Jake pushed away from the table before asking a single question. The old priest filled their goblets with wine. Jake clasped the delicate blown glass, marveling at the riches here.

"A toast to our new friends from America," said Father Duran. The three other priests seated before them raised their glasses and drank.

Jake followed suit, rising to his feet. He glanced at Emma, who held her glass aloft waiting. She looked thin beside the group of men and he realized that she had lost much weight over their travails. Looking at her, it would not be difficult to imagine she had suffered greatly on the journey, for so she had.

"Praise God for leading us to our salvation," said Jake.

The men beamed and drank.

Jake's backside had only just hit the seat when Duran cleared his throat.

"Perhaps you could enlighten us as to how you two came to be in our company."

Jake launched into his tale pausing only to answer questions.

The Father gave Emma a critical stare and seemed to find her the picture of a wretched survivor. Jake realized to his dismay that little of that was acting. He had put her through hell. He hoped to make it up to her, but he had no idea how.

"But the mountains of chalk—you crossed them?" asked Duran.

Jake kept his expression earnest. These Mexicans hugged the coast like seagulls. They had not even ventured far enough east to see that the white on the mountains was snow, not chalk and he would not enlighten them.

"Yes, Padre. Very arduous. A most inhospitable country. Only the knowledge that we would find Christians here in California kept us alive." He left out telling the men about the fertile valleys high in the Sierra Nevada range or the streams full of trout and meadows overflowing with elk, deer and buffalo.

"Like the Israelites of old, you have found the land of milk and honey and may now take your ease."

"We are most grateful to you all," said Jake.

Satisfied at last, Father Duran clasped his hands together and rubbed vigorously. "Please tell the *señora* that we will say a mass for her husband and all the others in her party, if you will give us the names."

"I will."

"And you know I must alert the governor of your arrival in our country. A formality."

"Of course." He spoke directly to Emma, pausing to allow Jake time to translate. "Now, my child, you must rest. We have prepared a room."

Jake relayed Duran's words and Emma smiled.

"Thank you, Mr. Turner." She rose and nodded stiffly to Jake. Her formality irritated him and he wondered if it was for the benefit of the others or as a way to distance herself from him.

She rose with all the majesty of an exiled princess and followed Father Duran from the room. She was no more loquacious at dinner than lunch and she retired immediately afterward.

Jake found he did not like that she could come and go as she pleased. He most especially did not like sleeping in the friar's quarters beside the snoring Father José.

Penned in beneath the tile roof and surrounded by walls for the first time in several years, he felt as if he slept on an anthill.

Breathing became difficult and the creak of men moving in their rope-strung beds kept him awake.

How did Emma fare? She had a private chamber, a converted storage area off the workrooms, with a window to the courtyard. Did she miss him?

Finally, he fell into a restless sleep. He woke several times reaching for Emma. When the brothers rose to the bells, he felt as if he'd been pummeled all night.

At breakfast he found Emma, her skin shining from a good scrubbing and her hair tucked neatly into a bun. He scowled at the formal style, preferring the central braid she wore on the trail.

"How did you sleep, Señora Martin?" asked Father Duran.

Jake translated and waited for her to answer.

"Never better. What a joy to rest on a mattress once more."

Jake ground his teeth together. She enjoyed her comforts, like every woman. Why had he thought her different? The fact that she slept well irritated him after his restlessness. Hadn't he woken many times to search for her? Then he noted the circles beneath her eyes and paused. The ridiculousness of his resentment hit him, replaced by guilt. No one deserved a bit of comfort more than Emma and he begrudged her even that. His scowl deepened as he relayed her thanks to the missionary.

Emma smiled as Father José poured coffee into her ceramic mug then leaned forward to inhale the aromatic steam.

"Hmm, heaven." She added honey and stirred. Then glanced at Jake.

Over the next week Jake and Emma enjoyed the brothers' hospitality before receiving escort to Santa Clara de Asis, some thirty miles west. This mission had more vineyards than cattle. The whitewashed walls of the church topped with a red tile roof reached two stories. Here Father Ignacio Martinez took charge of them for two days until a letter arrived instructing them south to Monterey to meet the governor.

Father Martinez graciously escorted them to the mission at Santa Cruz. Here Jake caught his first glimpse of the Pacific

Ocean. He sat on his horse on the gentle slope of a hill surrounded by the largest pines he had ever seen. The monstrous trees would take four men to reach around them and were covered in thick red bark.

He heard the surf first. Below the ridge, waves rolled into a perfect tube before crashing upon the beach.

When he turned to Emma, he found her eyes dancing with delight as she sat silent upon her horse. Their gazes met and held. She understood the meaning. His map to the Pacific was complete.

He breathed a sigh of relief and wished he could take her in his arms again. The happiness inside him seemed to spill out and he found it hard to sit his horse.

"Have you ever seen the ocean?" asked Father Martinez.

"Only the Atlantic and there the beach is flat and the water a dirty green, not this magnificent blue."

"Yes, yes, the lure of the sea. Just a little north, we have the port of San Francisco and also ships come to Monterey, though the harbor is not protected by a bay."

A few hours later, the brothers at Santa Cruz welcomed them warmly, but had no private quarters for Emma and had instead arranged for them to stay in a private home with the owner of a local mercantile, Señor John Price.

"Is he English?" asked Jake.

"No, once an American, like yourself. He married into the family of Peralta. A very good match, as they own two thousand head. He brings the business savvy and they the cattle. He is now a member of the true faith and a citizen of Mexico. I think Señora Martin would appreciate a woman's company after being so long in the wilderness."

Jake considered if this might be true. Emma had lived in a fort full of soldiers and these last two months he had been her only companion—a poor one at that. Guilt sparked again at his lack of control. Why had he taken her?

And why did he want her again?

Martinez turned his attention to the town. By the time they

arrived, Jake knew the names of all the prominent families. He filed this away and wondered why the Mexicans thought nothing of showing him the bounty they possessed. He had yet to see a single soldier or fortification anywhere in California. He was most interested to hear about their forts, which the Mexicans called presidios. According to his host, there was one in Monterey.

He turned his attention to the power structure.

"Is the governor in command of all of California?"

"No, *Señor*. The territory is broken into two territories, southern and the northern. We are in the northernmost section. Beyond the San Francisco Mission along the coast is Russian territory."

"How do you get on with your neighbors?"

"They tried to take the bay, but our missions deterred them. They grow nothing. They raise nothing. They are only interested in otter and seal pelts."

"I've done some trapping in my time."

"Perhaps you would like to speak with them. Here in California the only hides we deal with are cattle. The sailors call them Mexican banknotes." Martinez laughed. "It is true, for hides and tallow keep us well supplied. There is nothing the ships do not bring us."

"From Mexico?"

"No, from rest of the world—England, France and America. We welcome all."

Jake knew this, but did not understand it. Any vessel with commodities to trade was allowed ashore. The authorities set arbitrary taxes and lined their pockets. But they did not defend their ports. One American man-of-war could take any harbor on the coast. Such rich land warranted protecting. The Mexicans either could not or would not take the steps to populate and protect what was theirs.

It was their weakness, that, and their hospitality.

They reached the two-story adobe structure with a wide

front porch and upper balcony of wood. Standing in the shade, dressed as a Mexican in dark trousers, white shirt and a short coat, stood their host. Jake smiled to see he had even adopted the wide mustache of his new countrymen. Beside him, his wife, Francisca, stood like an exotic bird. One glance and he saw why Price was willing to leave his home and faith. The woman radiated lush beauty. Dark eyes flashed beneath raven eyebrows. It was a moment before he noticed she was heavy with child. A toddler, barely able to stand, clung to the red fabric of her ankle-length skirt.

"Mr. Turner." Price stepped down from the shade to greet him as Jake dismounted and gave him a firm handshake. "I am so happy to meet you, astonished, really. Welcome to my home. Let me present my wife, Francisca."

The woman moved gracefully for one so burdened. She raised her hand, palm down and Jake accepted it, dropping a kiss on the fine skin.

"Thank you for extending your hospitality to us, *señora*." He spoke in Spanish, but she answered in English, heavy with accent.

"I welcome you both to our home. I am so happy to practice English with Señora Martin." She turned to Emma and kissed her on both cheeks.

Emma beamed and blushed, before Francisca led her into her home. Price motioned with his hand and Jake followed the women. The missionaries trailed behind leaving the servants to look after their horses. Jake glanced back at Duchess and his saddle, containing his precious journal. Jake patted his bag, assuring himself that he had the map painted on the leather.

In the main room he found the table already set with a white linen cloth and silver candlesticks. Francisca waved a hand at the bees drawn to the sweet juice of the ripe fruit upon her table and they droned into the air.

"Please be sit," said Francisca.

"Thank you." Emma took the chair her hostess indicated.

An Indian with short hair, wearing a clean white shirt and gray trousers approached holding a ceramic mug of red wine, laden with slices of fruit.

Emma accepted a mug. "Oh, more wine." She glanced at Jake as if for rescue. "How lovely."

"This wine is from Spain."

Jake took his place. "Spain? When you have vineyards all about you?"

"Most of the mission wine never reaches town. Also, this is better."

Jake noted that everything in the room seemed to have come from a ship. Even the table looked to be of white oak, possibly from France. With all the wood in the forest, these Mexicans did not even make their own furnishings.

Emma sipped her wine and when the servant refilled her cup, she gave him another meaningful glance.

Francisca noted Emma's distress. "Perhaps you would prefer chocolate?"

A quick order to a servant and a mug of coffee laced with chocolate was set before Emma. She sipped and smiled. Jake found himself smiling, as well.

After the meal, the missionaries departed and Jake took a tour of the port with Mr. Price, leaving Emma with the effervescent Francisca.

He smelled the tannery a mile off from upwind. The reek of rotting flesh permeated the very clay of the adobe warehouse. He found that Price traded hides and bags of tallow with the captains, filling his mercantile with goods. The trade regulations once imposed by Spain seemed permanently suspended since Mexico took over the territory. The arm of the authorities in Acapulco was not long enough to effectively manage this outlying territory and these settlers seemed greedy for the goods the ships supplied.

From Price's warehouse, Jake could see the presidio. The fort was well situated on the highest ground on the north edge of the harbor on the wooded hill. To the south the harbor was sandy with gentle hills. In the center stood Price's warehouse along with the houses of the residents. Jake estimated there to be about one hundred structures including the tannery and warehouses upon the beach.

The harbor offered sheltered ports and deep water. One ship, the *Loriotte,* lay at anchor. According to his host, the brig sailed from the Sandwich Islands to the coast of Peru and then back to California again.

"The captain is an American, Charles Billings, but his crew is a mix of Spaniards, Spanish Indians, Sandwich Islanders and a few English sailors," said Price.

An American captain. Jake's lips curled. "I'd like to meet him."

Price nodded. "I assumed so. He'll attend the banquet tomorrow."

"What banquet?"

"The one my wife is holding in your honor. And in her condition, I indulge her. The entire town is invited."

Jake eyed the fort, seeing no evidence of heavy artillery. "What about General Vallejo?"

"Oh, the general never misses a horse race. I'm sure you will meet him tomorrow."

As it happened, Francisca invited the sea captain for supper. He was climbing the hill from the port as Jake and John Price returned from their ride about town. They dismounted to walk beside the man.

"A pleasure, sir," said Billings, shaking his hand with vigor. "It isn't often I have a chance to speak English here."

Jake judged Billings to be over thirty and bursting with strength and good health. His blue eyes shone clear and bright. He wore bushy sideburns and the thick black mustache of a New England captain as his accent made Jake believe him to be.

"Boston?" asked Jake.

"Aye, that's a fact."

"I'd like to see your ship, Captain. Would that be possible?"

Jake prayed it would, as he needed time alone with the captain in order to make his proposal.

"Wednesday evening?"

"Wonderful."

"I'll send in a boat before dark on the second tide."

Jake considered that everything was going wonderfully. He'd need this evening to make final additions to the second map.

Price's voice drew his attention.

"Ah, I'm afraid we will have to switch to Spanish. I see General Vallejo could not contain his curiosity until tomorrow."

Jake glanced to the wide shaded porch, which Price had furnished like a living room, with benches, tables and chairs. A slender man of some considerable height, dressed in the blue-and-red uniform of a Mexican officer sat beside Emma deep in conversation. Upon her lap lay her sketchbook. Jake felt the pit of his stomach drop. How long had he been questioning her?

Standing in the sun four more soldiers stood, bearing arms. Jake moved to full alert.

His step quickened, but then he forced himself to maintain the easy pace of his fellows, pushing down the dread. He should have known the authorities would find her first. Had she held to the story? His chest pained from the accelerated beating of his heart.

Francisca Price rose, beaming a great smile, which looked brighter for her red lips. Her thick black hair, now swept up in elaborate combs, lay partially covered by a veil of white lace.

"At last you come. General Vallejo growing tired of the company of women, I thinking."

Price kissed his wife, resting a proprietary hand on the swell of her belly for just an instant, then switched to Spanish.

"Nonsense, no other hostess compares to you, my dear."

Francisca flushed at the compliment. "Señora Martin has been sharing the story of your terrible ordeals. My goodness, what you suffered. I think you better both stay here. Certainly life in California is preferable to facing that desert again." She slipped her arm into the crook of her husband's elbow and led him to a seat. "Did you know that Señora Martin is a crack shot? She killed a pouncing mountain lion."

Jake found the general's eyes fixed on him as if taking his measure. Vallejo extended his hand, but his expression remained too serious for a friendly greeting and they exchanged only the slightest brushing of palms.

"Señor Turner, the missionaries sent word of your arrival in our territory."

Jake thought he overemphasized the word *our.*

"Do you have the proper papers to enter California?"

Price stepped in. "Señor Turner had no intention of ever entering California, so why would he have papers?"

Vallejo nodded, but kept his eyes focused on Jake. His smile was not friendly. "So Señora Martin has been telling me. Still there must be papers. To travel without them is not permitted."

"I'm sure we can write to Acapulco and obtain the blasted things," said Price.

"What about some proof that you are who you say?"

Francisca inhaled sharply, clearly insulted on Jake's behalf. "General Vallejo—"

"This is the least that is expected. I am executing my duties, Doña Price." He bowed to her.

She lifted her chin in a way that made Jake think she was not accustomed to being overruled in her home.

"I have already sent word to Santa Barbara of our visitors' arrival. I am confident that Governor-General Echeandia will be most curious to meet you both. As you might know, you are not the first Americans to appear from the East. Captain Smith left our company only three years ago." The general turned to Jake. "He violated the terms of our agreement, fleeing to the mountains when I sent men to apprehend him."

"I hope you do not judge us all on the behavior of one man."

"There were rather more than one. But you Americans have

to learn that proper protocol must be maintained, papers among them."

Jake nodded. "I will do whatever you deem necessary to see that protocol is followed."

"I should like to ask you a few questions, if I may. I have a good picture of your experience from Señora Martin already."

Jake turned to Emma and saw concern reflected in the swirling smoke of her eyes. He needed to speak with her, but how to do it?

The general turned to their host. "May we just borrow your study for a few moments?"

Price led the way and Jake trailed behind, pausing to drop his satchel beside Emma's chair. He watched her hand move so slowly it was barely perceptible until she held the strap firmly in her hand.

He turned to see if the general was out of earshot and noted he stood just inside the door, waiting like a cat for a mouse.

"Sergeant, bring me that bag," said Vallejo. He then motioned to another man to follow. Finally, he pinned Jake with a confident smile. *"Señor?"*

Jake followed him with leaden steps. Emma did what he had asked of her. He knew it in his heart. But had she embellished? Had she inadvertently set a trap for him to step into? The general was a fox and he the hare. He would ask for minute details, the kind two people could never match when questioned separately.

The general motioned to a doorway that Price held open off the main living area. His host waited for Jake to pass, his expression serious. The general entered first, then Jake, followed by Vallejo's two men. Jake turned to find Price withdrawing.

Jake would face this challenge alone.

Vallejo motioned to a chair, but as he did not sit, so Jake declined. The sergeant still clutched his possibles bag. Jake thought of the map secreted on the inner lining of his creation and forced himself to breath evenly.

The questioning began with the Indian attack, asking details about the Mojave which Jake readily supplied. He wanted specifics about the desert crossing and how they managed to break the barrier of the mountains.

"Until Captain Smith arrived in Santa Barbara, we thought the mountains invulnerable," said Vallejo. "You Americans must understand that this territory belongs to Mexico. We will defend it from invasion."

"I assure you, General, I am no invader. Only an unfortunate traveler asking for the hospitality of Christians in the wilderness."

"So you say, but I wonder if you are instead a scout."

"Strong words," said Jake. "You accuse me of subterfuge when I am only guilty of volunteering to help Señora Martin across a river. Nothing more sinister than chance brought us to you."

The general tugged at his mustache. "Perhaps. But what proof do you offer?"

"I have none, except the lion skin that Señora Martin shot, oh, and a sketchbook she kept of our journey."

"Yes, I have seen this. She has a talent. It does document your journey very well, too well, perhaps. It does not, however, document your purpose."

"As I said, we seek refuge from the wilderness."

"You look like a man who seeks refuge *in* the wilderness."

"Ah, but I have a woman in my care. I owe it to her husband to see she reaches civilization and returns to her people."

Vallejo laughed. "I believe her people are somewhat east of this position. Where have you been this afternoon?"

"Price showed me his warehouse and took me to the harbor."

"So you have seen three missions, counted our cattle, toured our vineyards and scouted our defenses. Not bad work for the ten days since your arrival."

Jake said nothing, fearing he would sound defensive.

"We will continue this conversation again soon. I am certain the governor-general will wish to meet with you."

"I await your pleasure." Jake thought his bow somewhat rusty.

Vallejo motioned to his sergeant who handed his commander

Jake's bag. The General dumped the contents on the desk and then glanced into the empty pocket. Jake could not keep his breath from catching. If he cut the seams, he'd reveal the map and his deception. In a moment Vallejo tossed the sack aside. He inspected the contents of his smaller fire-starting kit, seeming disgusted by the birch fungus and considering the flint, steel and tinder.

Next he fingered the telescope and compass.

Jake waited as he palmed his compass, feeling sweat dribble down his spine. Vallejo turned and lifted the item.

"Yours?"

"Common enough in the mountains."

"Also common in the military. Standard, in fact. Have you ever served, Señor Turner?"

"I've spent the last eight years trapping in the Rocky Mountains."

"And before that?"

"Trapped as a clerk for my father."

The general chuckled. "Why is your Spanish so good? This is not common, I think. Smith needed a translator for our meetings."

The men stared at each other a moment as Jake searched his mind.

"I went to an academy where French and Spanish were required, along with Latin. Do you speak Latin, General?"

Jake knew the man from Smith's stories. He had been educated here in California, with only what books could be borrowed.

"I'm afraid not."

He turned back to the items before him and carefully checked the contents of each pouch. When he finished, his expression held clear disappointment.

"Señor Turner, please remove your shirt."

"Is this how you treat all your guests?" asked Jake, letting his ire seep into his voice.

"Your arrival is very suspicious. You admit you are a scout. But for whom are you scouting?"

"I told you, I worked for Emma Martin's husband. Let me

ask you a question. If I planned to come here, why would I drag a woman over those mountains?"

Vallejo dropped to the chair. "This disturbs me. It is the question to which I find no easy answer. If you are what I think you to be then burdening yourself with a woman would be very foolish indeed."

"I agree. So maybe what I say is true."

Vallejo rested his knuckles on the desk as he leaned over the surface. "Take your shirt off."

Jake laid his powder horn on the desk and removed his belt. The General poured some of the contents from his horn onto his palm as Jake pulled the buckskin over his head. The corporal retrieved the garment and handed it to the general who searched the hide while the corporal swept a hand down Jake's legs, then stepped away.

"Your shoes," said the general.

Jake tugged off his moccasins and the sergeant pulled them inside out before tossing them back.

The general paced behind his desk, his agitation clear.

"Gather your things."

When Jake finished collecting himself, Vallejo smiled and glanced out the window. Jake noted the soldiers were missing. His teeth clenched as he considered where they might be. "Follow me, Señor Turner."

On the front porch lay all his belongings neatly displayed as if for sale. Jake's gaze raked the wooden slats noting his saddle, blanket, Emma's clothing, their bedding, her firearms and his. His gaze locked on his rifle, noting the secret compartment open. They had found his sexton and map, then. He glanced about. It was a moment before he realized the incriminating items were not in view. Confiscated already and he had not even managed to get a copy to the American sea captain. He had failed. The Mexicans' hospitality and lax defense had lulled him into a false sense of security. His mistake would cost his life. A fair exchange for his folly.

But what of Emma?

He needed to protect her. In that instant he knew he would do anything, including jeopardize his mission, in order to save this woman's life.

Chapter Seventeen

❦

Jake had underestimated his foe. He saw that now. Just because they lacked militia and arms, just because the friars and merchants of California accepted him at his word did not mean they were stupid.

He would have done the same in Vallejo's position. No, he would have taken him into immediate custody as a precaution.

Jake stared at Emma, who sat with a fixed rigidity radiating tension. Her face now a mask of alert caution, she said not a word, but seemed to be desperate to speak to him with her eyes. He noted the rapid breathing as she perched on the wooden chair, her army-blue skirt draping the porch like a rolling wave.

Francisca stood beside her, a scowl upon her forehead. John grasped his wife's hand and gave it a reassuring pat. Jake's instinct was to move to Emma and stand between her and the danger these men presented. But he held himself in check. Four men and the general—he was outmanned.

Vallejo now inspected their belongings, his boot heels striking the hollow wooden decking with an echoing thud.

He paused at Jake's rifle, then stooped and lifted the gun noting the open chamber in the hollow stock. He seemed unable to contain his glee as the corners of his mustache lifted.

"What was in this compartment?" he asked his underling.

Jake's stomach squeezed the contents of Francisca's excellent lunch and his skin grew damp. It would be only a moment now and they'd have him. Duchess, where was his horse? It didn't matter. He could not run, not with Emma sitting there before him on the porch.

The man snapped a salute and then pointed to the leather bag. Jake's forehead wrinkled in confusion.

The general lifted the pouch and peered inside. Then he upended the contents. Round lead balls struck the wooden planks like hailstones. Jake flashed Emma a look, but she remained rigid, staring at the general.

"What is this?" Vallejo scowled at Jake.

"Extra ammunition," he said, wondering if the ice in his gut would ever thaw.

"Why is it hidden?"

"Your men found it all right."

Vallejo threw the pouch against the wall and frowned as he lifted the red ribbon.

"Trade goods," said Jake. "So are the knife blades, awls, buttons and beads."

He lifted the lion skin cloak and thrust a finger through the bullet hole in the side. "A good shot, Señora Martin. Where did a missionary learn to shoot like a soldier?"

Jake turned to Emma, who did not answer. "She does not speak Spanish."

"Yes, I know. Doña Price has been kind enough to help me translate. Let me try in English then." He smiled at Emma and Jake's skin crawled. "Mrs. Martin, you learned to shoot where?"

Emma kept her gaze on the general. "I followed my husband's instructions. He thought it necessary that I learn to defend myself."

"Ah, of course. This gun, it is not the same as the party of Captain Smith. You purchased it where?"

"I did not purchase it. My husband did and, as you know,

he is not here to answer your questions." Tears welled and Jake felt a mix of admiration and unease at her performance.

Francisca released her husband's hand and faced the general. Her feminine attire did not completely diffuse the authority of her carriage.

"General Vallejo, we have done as you asked. Please complete your search. I am embarrassed to display my guests' belongings as if it were market day."

The general's mustache twitched as he faced the wealthy daughter of a powerful landowner.

"Don Price, I can deny your wife nothing. Just indulge me for a few more moments." Like a swooping hawk, he studied the items before him. He lifted the saddle. Jake's mouth went dry. Somewhere beneath the general's left hand lay the journal.

The general dropped the saddle on its spine and shoved it with his boot, then turned to the next item.

Jake found his breath again as Vallejo turned to Emma's things; his fingers brushing the lace on the hem of her bloomers.

Jake felt a shot of anger. Like whiskey in his blood, it made him rash. He took a step forward, finding his hand on the man's arm.

Vallejo smiled. "I would be careful, if I were you."

"Well, you're not me and I'd take my hand off Señora Martin's undergarments before I found myself lying on my back in the street."

Vallejo released the fabric. "So angry, almost as if she was your wife instead of a duty you have struggled to discharge."

Jake stepped away and let the general finish his search. When the man reached the end of the porch, he masked his disappointment poorly.

"This is all?" he asked the closest man.

"Yes, General."

"Are you certain?"

"We carried out all the things in the house then went to the barn for the rest."

"Did anyone stay with these things when you went to search the barn?"

The man blanched. "You were with Señor Turner, sir."

Vallejo spun about pinning Emma with the gaze of a predator. Jake understood in that instant that Emma hid his sextant and map. Vallejo knew, or at least suspected, as well.

Before Jake could intercept him, Doña Francisca stepped forward. "We have been very cooperative, General. I waited with Señora Martin while your men searched both my house and my outbuildings. Now, I think it is time for supper. Will you be joining us?"

Jake could have kissed her. He did not know why she stood between Emma and harm's way, but he was grateful.

The General stopped glowering first at his men and then at Emma. Finally, he bowed to Doña Francisca.

"I am sorry to inconvenience you. I will call again when the governor-general sends word." Then he descended the steps to the street and cuffed the nearest man in the head with his open hand. "Idiots," he muttered.

Jake hung on to a thick whitewashed post and watched the general mount up. Soon they were gone. Jake's shoulders drooped. He turned to Emma, finding her resting her head in her hands.

Doña Francisca already had her maids gathering up their belongings and setting things to right. She ushered her servants into the house, leaving Emma with the men. Captain Billings lifted his cap, holding it between a thumb and forefinger as he scratched with the other three.

"The man definitely has it in for you, Turner. Thinks you're a bloody spy."

"Because he came over the mountains. Until Captain Smith showed up, they thought the mountains impenetrable," said Price.

"Now you arrive and with a woman. Makes it seem anyone with a horse can make the journey," added Captain Billings.

Jake decided to feign ignorance. "So I'm a threat?"

"But not a spy," said Billings.

Jake said nothing and the captain lifted his eyebrows until they quite disappeared under his cap.

"Great blue blazes, you aren't, are you?"

"I am a guide, hired by the Martin party." Jake watched relief cross John Price's features, but the captain seemed less inclined to take things at face value.

The captain folded his hands behind him and gazed out at the dusty street. "What if you weren't?"

Jake said nothing, but his gaze flicked to Price, judging his serious expression as he rubbed his chin.

The captain continued. "In that case I would remind you that I have been away from America for nearly nine years, but I am still a loyal citizen. My allegiance lies with Old Glory. But I would not favor jeopardizing my harbor privileges."

Jake nodded. "I understand, Captain Billings, and I greatly look forward to our dinner onboard ship."

The captain nodded. "You might like to know that Mr. Price and I have long considered this territory underutilized. I'd say between the two of us, we have seen most of California, I, by sea, and my friend here, by land. Isn't that right, John?"

Price nodded, his expression still etched with worry.

"That sort of information could be very useful in the right hands. What do you say, John?"

Price sighed. "I say I would not endanger my family."

Jake understood. The man was a Mexican citizen.

"But I would favor living beneath an American flag," Price said.

Jake's head snapped up and his gaze shot from one man to the next. They offered support before he even asked. His confidence returned. He was not alone.

"I'm off," said the captain. "Matters on ship and all. I will see you both tomorrow."

"Won't you stay for dinner?" asked Price.

"Another time. Please give your wife my regrets."

The captain shook Price's hand and then Jake's. "Until tomorrow, then."

Jake watched him steer down the center of the street on sturdy legs.

Francisca returned and called her husband inside. Price followed her without hesitation, leaving Jake alone with Emma.

He sank on his knees before her and took her face in his hands. "How did you do it?"

Her red lips invited, but he held himself in check. Somehow she had saved him and the mission.

"Where is my sextant, the map?"

His fingers burned against her pale, cool skin. He felt her trembling begin, like a bowstring after the arrow is well away.

She leaned forward and he released her with reluctance. She grasped the hem of her skirts and lifted, revealing her moccasins. His sextant lay protected between her bare ankles, beneath the instrument rested the map.

"He caught me with the sketchbook, before I could hide the thing."

Jake threw his head back and laughed, then he pulled her up out of the chair and into his arms.

"You are the most wonderful woman in the world." He lowered her, letting her body slide against his. The relief of an instant before ignited into a bonfire. He wrapped his arms about her and determined to kiss her soundly.

He did not expect his advances to be greeted with such ardor. In an instant he whisked her across the porch and pressed her to the wall. She gripped his neck fiercely as she drew him to her.

It was the ringing of church bells that finally broke into his awareness. He pulled away, blinking down at Emma, who panted, openmouthed. He dipped to taste her again, but she turned away and he was met with the soft skin of her cheek.

Broad daylight. His surroundings rushed back. She's a widow and he, her guide. He glanced back, embarrassed to see the map and sextant lying in plain view.

Jake released her and stepped away.

"I'm sorry," he offered.

She said nothing, but turned to retrieve his treasures.

"How did you do it?"

"One of the men tossed your rifle to a second and there was a rattle. The soldier held the stock up to his ear and shook your gun. Before he could investigate, the officer called them to the barn. I waited until they rounded the house and then I retrieved it."

"Didn't Francisca see you?"

"She did. It was her idea to put it under my skirts."

Jake absorbed the surprise of this. "Why did she do it?"

"I don't know. She just joined in."

"And you switched the lead balls into the stock?"

She nodded.

"Damn clever."

"The men came back in a big hurry, ignored your saddle and went right to the rifle. The soldier must have told them about the noise. It took time to release the mechanism."

"And all they found was lead." He laughed. "I have to find a new place to hide these." He slipped his map and sextant into his moccasin.

"I could make a pocket in my petticoat."

That would keep the thing out of sight, but if they searched her person as they had his, she could not deny involvement.

"No."

"Why not?"

"If they find it, they will hang you beside me."

"I know the importance of this. I can be as brave as you. Let me help you."

He paused as his mind and heart battled. She proved trustworthy over and over. She was resourceful, smart and an actress of the first caliber. But she was a woman, fickle and unreliable.

"I can do it," she urged.

He met her beseeching gaze and nodded. She could. She would. "All right."

She sighed and placed a hand over his heart. "Thank you."

"How long did the general question you?"

"Seemed like hours."

"What did he ask and what did you tell him? I have to know exactly."

"I told him what we agreed upon."

"What about details?"

"He asked me to describe John Martin. I did."

"Tell me what you said, so my description matches yours."

"I described you."

He straightened. "I thought you said he was your first love?"

"I made that up to make you jealous."

"What?"

Her complexion brightened to an alluring shade of pink. Her ploy had worked, too, as he recalled. News of her involvement with the fictitious Mr. Martin irritated him as much as sand in his eye.

"I can't tell when you're telling the truth any better than General Vallejo."

"He asked me about the attack, what direction did they come from, what were they wearing, what color were their horses, how did they wear their hair."

Jake's stomach knotted and reknotted at this. "What did you say?"

"I told him I was too distraught to notice such trivialities and I refused to relive my husband's death for his benefit."

Jake gave a low whistle. "Bet he didn't like that."

"Not a bit. He pressed me, so I cried."

"Women usually do."

She dug a fist into her hip. "What would you suggest?"

He knew a kettle when it was about to boil over. He chose to remove it from the heat.

"I'm proud of you. You thought quickly and pulled my fat from the fire. I'm indebted to you."

The fist remained planted. "I don't want you indebted."

"What do you want?"

She continued to stare until he needed to resist the urge to shift beneath her regard. Those damn smoky eyes again.

"I'd like you to treat me with a little respect and allow that a woman handles problems differently than a man. That doesn't make it wrong."

"I don't know what you mean."

She rounded on him, finger aimed like a pistol at his chest. "Oh, yes, you do. You lie to the general and it is clever. I lie and it's deceitful. You are a hypocrite."

That brought him up short. He gritted his teeth and stared at the mouth now pinched and realized that only a moment before the tender flesh yielded to him. Not now. Now she looked capable of pressing grapes between them.

"I am not a hypocrite. I just don't think using tears is fair."

"Oh, you don't."

He shook his head and watched her lower lip thrust forward as she prepared for battle.

"And just how do suggest I fight a man, with my fists? Perhaps I should wrestle. Would that be fair? I know, let's have a footrace, me in my skirt and three petticoats and you in your breeches."

"What are you blathering about?"

"I'm trying to come to terms with what weapons a woman, who is smaller, weaker and legally dependent upon a man, has in her arsenal. I'd say tears are a poor substitute for all the advantages you enjoy."

He frowned at her, but could find no retort.

"I won't be manipulated that way."

"Did it ever enter your mind that a woman might not be dead set on entrapping you, but only trying to live with you peacefully without being crushed beneath your boot heels? I am tired of being cast as the sly fox and you as the hapless hare, when the truth is you call all the shots, you make all the decisions and you do most of the lying."

He gaped at her as she leaned toward him.

"You should try a step or two in my shoes and see how you like it."

He'd never considered any of those things and the truth of her words lifted his defenses. "Just don't try tears on me."

"I won't waste the water."

She turned away, but he snatched up her arm and spun her against him.

"I'm not through yet."

"Well then I suppose I'm not, either, since you have me captured. Perhaps I should cry on you. The water might work like scissors worked for Delilah."

He found his grip relaxing as the truth of her accusations sank in. He could hold her for as long as he liked and she could do nothing about it. He could take advantage of her person whenever he chose and she could not avoid him.

"Is this how your father treats you?"

"Multiply this by a thousand and you still will fall short."

His hands fell away. "I don't want to hurt you."

"Well, it is too late to prevent that. I believe I saved your sextant from confiscation. But you still don't condone my crying for the general. Is that about it?"

His head sank. "What can I do to make it up to you?"

"Stay away from me."

She spun so quickly, her skirt flared out behind as she stormed away. He let her go, knowing he could retrieve her whenever he wanted and suddenly feeling quite disgusted by the fact.

Chapter Eighteen

The morning of the feast, Emma put aside her annoyance long enough to walk with Jake to the barn on the pretense of checking the horses. The silence stretched as they entered the stuffy barn.

He knew she still smarted from their discussion yesterday. The entire conversation sat in his stomach like old cheese.

"Emma, I regret my harsh words. I want to thank you for all you've done. I'll not make excuses, but I'd like to say that I've never met a woman like you. All the others, they were tricksters, so I'm naturally suspicious."

"Rather a blessing in your chosen profession." Her tone held none of its usual warmth.

"Do you forgive me?" He found himself holding his breath waiting for the opinion of a woman and the fact astounded him.

"Apologies are less appealing than actions. A change in your attitude would go a long way toward a change in mine."

What did that mean? "So will you forgive me?"

"I will, if you cease to treat me as if I were contagious."

He nodded. "Fair enough."

She turned to go and he flanked her, not ready to leave her yet, but unwilling to restrain her. He reached out with his voice.

"Francisca told me there will be horse races."

"Bearbaiting, too. If the bear wins they cook the steer," she observed.

"I'm not anxious to see that. Grizzlies deserve more respect."

"What about the cockfights?"

"I don't have much regard for chickens. Stupidest animal and dirtier than pigs."

"I understand they have wild horses and some of the younger men will try to ride them. It's called a rodeo."

Emma led him to the horses as she led the conversation. Another trick women used. When they reached Duchess, he paused and she drew to a stop. He turned to the matter that required privacy.

He patted the pouch he'd constructed to hide his copy of all the maps in his journal. "I want to get this to Billings, but it must be done in private. I'm going tomorrow to his ship. After that, I'd like to gather supplies and get out of here before we outstay our welcome."

"General Vallejo said we need papers to travel. He said we have to remain here until the authorities allow us to go."

"He's got only twenty-nine men, most of them funded by the local businessmen, which is why he can't restrict trade. It seems Mexico has no coin to spare for maintaining armies. We can't outrun him if he chases us. But I don't think he will. The General can't afford to leave the coast unprotected."

"So we will just leave?"

He nodded. "At night. Smith tried to follow the regulations. It took months of dithering to finally grant permission and then they rescinded his letters of transit. Of course, he had forty well-trained, well-armed men. Easier to delay two people and we can't wait months. We need to cross that desert in the winter."

She gave him a doubtful look. His mind flashed back to Emma in the desert the day she nearly died. How much more terrible to face the wasteland a second time after barely surviving the first?

"We'll be ready this time," he assured. "I'll carry more water."

"You said yourself you can only bring so much and we have two less horses now. Will you follow the same route?"

He shook his head, keeping his gaze fastened upon her, asking her to be brave with his eyes.

"Well then, best face that in the winter."

"We have to leave within the month."

"All right then." She turned to go, but he stayed her with his hand.

Her eyebrow arched, challenging him and he released her instantly.

"Emma, if I am arrested, take these to Captain Billings." He extended his satchel and an envelope constructed from paper, tied with red trade ribbon and sealed with wax. She read the name of the addressee and the queer feeling returned to her stomach, as if some crawling thing wriggled within her. Neat blue letters spelled President Andrew Jackson, President, United States.

Jake retained his grip on the document as she accepted the other end. His gaze met hers and locked as her breath came in short panicked breaths. Why did he talk of being arrested?

"Will you?" he asked.

"You know I will."

He released the letter and she stooped to open the secret pouch beneath her skirts. She tucked in the papers then dropped the hem of the bright green skirt Francisca had lent her. The hem fell short by American standards, just brushing her ankles. When she straightened she found him staring at her.

"What?" she asked.

"Seeing that much leg does something to my insides. Damned if I don't want to kiss you again."

A tingling awareness danced over her skin as she considered how very much she wanted to kiss him, as well. But she wouldn't. She was a widow and they stood in a barn that was nearly as public as the street where he'd kissed her yesterday.

She lifted her chin. "I'm still in mourning."

"Of course. I wonder if you might take charge of this, as well?" He draped the satchel over her shoulder. "The sextant is within."

She understood this act as a peace offering and a validation. He told her without words he trusted her with matters of importance. But there was something else. He didn't think he'd be here to do it. He talked of escape and planned for capture. Bands of fear squeezed the breath from her.

"I'll keep it safe," she whispered.

"I know." He glanced toward the sun streaming into the barn. "Best get back, before we are missed."

"Jake? Will it be all right?"

He did not offer assurance. "If they take me—go to Billings."

He stroked her cheek and her eyes fluttered shut. She waited. When she opened her eyes, he was gone.

Emma went to help Francisca with her party, tamping down her dread with each step. Soon Emma sat upon her horse beside a great two-wheeled cart, laden with food. Price had his men setting up tables upon wine casks on the hard-packed sand beyond the sea grass at the edge of town.

"Perfect for horse racing. You will see," said Francisca.

Emma noticed the spits set up upon the beach and wandered down the path to the sand. Great hollows had been dug. Several men carried shovels full of hot coals from the bonfire to lay beneath the roasting meat.

Emma counted three lambs and a steer, split in two like a chicken carcass. She watched four men turn the thing, using metal poles.

Francisca laid out bowls and utensils. Kegs were placed and readied for the tap. Three musicians holding guitars began to play. This seemed to be the signal for the party to commence. The town turned out to celebrate.

Women gathered at the tables to arrange the meal. Her hostess introduced her in English and Spanish, but none of the women spoke anything but Spanish.

Emma spent the early afternoon nodding and being dragged to and fro. Francisca led her down the path to watch the races.

Far down the beach a group of men sat on agitated horses waiting. The crack of a rifle shot signaled the start. The men kicked at their horses. Sand flew from hooves as they thundered down the beach. She recognized Duchess on the ocean side galloping along and found herself cheering and waving a kerchief with the rest of the women.

The finish line loomed and a pinto nosed forward, beating Duchess by half a length. The woman beside her, draped in a shawl embroidered with pink roses, yelled and ran toward the victor. The rider dragged her up before him for a kiss, and then paraded about before the cheering crowd.

Emma found Jake sliding down from Duchess.

His grin warmed her.

"Close one," he said.

She laid a hand on Duchess, whose ribs heaved as she blew great breaths. "I blame the rider."

He laughed. "I think I could have taken them if she'd had a little more rest. The journey has been tough on all of us. The blacksmith looked over the horses."

Emma glanced down at the horse's neatly filed hooves. "You had her clipped."

"And I bought another mule and a good saddle for you."

Emma's heart pounded. "Readying for departure."

He nodded. "Soon. I don't think I can see much of the southern coast. I'll have to rely on Billings and Price for that. North of the bay is the Russian outpost. I've a mind to have a look."

An unwelcome voice broke into their conversation.

"I found you. A good race, Captain." General Vallejo spoke in English. Behind him eight soldiers watched with somber expressions.

Emma's defenses snapped up. Something was very wrong. Had the general gotten word from Santa Barbara so soon?

"My horse is no match for the Spanish ponies."

Vallejo's smile did not reach his eyes. Emma noted that he kept the palm of his hand resting on the butt of his revolver.

"Perhaps you only had the wrong horse."

Emma knew the general toyed with them, but she could not understand the game. She glanced around for some help. Perhaps Doña Francisca would appear, or her husband. She found them standing by the tables beside two soldiers. The worried expression on Francisca's face made Emma's stomach clench. Then she saw him.

A young soldier led forward a familiar horse, a big chestnut gelding. Her mouth went dry and small spots erupted before her eyes. It was Scout.

"Don't faint," she told herself.

Jake glanced her way. "What?"

Then he spied her horse, led forward by a man who looked none to happy with the honor.

"Your horse, I believe," Vallejo said.

Emma was about to deny it, when she saw the general's gaze fastened on Jake.

"Not mine," he said.

Emma marveled at the relaxed tone, the easy posture. She felt like an icicle about to shatter on rock.

The triumph in the general's stare gave Emma strength, turning her terror to resolve. The man looked so smug, so certain.

"This horse is captured to the east. The rancheros is surprised when he see him already gelded. More interesting is this brand." The General moved to Scout's hindquarters and traced the incriminating mark. Scout lifted a hind foot but the general moved away too quickly.

Regret burned into Emma as she recognized that her softhearted nature, her unwillingness to sacrifice her horse's life would cost theirs.

"U.S. How you think this creature came here?"

"Walked?" said Jake.

Vallejo seemed to only like sarcasm when he dealt it. "This is your horse, Turner."

"Not mine. Maybe it got away from Smith's party."

A flicker of doubt crossed Vallejo's face, then he frowned, setting his lips until they whitened.

"Saddle this horse," he shouted.

Two of his men sprang to do his bidding. Scout flattened his ears and nipped at the closest soldier landing a bite that caused the young man to howl and leap away.

A smile crossed her lips and she forced it back. Silly to feel proud of her horse, but she did.

"Mount up," said Vallejo.

Jake shrugged. "I don't know what this will prove."

"No one can ride this horse. The rancheros tried and they are the best riders. This animal belongs only to one man—you."

Jake lifted a foot to the stirrup. Scout swung his head around and Jake slapped him with his hat. Scout's ears flattened as Jake mounted. Emma held her breath as his seat hit the saddle with more force than necessary.

Emma noticed he left the reins very loose allowing Scout to immediately drop his head. For a moment, the horse stood motionless and then erupted into wild bucking sending them all scurrying for safety.

Scout wheeled on his front feet, kicking his hind legs high in the air. The crowd gasped as Jake clung to the saddle horn. Scout crow hopped as sand sprayed in all directions. Finally, Scout succeeded in getting Jake out of the saddle. He bounced once on the creature's hindquarters before soaring through the air in a spectacular arch and landing on the beach hard enough to leave a divot.

Emma rushed to Jake, kneeling as Scout took several more unnecessary kicks. He came to a stop then and stared at Emma, his ears pricked.

Her heart gave a shudder and she glanced away.

Francisca and John now reached Jake.

"Are you injured?" asked John.

Jake shook his head.

"Well, I hope that satisfies you, General. That—" John pointed at Scout "—is most definitely not his horse."

But the general was watching the animal as he nickered.

Emma felt her face heat.

"I fear I make a mistake." His mustache twitched. "It is not his horse. But the Señora's."

Emma felt pinned to the sand. She could not have risen if her life depended upon it. Then she realized that it did.

"I would like to see her ride this horse," said Vallejo.

Francisca stood before her. "Are you mad? That devil will kill her."

John faced Vallejo. "You said yourself that none of the rancheros could ride him. I cannot permit a woman, my guest, to try."

The general faced off with John Price as Emma cowered in the sand trying to look terrified, which she was, but not for the reason they supposed.

"Think I broke my elbow," said Jake, lifting his sleeve to reveal a purple welt upon his arm. "And that fellow needs attention."

Emma glanced to the soldier Scout had bitten and noticed he held his hand over a bleeding wound.

The general scowled at the group before him. "Take that horse to the corral." He stared at Price. "You should remember what country accepted your citizenship."

Price did not blink. "And you should remember that my funding pays the salary of six of your twenty-nine men."

Vallejo's forehead wrinkled further as he pointed at Jake. "I am detaining this man until the governor-general sends word." He waved to his soldiers who quickly grasped Jake's arms.

Emma found her legs beneath her and she beat her fist on the chest of the nearest soldier. The man looked horrified and released Jake to step away.

Jake grasped Emma's arms. "Stop now."

She gazed up at him.

"Remember what we talked about earlier?" His voice was low, barely more than a breath. He lifted his satchel from the sand and draped it onto her shoulder. Beneath her skirts the letter and sextant rested. She understood. The maps, he wanted her to go to the captain.

She nodded.

"There's a good girl." His voice was louder now. "Just like a woman to get hysterical over such a thing. They are such emotional creatures, God love them."

The general gave Emma a dismissive look and she understood. Jake expected her to act like the spy she had asked to become. She set her teeth and lowered her gaze to the beach, making her posture look the picture of defeat. After all—what could one woman do?

Chapter Nineteen

Jake turned from the barred window of his prison cell within the fort and handed the letter to John Price.

"Please give this to Emma and see she gets aboard the *Loriotte* today."

John scowled. "Certainly, but are you sure that's what you want?"

It wasn't. He admitted it to himself. He didn't want to lose Emma anymore than he wanted to lose his life. But he saw no other way to keep her safe than to send her into another man's keeping.

"I dragged her into this mess."

"Good thing, really. She's the only reason Vallejo hesitates. No one in their right mind would bring a woman on such a journey. But if what you say is true and Miss Lancing is your unwilling companion, why has she not sought assistance from my wife or Captain Billings? For what reason does she risk her life to guard your secrets?"

Why had she? "I don't know."

"There is the possibility my wife favors."

He could use a woman's perspective, as he was at a loss. He didn't understand why it was so difficult to do what he knew was right. For Emma's safety, he must get her out of California.

Price continued. "But first I have a question for you. How do you feel about Emma?"

"What do you mean?"

"Simple question, Turner. Would you die for her?"

He nodded without thinking.

"Well, then I'd say my wife is correct. Emma is in love with you. And it appears you are in love with Emma."

Jake stared in silence as that possibility seeped into his brain like water through cracks in the earth. Was it possible? He gazed at the bars of the cellar window. What difference did that make now? His teeth gnashed together and he snapped at Price. "Will you give her the letter or not?"

"I'll be happy to. Also, I have word that Governor-General Echeandia has arrived. Whatever they will do should begin shortly. I am urging that they deport you at your own expense. I, of course, will be happy to fund your passage home." Price grinned and the edges of his mustache lifted.

"Thank you for your efforts."

John extended his hand. "I'll come again tomorrow."

Jake listened to his friend's heels ring along the passage and his knees gave way. He sank to the cellar floor. Could it be true? Could Emma love him?

A wave of longing swept through him. This was best for Emma, but how he ached to hold her in his arms one last time.

He stared at his small rectangle of daylight and wished he could slip between the bars like a sparrow.

When had he fallen in love with her?

What did it matter? He'd turned her life upside down and dragged her nine hundred miles over mountains and deserts. She would be lucky to be rid of him. He smiled.

They'd had a hell of a ride.

"He wants you on that ship," Price said again.

Emma's insides coiled and clenched like an injured snake as she balked against what Jake asked of her.

"But he needs help."

"I am writing to the American ambassador in Mexico, the president of Mexico and to the president of the United States demanding Turner's release. He has friends here."

"How long will that take?"

He glanced away.

"Months?"

"With luck," he admitted.

"Can you assure me that they will not harm Jake?"

Price stared at the floor. She had her answer.

"We have to get him out."

When he met her gaze, she recognized the fear in his eyes. How many times had she sat impotent, frozen by her doubts? Now she witnessed the palsy in another. He would not act.

"You have to understand. I have a wife and children. This is my home. I must live here after you have gone."

"I understand." She was alone.

"You must appreciate my position."

Emma inclined her head. "Yes, Mr. Price. I wonder if you would do me one favor. You gave Mr. Turner a tour of the town. Would you do the same for me? I should like to see all the streets, know every house and business."

"Certainly."

"And the fort?"

"They will not permit you inside."

"You have been to see him. You know where he is."

"I could draw a map."

She smiled.

Perhaps she was not alone after all.

Emma suffered the indignity of being loaded in a sling and hoisted up to the decks of the *Loriotte* like a load of tallow. As netting descended to puddle on planking, ropes fell upon her and she lost her footing, sprawling on the deck like some catch of the sea.

Billings cleared the lines and helped her to recover herself. She accepted his callused hand as he led her to his cabin. The door clicked shut and he offered her a chair. She realized once seated that all the furniture was anchored to the floor. The captain poured her a cup of tea and waited until she took a sip.

"Now then, Mrs. Martin, how can I assist you?"

Emma turned aside and lifted her skirts drawing out the letters entrusted to her. Then she laid them with the empty satchel upon the table.

"Mr. Turner asks that you take charge of these. The inner lining of this leather bag is a map of our passage. The letter is for President Jackson. Mr. Turner requests that you see they find their way to a friendly ship headed for the East Coast."

Billings collected the items. "I will see it done. Now what about you? I could transport you to Vancouver, a British port."

"I have decided to stay in California."

"You realize that if evidence implicating him is found—" the captain stared hard at her "—they'll hang him."

"You mean if they get me to admit to our purpose."

Billings nodded. "I agree with Turner. Your presence here jeopardizes him. The safest thing is to get you clear of this mess."

"Turner thinks that Monterey is vastly underdefended. What is your opinion?"

The captain gave her an assessing look. "He is correct."

"What would Vallejo do if Mr. Turner escaped?"

Now the captain's eyebrow quirked as his interest peaked. "What are you up to, Mrs. Martin? Because I won't risk my ship."

"Nor would I ask you to. I just wondered if some diversion might not draw men away from the fort. Then perhaps a person could enter and release Mr. Turner."

"You?"

She nodded.

"Do not think that being a woman will protect you in this matter. If captured, you will certainly both hang."

"I cannot assure my success, but I can assure you that I will not be taken alive."

The captain choked on his tea. He stared in amazement as if she had changed color before him. Then he nodded. "I see why Turner brought you along. You are not at all what you appear."

"What do I appear?"

His forehead lifted. "Biddable."

She smiled. "I was once. But I cast that off, as a snake sheds his skin. Perhaps appearing to pose no threat makes me a greater one."

Billings pinned her with a look of uncertainty. "Do you have a plan?"

Emma leaned forward and explained her scheme.

The captain's expression changed as she talked, the scowl gradually lifting from his face.

"Risky." He scratched beneath his chin. "Might work." He stared at the cabin ceiling for a moment than slapped a hand upon the table, making Emma jump. "All right then. We'll do it."

Emma smiled, breathing her relief away.

He rose and extended his hand. "We shall sail to Santa Barbara tomorrow night on the second tide. Whatever the outcome, I will not see you again."

Emma accepted his hand. "Thank you, Captain Billings. I hope your voyages continue to bring you good fortune."

Billings held open his cabin door. "I will make the delivery you requested. Fair winds, Mrs. Martin. I will add you to my prayers."

"Fair winds to you, as well, Captain."

Francisca presided over her table like a queen. Emma sat alone as the only guest, beside John. She stared at Jake's empty seat.

"So you see the town and visited the Captain Billings," said Francisca.

"Yes, I have had a busy day."

Francisca waved away the servers, waiting until they left the room. "How will you get inside of the fort?"

Emma stared at John who shrugged. She returned her attention to his wife.

"I plan to take a uniform at gunpoint."

Francisca made a face. "You don't speak Spanish. How will you tell him to disrobe?"

"I feel the gun will help with communication."

"Do you remember Maria Pardo? You meet her at the banquet. She is wife to the candle maker. She has nine children, do you know? A lot of mouths to feed on the candles. Peoples here are making their own candles. Only the ships buy from Pardo. And you know, sometimes the ships, they do not come. Señora Pardo makes the sewing to help bring the money."

Emma stared wondering what in the world Francisca was babbling about sewing and candles.

"Maybe you like to know what Señora Pardo is sewing? New coats for winter soldiers. I see a hat there, too. Is not that better than taking at gun pointing?"

Emma's eyes went wide as she gaped at Francisca.

"Now dear," said John, "I told Emma we could not get involved."

"No, you said *you* could not involved. I am listening to you on the porch. And you are not get involved. I am."

She stared her husband down. Emma was impressed.

But she did not understand this woman. She was born in Mexico. This was her country. She must not want her homeland to lose this territory. John Price was American despite his change in paperwork. His allegiance she understood.

"Francisca, America is not your country. Why are you helping me?"

She laughed. "Is that why you risking your neck, for your country?" She shook her head. "I do not think so. You risk for love of this man, yes?"

Emma lowered her gaze. She could not deny her feelings. "I don't know if I love him, but I don't want him to hang."

"I don't want him to hang, too, but I am not rescuing him.

You don't wanting him to hang enough to risk your life. That is love, Emma."

She gaped, knowing in the marrow of her bones that Francisca was right. How had it happened? She once thought him an ogre like her father. But he had changed, hadn't he? Yes, he respected her enough to tell her the truth and to trust her.

Francisca interrupted her thoughts. "I am helping a woman rescue her man. I cannot stop myself. I am such a romantic."

Emma found tears on her cheeks. "I'll never be able to thank you."

"You name a baby after me. That is the best thanks."

"A baby!" Emma gasped.

Francisca laughed. "You do not think there will be babies?" She waved her hand at the ridiculousness of that.

"She'll have to get him out of the fort first," said John.

"Yes, yes. First the fort, then the babies." She wrapped an arm about her husband and one about her swollen abdomen. "Everyone should have babies."

Emma drained her wineglass. She could not think beyond tomorrow evening.

Chapter Twenty

Emma pulled the leather brim of the navy-blue cap low upon her forehead and next tugged at the short coat. She kept her gaze on the ground as she approached the fort.

The doors flung open and men ran from within. Motionless beside the shadowed wall, she saw a man rush up the hill and through the doors. She decided to do the same.

The tight-fitting pants clung to her legs. She felt exposed, but the freedom of movement made running nearly effortless. She dashed through the gate·and past a man running with an armload of shovels.

The smell of smoke clung to his clothing. It was hard to wait until the tannery was in full blaze, but she forced herself. Now all seemed in disarray.

Running across the courtyard, she searched for the correct doorway. Her heartbeat echoed her pounding feet as she reached the archway and ducked within.

Nearly there.

She found the stairs and raced to the bottom colliding with a man running up. The impact drove Emma back and she fell before him on the step.

He dropped the rope he carried and shouted at her. She understood not a word but quickly sprang to her feet, keeping her head down and trying to slip past him, but he blocked her way.

His fingers gripped her arm. Emma drew her pistol. The man still shouted as she pressed the steel barrel into his stomach and cocked the trigger.

Their eyes met and he stilled, gaping, his black mustache framing his pink mouth.

"Get back or I'll kill you."

He descended the stairs backward. At the bottom she let him inch away, feeling safer with some distance between them. Already his gaze swept about for some means to disarm her. She knew at close range he might easily wrestle the gun away. But at four feet, she had the advantage. When they reached the door she sought, she motioned with the tip of the pistol.

"Open it."

His hand trembled as he slid back the bolt. With a tug, the door swung out.

Another sweep with the gun. "Inside."

He backed in, hands raised. She could not see into the blackness beyond.

"Jake?"

He pushed past the soldier. "Emma? Damnation! You're supposed to be on that ship!"

"Get his clothes."

Jake had the coat and hat on in a blink. The rest he left, pushing the man into the darkness and sliding the bolt home. Then he turned and grinned at her.

"Never been gladder to see anyone in my life." His hug was quick and brutal, making her ribs pop.

"We have to go."

She handed him his pistol, retaining her own, then dashed up the staircase.

"Grab that rope," she ordered. To her astonishment, he did. Together they raced across the open yard and through the gate. They darted down the hill, first toward the fire and then veering off between two houses.

"Drop the rope," she shouted and heard it fall behind him.

He ran beside her now. "Who set that fire?"

"Billings's men."

"Brilliant."

Behind the houses Emma slowed. On seeing the shadowy figure before him, Jake drew his weapon.

Emma lifted her hand. "No."

Jake lowered his pistol.

Francisca stepped forward, dressed in black skirts and shawl. She looked like a living shadow as she kissed Jake.

"She did it." Then she turned to Emma and handed her the reins. "I knew it. Go quick before you are missed."

"Did Scout give you any trouble?"

"No. I think he likes the women." She patted Emma's horse.

"How'd you get Scout back?" asked Jake.

"I rescued him first." She grinned.

Jake scowled, but wasted no time swinging up into the saddle as Duchess nickered her welcome. Tied to his saddle were the packhorse and the two mules.

"Good luck," whispered Francisca and she kissed Emma. "Remember, the first girl."

Emma nodded, pulling away, then hurrying into her stirrups. She led the way from the town, skirting past the rear of houses. Behind them the shouts echoed in the night.

The wind in Jake's hair pleased him more than he could say. He had Emma to thank for that. Imagine *her* rescuing him. The thought made him laugh. He wondered whose idea it was to dress Emma like a soldier. Even in the dark, her curves revealed her. He expected it was John. He should have come himself. He had strange ideas about women that Jake did not share, including allowing Francisca to walk all over him. Why on earth had John allowed his wife to hold the horses for them, and in her condition? Emma pointed toward the grove of redwoods and they galloped across open ground.

Once out of the city and hidden in a grove, he pulled to a walk. The horses could not maintain that pace for long. Emma slowed Scout. He couldn't wait to hear all about the rescue. He glanced about.

"Where are the others?" he asked.

Her forehead wrinkled at his question. "What others?

"John and Billings."

"Captain Billings is preparing to sail and John refused involvement."

"He what? That's impossible. How did you get in? How did you get the horses and the uniform?"

"I stole the horses from the corral and the uniform from a seamstress."

He gaped. Words would not come. She had done this? Emma Lancing, who, by her own admission, lived under her father's boot heels until he found her. Impossible.

"But, but who made the plan?"

Now her expression changed from confusion to irritation. "I did."

"The fire?"

"My idea, accomplished with the assistance of Captain Billings's third mate."

"Yours?" His voice challenged.

"You act as if I never had a thought of my own."

He stared at this stranger before him. There would be no outside assistance. Emma organized and accomplished their escape single-handedly. Another thought struck him and a ripple of fear washed cold down his spine.

"You could have been killed!"

She lifted her chin. "I know."

"Or captured."

She nodded and he realized that she fully understood the ramifications of her action. And she did it, anyway.

"But why?"

She dropped her gaze and then shifted it back to him. "They were never going to release you. I had to do something."

"No, you didn't. Billings didn't, neither did Price."

"I'm your partner."

She was, in every sense of the word. That realization forced him to swallow hard. He owed her more than he could ever repay.

"Thank you, Emma."

Her smile curled and his heart squeezed. She was remarkable.

"They underestimated you. We all did. Why is that?"

She shrugged. "I am a woman."

He knew the truth in this. Formidable, resourceful and a woman. "That makes you the perfect spy—the perfect partner."

She cast him a look of such longing his heart ached. Obviously, Emma took partner to mean something quite different than he'd intended. Her eyes glowed warm and a smile curled her lovely mouth. He wrestled with his breathing, which began galloping like a wild mustang.

She nudged Scout forward until her leg brushed his.

"You sure got us out of a fix," he said.

"A fix that I got us into. It was entirely my fault you didn't shoot Scout."

He watched her lips as she continued speaking, showing flashes of white teeth and the sensual curve of her mouth as she formed the words like a kiss and, God help him, he wanted that kiss.

"How do you do it?" he asked.

She cocked her head, puzzled. "Do what?"

"Make me want to kiss you?"

She drew in a sharp breath and held it, but did not retreat as he leaned toward her, grasping her arms. She stiffened for an instant and then something seemed to break loose inside her. Somehow she was in his arms, sitting before him on Duchess and her arms pulled him down for another kiss. He dipped his head relishing the warmth of her lips and the sweet tugging of her arms as she urged him on.

Something brushed her leg and Jake jerked. Emma found Scout preparing to take another hunk out of him. Jake dragged the military cap off his head and swung at her mount.

"I should have shot you when I had the chance."

Emma laughed. "He's jealous."

Jake looked doubtful. "More like he noticed my distraction and thought it a good opportunity to take another piece out of me."

Emma slid to the ground and collected Scout's reins. "Is that what I am, a distraction?"

Jake sighed. "We best get on. Where were you heading?"

She mounted up and shortened the reins. "East. Vallejo has to handle the fire and he only has twenty-nine men. He can't spare them for a search."

"Oh, yes, he can, if the task is important enough. I believe he'll send some of them after us. They'll alert the missions, as well, so we'll find no help there."

"Can we outride them?"

"Not with pack animals."

Jake considered his choices. Billings would be sailing before he could reach the ship. To the east, the missions would be on watch.

"We go north to the Russian settlements."

"Will they aid us?"

"Doubtful, but it is the only direction in which the Mexicans cannot follow." Jake glanced up at the three-quarter moon filtered through pine needles. "Let's ride."

They set off following the trail along the bay. The moon turned orange as it prepared to set and they skirted past the mission of San Francisco. This was the northernmost outpost of the Mexicans and Jake breathed a sigh of relief to have it behind him. The river stopped them and they rode ten miles east before he found a place narrow enough for the horses to swim across.

Late in the night, as they climbed along the cliffs to the north, fog rolled in from the bay blanketing them in a white mist.

"We have to stop," Jake said.

Emma stood three feet from him, but she seemed only a ghostly outline now.

"We could fall over the cliff in this. We'll rest and see if the morning burns off the mist."

"Won't the Spanish catch us?" Emma asked.

"Fog will hinder them, as well, if they even know to head this way. Lead your horse and follow me."

He picked his way inland, through brush and between trees. The mist collected on his clothing and the shaggy coats of the horses, beading and running off. Soon he was as damp as if he stood in the rain. He halted at last, unable to see to go farther.

Soon he had the deer hides down for ground cover and the buffalo hide staked up on sticks to form a small shelter. Emma unsaddled the horses and joined him in the nest. She stripped out of her military costume and into her buckskin shirt and faded blue skirt, as Jake transformed back to a trapper.

With the wolf-skin blanket thrown over them, a calm filled him.

"I was so worried about you," she whispered.

"Why didn't you do as I told you and get on the ship?"

"That wasn't best for you."

"It was best for you."

She didn't deny it. Instead she snuggled closer, wiggling her bottom into the curve of his waist. Now it was too hot and he no longer felt like talking.

"Night, Jake," she said and breathed a long sigh of contentment.

He gritted his teeth at the involuntary response his body had for this woman. Try as he might, he could no more control it than stop the beating of his heart.

This partner business was driving him crazy. He wondered again if she would agree to be his woman. He did not know which prospect scared him more, that she might say no or that she might say yes. John Price's comment about having feelings for Emma started him thinking. Accepting that he did not want to part from her was shock enough. He had no notion as to how he should proceed.

Her words returned to him and now they suddenly seemed a stumbling block. She'd told him she did not want to marry. Having escaped her father's house, she never wanted to put herself under a man's control again. At the time he'd thought, so much the better. Now her wishes disturbed him greatly.

After much restless shifting, the fatigue of his body won the battle over his mind and he fell asleep.

The morning proved only to be a brightening of the fog. They broke camp and continued on foot, leading the animals along the path above the water. When he reached another river, he paused.

He could not see the other side.

Chapter Twenty-One

Jake knew Vallejo was back there. With luck he was searching to the east giving them the time they needed to reach Russian territory. The journey took longer than Jake guessed because of the backtracking up rivers to find a place to ford.

They located the Russian camp on the morning of the fourth day. Jake lay on his belly on the bluff above the crude log cabins, roofed in split cedar shingles with a hole to allow the smoke out. The camp stood on the high ground beside a wide river, close enough to the sea to allow hunting, but not so close to suffer the brunt of the storms and high water. Low clouds hung just above the sea cliffs, waiting to drop upon them once more.

Emma stood fifty yards behind with the horses. Jake glanced back to check on her then focused on the camp. After seeing a trapper drinking from a jug and then shoving a fellow to the ground, Jake decided this outpost was too rough for a woman. He inched back to Emma.

"I'm getting a bad feeling. Might be safer to head inland, avoid them entirely."

Emma absorbed this. "If you think that's best."

"I do."

The distinctive click of a trigger locking stopped Jake in his tracks. It came from behind him. Emma faced their attacker.

Jake slid his revolver from his holster and then glanced over his shoulder.

A group of eight rough-looking trappers stood with hands on their weapons. Jake slid the pistol home and glanced at Emma.

"You're my wife, Mrs. Jake Turner."

She nodded, her eyes round with fright.

Jake faced the men with open hands. "Hello, friends. Anyone speak English?"

The men exchanged startled looks and rapid-fire Russian darted between them.

Jake noted the dead deer slung over one man's shoulder and realized their discovery was due to bad luck. Generally, these men stayed close to the water and the precious otter they hunted. He tried again. "What about Spanish?"

A giant of a man with a bushy red beard stepped forward. "I do."

Jake smiled, though his insides felt tight as the head of a banjo. "I'm Jake Turner and this is my wife, Emma."

The man's gaze flicked to Emma and then over her body in a way that made Jake consider shoving him onto his ass.

"British?" asked the leader.

"American."

The man's bushy eyebrows lifted causing the nasty scar that bisected his forehead and cheek to pucker. The old injury caused his right eyelid to droop and brought a stripe of white to his otherwise remarkably red beard. "What are you doing here?"

Right to the point, Jake thought.

"The Mexicans wanted to lock me up, so we decided to try the hospitality of our Russian brothers."

The man chuckled and then translated. The men behind him laughed. When he turned to Jake the smile upon his lips looked predatory.

"Of course. A wise choice. As you see, we are much more civilized." He translated and the men laughed again, doffing their hats and making a mockery of bowing.

"I'm glad to hear it."

"But just one question. Why were you in Mexican territory?"

"I'm a merchant. I thought to settle in California, but could not secure the land I had hoped for. What is your name, brother?"

"I am Nikki, these are my men." He waved his beefy hand and Jake prayed he would not have to fight this giant. "If you are looking for land, we have plenty." His gaze fastened on Emma, who shifted beneath the scrutiny. "Women, on the other hand, are in short supply."

Jake stepped between them, bringing the big man's attention back to him.

"I'm sure seeing Emma is quite a shock. My wife is accustomed to civilized treatment from men of honor. Will we find that in your camp, or should we move on?"

Nikki's leer could not be mistaken for a smile. "We cannot allow you to leave." He turned to his men and barked an order. The weapons were lowered, but kept ready. "Please, join us for dinner."

Jake would rather have wrestled a grizzly, but he saw no other way. He turned to Emma. "They want us to follow them."

"I don't want to," she whispered.

He grasped her cold hand. "Neither do I, but I can't figure a way out just now."

"Did you see the way he looked at me? Like he wants to gobble me up."

He squeezed her hand. "Eight to one."

Her breathing revealed her disquiet. "Eight to two."

"Can you kill four before they shoot you?"

"No—but I'd rather die here than go with them. They'll kill you and take me."

"The same thought occurred to me."

"We have to get away."

He nodded and they descended the trail, sandwiched between Nikki in front and his men, behind. Jake cast a glance over his shoulder. The Russians looked like a pack of wild dogs.

At camp, Jake found their numbers increased to ten. The reek of unwashed bodies and otter hides made his nostrils burn. The men roasted the deer over an open fire and drank whiskey while Nikki collected Jake's guns. It was not long until the first fight broke out.

Jake sat close to Emma, watching the men grow more raucous and wondering if they might, by some stroke of luck, drink themselves insensible, allowing him to slip away with Emma.

Two men began to dance to a tune only they could hear. Others soon joined. One of the younger men grasped Emma's hand in an effort to draw her into their circle.

She resisted, leaning away and tugging to no effect. "Let go, you beast."

Jake sighed, wishing for better odds, stood and prepared to fight. He stiff-armed the man, who toppled over backward and then sprang to his feet. Jake needed no Russian to understand the curses issuing from the trapper's mouth.

The man cocked his fist in a sloppy, off balance move, the whiskey making him clumsy. Before he could swing, Nikki gripped the man's fist in his own, completely enveloping it.

Jake gritted his teeth, realizing that Nikki did not drink nearly the amount of whiskey as his fellows.

He shouted at the man, who opened his mouth to argue and then screamed as Nikki squeezed his fist. The distinctive crack of bone breaking came next and more howling. He released the man, who fell to the ground clutching his hand.

The others stopped their dancing. Emma moved behind Jake as Nikki faced him.

"My men are a rough band."

Jake did not take his eyes off the threat before him.

Nikki turned to the others and waved them away. They did not go. Jake thought of a wolf he once had watched take down an elk to get to her calf. Emma was the calf.

Angry words flew and at last Nikki said something and his men reluctantly withdrew.

"He's offered me to them when he is done," whispered Emma.

Jake scowled. "You understand Russian?"

"No. I understand men."

The men went slowly, pausing often to gaze at Emma then halting at their cabin doors. Jake knew she was right.

Nikki smiled. "I think your wife should sleep in my cabin for her safety."

Jake tried not to smile. "We'd be grateful."

Nikki's wolf eyes glowed in the darkness. "This way."

Emma gripped Jake's shirt. "Careful now. He means to kill you first."

"Sounds right."

Nikki disappeared into the cabin. Jake waited outside the door, knowing better than to meet a wolf in his den. Nikki had the advantage and might right now be pointing a gun at his belly.

"Come in," he called from the darkness.

"As soon as you light a lamp."

Nikki exited to the fire and carried a burning branch inside. The fog crept along the ground, making the watching men seem menacing spirits. Water beaded on Jake's shirt as he waited, Emma huddling beside him.

"I think we should run," she whispered.

"Not yet. We have to overpower Nikki, quietly. Then recover our horses and guns."

Orange light issued from the cabin and Nikki appeared in the door grinning like a man with something to look forward to.

"Come in, friends."

Jake wondered how to pass him without coming within range of his grasp. The man outweighed him and topped him by at least five inches. In a fair fight, Nikki would win.

Jake knew neither man wanted a fair fight.

Nikki slapped at the filthy pile of bedding. "Your wife can have my bed. I'll sleep by the fire."

Jake glanced about the cabin and saw only a table littered

with stretched otter pelts. On the walls traps dangled from their chains. Jake thought the bench beside the table was his easiest weapon. The sturdy planks might give him the edge. Nikki closed the door behind them.

"We've decided not to spend the night."

Nikki's eyebrows lifted, stretching the scar. "I insist."

Jake stopped playing games. "You mean to kill me and have my wife."

The man's smile twisted, his voice calm. "I don't have to kill you."

Jake squared his body, gathering for the fight. "Yes, you do."

The giant curled his hands into meaty fists. "Have it your way then."

Jake scooped up the bench, landing a blow to the man's shoulder. He staggered as the bench leg snapped.

Now Nikki came at him with his hands open as if to tear Jake in two. Another swing and the bench thudded into his ribs buckling him forward.

Raising the remaining plank over his head, Jake prepared to strike at his opponent's head, but Nikki lunged forward like a wrestler, carrying Jake to the earth floor.

The impact of the giant driving him into the ground made Jake see stars. For an instant he was insensible and that was all Nikki needed to wrap his thick hands about Jake's neck.

He lifted Jake as he squeezed then thudded him against the ground, simultaneously choking and beating Jake's head.

The edges of Jake's vision blackened as he sought release from the crushing grip. His lungs burned and he floundered, unable to remove the heavy man from his chest. Locking both fists as one, Jake swung, landing a blow to the Russian's temple. Nikki slumped to the side and Jake was upon him in an instant. They rolled together. Jake saw the knife, a skinning blade, gleaming with a razor's edge.

The Russian slashed at his throat, but Jake deflected the blow, sending his attacker's arm sweeping above his head.

Nikki straddled him and locked his fists around the blade lifting his arms to plunge the weapon into Jake's chest.

Jake caught the descending wrists. He strained and the Russian grunted. With the point only an inch from his heart Jake lunged to the left and felt the blade cut into his shoulder joint. The crunch of cartilage echoed in his head as the pain sliced, poker hot into his flesh.

The Russian withdrew the blade and raised his arm for another attack. Something moved above Nikki's head. Jake could not make out what it was, but heard the sickening thud. The knife dropped beside Jake's ear.

Nikki fell, giving Jake a picture of Emma gripping the ring of the closed trap in her fist. The chain swung gently to and fro.

Nikki rolled to his knees and sprang to attack. Jake lunged for the knife stabbing it into the man's chest.

Jake rolled to the side, clutching his bleeding shoulder as the giant toppled forward. Beside him, Nikki lay inert as blood poured from his chest wound.

"Is he dead?" Emma asked.

Jake grimaced from the pain. He was dizzy from it. "Not yet."

He struggled to sit as Emma gasped and fell to her knees beside him.

"Oh my God!" She reached for him pressing her hands to the wound. "Lie down. Don't move. Oh my God, has he killed you?"

"My shoulder, I think."

She pressed harder and a wave of nausea rolled through him. Sweat broke out on his forehead.

"Did he hit your lung?"

"I'd be bubbling from the mouth if he had. Check it."

She removed her hands and peered beneath the slice in his buckskin shirt. "Oh, it's deep. Jake, you're bleeding so fast."

He knew it. The black spots flitted like dragonflies before him.

"Emma, I'm sorry," he whispered. Then she disappeared behind the fluttering moths as he fell into the darkness.

Chapter Twenty-Two

Emma crouched on the floor, both hands pressed hard to Jake's wound and still the blood welled like groundwater between her fingers.

It had to stop. It must.

She searched the dirty cabin for something to staunch the flow, but found only filthy skins and greasy rags. Mud caked the blankets on the man's bed.

Finally, she decided on her petticoats, lifting her hands from him to clutch the drawstring with bloody fingers. Fumbling, she stepped from the garment. She gasped at the blood lost while she disrobed.

Wadding the linen, she leaned on straight arms with all her strength. Her fingers went numb and the fabric turned crimson.

The big Russian groaned, startling her. Her gaze flicked to him and his eyelids moved. *Oh, no, don't let him wake up now, not now. Not when the bleeding is finally stopping.*

She held the garment and kept her gaze on the Russian, but he did not move again. Jake's blood darkened as the clotting began. In infinitely slow degrees, Emma released the pressure and waited, holding her breath.

Jake's pale sweating face made her tremble in terror. She found the knife upon the table, cut her second petticoat into a bandage and used it to hold the wadded petticoat in place. Sliding the bandage beneath his inert body took all her strength.

What will I do next? How will we get away?

She gritted her teeth, focusing on the task at hand. When she finally finished she sat beside him, her aching back pulsing with her heartbeat.

The Russian's breathing changed. Emma grasped the beaver trap, prepared to hit him again if he stirred. Rasping, his chest rose with unnatural slowness. She studied his blue lips and let the trap slide from her fingers, turning to Jake.

What should she do? As she sat in the light of the fading fire, the sounds of laughter and singing died away. She held her breath. Footsteps.

She reached the door in an instant, lifting the solid redwood plank into the slot to bar entrance.

A moment later came the pounding. Not all the men were asleep. One of them wanted his turn with her. She stood frozen to the spot facing the door as the thumping went on and on. The man shouted something in Russian.

Emma seemed to become aware again. She ran about the cabin until she found the Russian's rifle. If she shot him through the door, the others might hear.

She stood, pressed to the wall, the rifle aimed at the entrance. *When would he stop?* The pounding echoed in her ears.

More cursing. *Was he kicking the door now?* She glanced about, suddenly grateful there were no windows. The hole in the shingled roof would not admit a man.

He could not get in and she could not get out. Trapped. How long until he roused the camp?

As suddenly as it began, the pounding ceased. She held her breath in the silence that ensued. Then came the sound of his footsteps as he staggered away.

She could breathe again. Her knees failed and she sank to the earth floor, then she crawled to Jake now lying motionless in the near darkness.

She added more wood to the fire and soon could see about her. What now?

Jake lay unconscious and Nikki's men waited just beyond the door. How long until they came again?

Her heart thudded in her temples as she patted Jake's face, hoping he might come to and help her. Fear tasted metallic in her mouth as she worried over what the trappers would do when they found their leader. She had to get away.

How?

She folded her hands in an effort to ask God's help, but found she could barely think for the uncertainty. Attempts to rouse Jake with water sprinkled on his face also failed. If she somehow managed to drag him out of the cabin, how would she lift him onto the horse?

It was impossible. But to wait here until they came—she would not.

Their things lay in a pile beside the door. She found her pistol and replaced it in its holster. Their guns rested beneath the Russian's filthy bed with Jake's sextant. He stole everything of value. She had stolen it back, along with his blankets and then added his otter furs for good measure.

Emma stood beside Jake wondering how to drag him. Lifting behind his shoulders would surely tear open the clot and begin the bleeding once more. She tried his feet and first could not budge him, but then managed to pull him a few inches.

She laid the blankets on the earth and dragged him onto them. Then she wrapped the wool about his body and lashed them shut, forming a large cocoon. Only his pale face with several days' growth of whiskers showed now. She crept to the door.

Uncertainty rang in her ears. There was no other way out except turning her pistol upon herself and she was not ready to admit defeat. Her trembling fingers lifted the plank and lay it beside the door. They could come in now. She couldn't stop them.

She cracked the door and gazed out. Something was wrong.

She could not see a thing. The white mist rolled into the cabin, swirling with vaporous fingers across the floor.

Fog. Fog so thick she could not see her own feet. In a moment her legs disappeared and she was enveloped in a white blanket. She turned back. Jake vanished in mist.

If she could not see them, then they could not find her. She took a step from the cabin and then paused. How would she find her way back to Jake?

She retraced her steps, colliding with the door frame, already lost. The door slammed as she leaned against it. Soon she collected all the rope in the cabin. She tied a knot around the latch and headed out into the fog.

Stumbling about she managed to find the tree where they had tied the horses. Scout nickered and she stroked the velvet of his nose. Mist beaded upon them, making their coats slick as any rainstorm. Her hand paused.

"Why they left the saddles on. What kind of men leave horses saddled overnight?" She felt about Scout's barrel. "The girth is still tight! I suppose they didn't feed or water you, either." Her fingers worked the rope as she tied a knot about the tree. Then she retraced her steps to the cabin. If not for the rope, she knew she would have already headed in the wrong direction.

How many trips to the horses and back? She lost count. She had packed the mules so often she thought she could do it in the dark. Now she found the task difficult beyond measure.

On her next trip, a sound halted her. One of the men called Nikki, over and over.

She ran the distance, the rope sliding through her fingers as she raced to the cabin. The man was near, but he had not entered yet. She grabbed Jake's feet and yanked. He moved a few inches.

"Nikki?"

Nearer now—or was it only the fog, tricking her, distorting the sounds?

Emma looped one arm over the rope until the hemp rested

beneath her armpit then grasped the blanket at Jake's feet and pulled with all her might. Scuttling like a crab, she succeeded in exiting the cabin.

"Nikki?"

The man was right beside her. She dropped to her knees next to Jake and felt the rope vibrate as the man stumbled into the line.

He spoke in Russian, his angry voice coming from just before her. He could find her by the rope. But if she moved away, she would never reach the horses.

His voice came again. She held her breath. The rope danced as he moved along it. This time his voice was farther off. He went to the cabin. In a moment he'd find their leader and then he'd follow the line straight to her.

Springing to her feet she tugged at Jake's inert form, dragging him backward. She could hear the horses shuffling their feet now.

A cry came from within the cabin and then shouting. More voices joined in as the camp roused. Next came the pounding of feet as the line before her shook.

She drew her knife and sliced. The rope dropped beside her. Emma stared into the blinding whiteness before her. They could still find her if they traced the direction of the line. She clutched the end of the rope the Russian followed and threw it. Then she tied the other end to her wrist and set out at a ninety-degree angle from her current course dragging Jake with painful slowness.

Moments later they came, hesitating, perhaps when they reached the rope's termination, then charged forward. She ducked low and felt their footsteps as they ran past, falling over rocks and logs.

"Emma?"

She pressed her hand over Jake's lips and leaned over him. "I'm here. You must be quiet."

He spoke in a whisper. "I can't move."

She sliced through the ropes lashing him into the blanket. "Where am I?" he asked.

"Near the horses, in the fog. The men are searching for us."

They were gathering. She could hear them shouting and moving together.

"We have to get to the horses," she whispered. "Can you ride?"

He sat, swaying. She thought he'd faint again.

"Help me up."

She wrapped an arm around his waist and he hugged her shoulder. She strained as he drew himself to a stand. In this instant, she realized how weak he was and it terrified her.

She handed him the rope, so she could use both hands to help him along. "Follow the line. It leads to the horses."

He pulled it toward him and they crept along. Scout nickered at their arrival as Emma untied the line from her wrist. She found Jake with one hand on the saddle horn, trying to lift his leg to the stirrup. She guided his toe into the slot. When he pulled she pushed, pressing her shoulder into his thigh and somehow he got his leg over the saddle. He slumped then, gripping the horn.

"Jake?"

Nothing.

She shook him. "Jake."

No answer. She wrapped the rope around the saddle horn and over his back. She was not sure it would keep him up. The thought of him tumbling off the horse onto his injured shoulder sent a chill through her.

She tied Scout to Duchess and then added the packhorse and mules behind them. Then she grasped the mare's reins and led her away from camp toward the sound of the ocean along the sandy riverbank. The shouts of the men disappeared in the fog.

Would they follow?

Emma stopped frequently to check Jake. He moaned now and then, but never roused. She paused to find his wolf-pelt blanket and threw it over his shoulders to keep the worst of the mist from settling on him.

When she reached the sea, she skirted the base of the cliffs

looking for some access to the top. She did not find one. Her
skirts were saturated and her buckskin shirt no longer kept the
water at bay. Onward she trudged. Visibility improved making
it possible to see forty feet ahead now.

She paused at a place where the ocean crashed against the
rock, safe for the moment in this alcove. She glanced toward
the cliff finding no access. The tide was rising. Judging from
the logs tossed in piles against the stone face, they soon would
be in peril.

With tired fingers she tied her skirts up at her waist, preparing to cross the tide line. For a time she studied the waves, but
found no pattern to them, so she waited until a breaker hit and
tugged Duchess's reins, venturing out into the retreating wave.
The team moved forward, with Emma trotting before the horses,
urging them on. She reached a little past the midway point
when the wave struck, taking her legs from beneath her. The
bridle bit into her hand as salt water tossed her. When the water
retreated, she lay on the sand, dangling from Duchess's reins.

Scrambling to her feet she rushed on reaching dry ground
before the next breaker struck. Once safe, Emma rubbed his
mare's head and praised her, feeling guilty for yanking on the
poor creature's mouth as she bounced about in the water like a
rubber ball.

She glanced down at her sodden skirts. So much for hiking
them up. Water streamed down her face from her drenched
hair, burning her eyes. She glanced at Jake and found he lolled
left in the saddle.

The wolf hide!

She turned to the sea and saw it rolling in the waves. The
breaker brought the hide to shore and then snatched it off the
beach once more.

Emma moved the horses up the sand and left them in an attempt to recover his blanket. She waited until the wave broke.
Long fingers of water pushed the pelt along. She dashed to the
hide and grasped it, running toward the high-water mark as the

next wave broke behind her. Just two feet of water hit her, but enough to sweep her feet away again. She fell hard. The retreating wave dragged her toward the sea. Clawing at the beach, she managed to hold her position until the ocean released its grip. Emma staggered clear of danger.

There she sat watching the waves break with terrifying force taking his wolf-pelt blanket far out to sea. When her heartbeat ceased to pound in her chest, she recovered the horse's reins and set out once more, her legs feeling all the heavier for the sodden skirts. She checked Jake, righting him in the saddle, then pressed on.

The wet fabric chafed her skin. The stress and fear of the terrible night dissolved with the last of the mist. Weariness overwhelmed her. Glancing behind, she realized the Russians could not follow her past the waves now crashing high upon the cliffs. Neither could she turn back. There must be a way to the lip of the escarpment.

By the time she found a break in the rock, her knees bled. The deer trail led through brush and prickers. Certainly these did not bother the deer, but they tore Emma's skirts to ribbons and then attacked her legs.

Once on top, Emma paused to look at the ocean. From here the waves seemed gentle as they rolled endlessly to the shore. The water sparkled with points of light on a deep blue sea. She had seen the Pacific and now it was time to leave it.

Would she ever see these waters again?

A lump formed in her throat and she swallowed hard to remove it. No time for tears, she must press on.

Emma led the horses inland until exhaustion and her bleeding knees forced a stop. Before her, a forest of giant trees loomed. Here at the edge there was grass for the horses.

She hobbled them first and then slid off packs and saddles, coming last to Duchess, who waited patiently, still carrying her burden.

How would she get Jake safely down?

"Jake?"

He moaned, but did not rouse. She unfastened the ropes, tossing them aside. Then she stood on her toes and latched her arms about his waist. He tipped in her direction. For a moment she thought she controlled his descent, until his far leg dragged free of the stirrup and she held his entire weight for an instant, before toppling.

She fell on her backside with his torso in her lap. Her bottom stung. Her thigh cushioned his head, but Emma knew she'd have a brutal bruise. His near leg still hung in the stirrup. Duchess took a side step and his foot fell free.

"That was ill conceived," she muttered.

Now he was down in the meadow, in an open area where anyone or anything could easily find them. She dragged herself from beneath Jake and checked him. His breathing was regular and his pulse even. The pallor of his skin disturbed her greatly. Why wouldn't he wake up?

Duchess grazed nearby and Emma decided only to remove her saddle. The process of dragging their gear to the cover of the trees took some time. She wrapped Jake in a buffalo hide. Finally, she fell beside him and gazed out at the horses and mules munching happily on grass. She lifted the water skin and dribbled the contents onto her raw knees, then held the opening to her lips until sated. She drew out a bit of jerky. Before she could bring it to her mouth she fell asleep beside him, still swaddled in her damp garments.

The hoot of an owl brought her awake. She sat up, unsure of her surroundings. The forest, she remembered. Where was Jake? He lay beside her. His stillness made her scramble to him. A hand pressed to his forehead brought a wave of relief. He was warm.

Her shoulders slumped as her breathing returned to normal. An uneasy tension followed. Too warm. She returned her hand to his skin confirming his fever.

Tears stung her eyes. *What else?*

Then her head swiveled. Where were the horses?

She sprang to her feet and raced about the meadow, her knees burning with each step and finding the two mules, head to toe near a holly bush. She grasped their halters and brought them to her camp.

Duchess and Scout were nowhere to be seen. She did not know if she should call or even whistle, afraid that to do so might reveal them to predators.

Finally an idea struck. She found the grain bag and shook some in Jake's hat, as she'd seen him do.

The sound of hoofbeats greeted her immediately. In her relief she gave all the animals grain, then tied them to a tree.

It was there that the Indians found her.

Chapter Twenty-Three

Scout's whinny brought Emma to her feet. She found an Indian boy in the midst of untying her horse's lead while another boy spirited Duchess away. Scout lashed out, kicking the thief viciously in the thigh, sending him to the ground.

That threat removed, Emma drew her pistol and took aim, shooting cleanly through the lead line. The boy gaped in astonishment and then ran toward the bushes, leaving his companion rolling on the ground.

Duchess trotted to Emma who patted her neck and praised her highly, then slipped the hobbles on her front legs. Now she aimed her weapon at the injured boy.

He stilled, obviously knowing about guns.

Now what? She had no wish to shoot a boy. But if she released him, he might return with others. The second boy escaped. He would bring them.

She holstered her weapon. The boy took his opportunity to spring up, took one step on the injured leg and fell to the ground howling again.

This time she kneeled beside him and touched his leg. He stilled, lifting up upon his elbows to watch her. Then his hand reached for his knife. She laid her palm on the empty pistol. He stopped and released the blade.

Her gaze swept his leg, noting the raised purple welt grow-ing on his thigh. He would be lucky not to have broken the bone beneath. She left him to find wood for a splint. When she returned he had crawled under a nearby bush. Sweat ran down his face and into his thick black hair and he panted like a dog in August.

She quickly tied the branches on each side of his leg. He seemed very much astonished at her actions. Then she offered him water and waited as he drank. He was suspicious of the meat until he saw her take a bite. Then he devoured that, as well. His appetite reminded her of the soldiers at the fort, always hun-gry. That thought made her sad and she wasn't sure why.

Through the afternoon she washed Jake's fevered body with a damp cloth and waited for the Indians to come. The boy watched her check Jake's wound, but she feared lifting the clot-ted cloth from his shoulder. Thoughts of fleeing came and went. Even if she determined to escape, how would she get Jake onto his horse? He burned with fever. Without help, he would die.

They came before twilight, creeping slowly forward from the bushes. She kept her pistol ready, thinking she might save a bullet for herself.

Before they reached her, the boy called out. At first he re-ceived no answer, but at last the response came. She waited be-side Jake, realizing she could not leave him, even to save her life.

Finally a group of seven men appeared, approaching cau-tiously, their eyes nervous as they held their bows in tight fists. The large-nosed man in the center smiled at the boy. Emma thought this might be his son. The tallest warrior noticed Jake and stepped forward to stare down at his pale, sweaty face.

He cried out and dashed away. The others followed him. From a distance they called to the boy and motioned for him to come. He shook his head and shouted back.

She could not understand why Jake struck such terror into the Indians. His condition rendered him harmless. Finally, the man with the large nose ventured forward to study Jake. With the tip of his bow, he flicked away the hide covering his upper body.

Emma watched him breathe a sigh of relief. Then he stooped to try to lift the bandage. Emma stopped him by placing her hand over his. He stared at her a moment and then smiled.

He stood and motioned for the others. Soon the men checked their own, noting the violet bruise blooming upon the boy's upper leg and the splint Emma fashioned from the tattered hem of her skirt and two stout sticks. The tallest nodded his approval.

Then they turned their attention to Jake. They soaked the bandage and peeled it away. She gasped at the yellowish pus issuing from the wound. The men exchanged serious glances and spoke in low whispers.

Emma clutched the tall one's arm. "You have to help him."

He replied, his voice even and level, but she could not understand his words. He patted her cheek.

The men constructed a stretcher by tying together the ends of two long branches and then adding a crossbar to form a rough triangle. They draped the buffalo hide around the poles in such a way that the leather supported Jake's weight without bowing. Then they repeated the process creating a second platform for the boy.

With the rope she used to tie him into his saddle, they strapped each stretcher to a mule. Emma loaded their gear onto Duchess and Scout. Each man took the reins of one of the animals. Scout began to buck and the boy shouted to the man holding the horse. He leaped clear before the front hoof lashed out. Emma took the reins and Scout settled down to walk behind his mistress.

She wondered what kept them from stealing everything and realized the answer was *nothing*. Strangely, they did not disarm her, as the Russians had. She trusted the tall one's kind eyes and the one with the broad nose seemed grateful for the care she gave the boy.

She sighed in relief realizing that she had made the right decision in not harming him.

They crossed through the forest, as the shadows grew deep. When she recognized that they descended toward the water, she wanted to howl in frustration. The entire day, she had struggled to find a gap in the cliff. Now, not only was she forced to backtrack, the Indians took her on a simple route that made her arduous passage seem ridiculous by comparison.

She stood at the shore of the Pacific and laughed.

"Turns out I did see it again."

The men watched her in silence, then continued down the beach. Moonlight glittered bright over the rolling waves. The first to greet them was a skinny yellow dog appearing from the night to run beside the horses, yapping all the way.

Smoke rose beyond the bluff. As they crossed beneath the large boulders on the beach, she saw their village. Large houses stood, unlike anything she had ever seen. Lodges of redwood bark flanked a central building large as a dairy barn.

A woman tending a long row of fish smoking by the fire rushed forward and, like an arrow, went straight to the boy. Emma had no trouble recognizing her as his mother from the concern in her eyes.

These people wore their long hair braided like the Sioux. Their furs and tanned leather seemed painted in unfamiliar patterns. Giant creatures with big eyes ogled out at her from the cape of an approaching man. Beyond him, on the beach, rows of boats rested above the tide line, each one carved from a single hollowed tree trunk. From the bow, elaborately carved animals guided their vessels.

The woman and boy spoke rapidly and Emma studied the pair. His mother looked startled and then stared at Emma, pointing. The boy nodded and the woman rushed to her, throwing her arms about Emma's shoulders and hugging her tight.

The words were strange but the sentiment familiar. She thanked her for saving her boy.

"You're welcome," said Emma, as she patted her back.

Four men carried Jake into a lodge and Emma followed. They laid him on a raised platform, heavily padded with thick brown furs.

"I understand we have a visitor."

Emma stiffened at the voice speaking English, here in this wilderness. The accent seemed British. She turned to find a man dressed from head to foot in tanned buckskin. A bushy brown beard hid most of his face and marked him as a white man.

She gaped as he chuckled at her astonishment.

"Alexander MacInnes at your service." He swept his fur hat away and bowed.

Even seeing him, hearing him, she could not believe her eyes. "You're English."

"Oh, my poor mother would roll over in her grave. I'm a Scot."

"How did you come here?" she asked.

He grinned making the crow's-feet more obvious. His eyes were pale, but in the firelight she could not make out their color.

"I was about to ask you the same, lass. I'm a trader from Fort Vancouver. And who might you be?"

"Emma Lancing and this is Jake Turner. He's been wounded."

"Your husband?"

She shook her head and then cursed herself. In her befuddlement she'd forgotten to claim to be Jake's wife, or should she be a widow once more? MacInnes grinned broadly.

"I am widowed. Mr. Turner is my guide." Emma looked him straight in the eye and did not fidget.

He laughed. "Guiding you where, may I ask?"

Jake had not prepared her for this eventuality. Retreat was the best option.

"Jake was stabbed. He lost a great deal of blood. Now the wound is infected. Will these people help him?"

"You treated the chief's son, even after he tried to steal your horses. They're indebted to you, lass."

Emma returned her attention to Jake, resting a hand upon his chest to measure his breaths. "He won't wake up and the fever is worse."

MacInnes frowned down at Jake. The Indian with the large

nose arrived with a white-haired elder. Deep wrinkles etched his face. MacInnes spoke to the men for a time. Then the Scot turned to Emma.

He indicated the man who came for the boy. "This is the chief. He's called Brings Many Pelts. He thanks you for looking after his son. The man beside him is the medicine man, Talks to Wind. He'll have a look at your man now."

Emma moved aside.

Talks to Wind felt Jake's forehead and cut away his shirt, exposing his chest. Emma's stomach clenched as she watched Jake's rapid, shallow breathing. Next the medicine man probed the wound, causing Jake to moan and thrash. Finally, the Indian sniffed Jake's shoulder, made a face and spoke to the others.

MacInnes translated. "He says the wound is putrefied and his fever is high. He will make a poultice to draw out the poisons. He also will make a healing tea.

"Will he live?" she whispered.

MacInnes translated the question. Emma saw the doubt on the man's face before the answer came.

"This man is very ill."

Emma stayed with Jake while they cleaned the wound. She held his hand when a wet poultice, smelling of moss and earth, was pressed to his wound.

Most of the tea dribbled down Jake's chin, but the medicine man seemed satisfied that Jake swallowed some of the brew. MacInnes came and went, finally insisting she eat.

"I'm not hungry," she said.

"Little Otter prepared a meal. You're being honored. If you don't come, you'll insult your hosts."

So she went to the lodge of the chief. The smiling woman was indeed the boy's mother, Little Otter. She patted the pelts beside the fire and filled a bowl for Emma.

The meal seemed to take hours. Her hosts wanted news of her travels. She told them the story they had given the Spanish. Alexander MacInnes sat too close to her and then walked her to the lodge of Talks to Wind. He clasped her elbow, halting her before she could enter the lodge.

"Your man might die. Have you thought of that?"

It was all she could think of, but hearing this stranger echo her fears made her tremble with uncertainty.

"I have."

"What will you do then, do you think?"

She pressed her lips together refusing to cry.

"You're a long way from home, lass. I'm sure this tribe would adopt you, if you've a mind. If not, I hope you'll consider coming with me."

"What?"

"I'm asking you to marry me, lass."

"Marry you—I hardly know you."

"I don't see that as an obstacle. I'd take you to British territory. I've a mind to trap as long as possible, then settle in Oregon."

"Mr. MacInnes, you can't be serious."

"I am. If your man dies, you'll consider my offer?"

To say yes felt like a betrayal to Jake. To say no, seemed rude. "I have to see to Mr. Turner now."

He accepted this, nodding and withdrawing. She watched him go, wondering what kind of man proposes marriage to a woman he has known only half a day?

Emma slept at Jake's side upon their buffalo robes. In the night, she reached for Jake and, instead of skin as hot as a stovepipe, her fingers brushed cool, moist flesh. He was sweating! She knelt beside him and offered thanks to God.

In the morning, Talks to Wind changed the poultice. The angry red around the wound was gone and the discharge ran clear.

"This looks much better."

The man nodded, poking the skin near the ghastly laceration. He spoke to her in his tongue and then lifted Jake to try to force more tea into him.

That afternoon, Jake woke.

He blinked at Emma. "What happened?"

"You've been ill, a fever."

His gaze scanned the ceiling, taking in the rough-hewn logs. "Where am I?"

"An Indian fishing village."

She grasped his hand.

"Are you all right?" he asked.

How could he ask after her welfare when he'd nearly died of fever? She cried and he knit his eyebrows.

"I'm fine, now that you're better."

He smiled. "I feel weak as my mother's tea."

The relief flooding through her made words nearly impossible. "I'm so glad to talk with you again. I thought, I mean, I have so much to tell you." She gazed down at their clasped hands. "I thought I'd lost my last chance."

"What did you want to tell me?"

She hesitated. She meant to tell him how worried she'd been. How, in the hours of the night, she accepted that Francisca was right. She loved this man and wanted to stay with him.

Now she remembered his aversion to marriage and doubt crept in. How could she make him understand that she would not ask him to settle? She would wander with him forever if he'd let her.

Sparrow, Talks to Wind's wife, arrived and gasped, obviously surprised to see Jake up. She called to her husband, who appeared a moment later beaming a great smile.

The two spoke and he checked Jake's wound. His wife changed the poultice as he prepared some tea over the fire. Mac-Innes appeared and hesitated as he noted the change in Jake's condition.

Emma thought she saw a look of irritation cross his face before he greeted Jake.

"Awake at last, my friend. How do you feel?"

"Hungry," said Jake.

MacInnes laughed and spoke to Sparrow who fetched fish chowder for Jake. Emma was uneasy as she noted that Jake could not hold the spoon or bowl. The fever had weakened him. Seeing him awake made her think all was well, but the recovery had only just begun. Emma fed him like a child. Then Sparrow brought tea. The sweet aroma sickened Emma's stomach and she wrinkled her nose.

"It's medicinal tea," said MacInnes. "I had it when the piles struck me. It clouds the mind but heals the body."

Jake seemed exhausted from his meal. Sparrow held his head as Jake drank.

Soon he slept. Now Emma felt the weight of her sleepless nights press down on her. Exhausted from worry and tending Jake, she curled beside his platform and slept soundly.

Over the next three weeks Jake ate, slept and drank the medicinal tea. He seemed relaxed and happy.

As he recovered, Emma felt anxious to begin their return trip. The New Year arrived tomorrow and she remembered Jake's determination to cross the desert in the winter months. But when she mentioned it to him he only smiled and nodded.

He did not seem himself at times. Though they talked at length about the journey, he made no preparations and left his bed only when necessary.

His wound knit leaving a nasty scar, running from the top of his shoulder to below his collarbone.

This cabin by the sea became their home, but she knew they could not stay forever. Restless, she paced the packed dirt floor.

"Do you think you should get up and move about? You need to regain your strength."

He lifted his hand to her and she sank on the bed beside him. "Why so anxious?"

"Do you feel better today?"

He smiled. "Emma, how do you feel about me?"

"What?"

"How do you feel about me?"

She stared at him, unable to understand the transition in their conversation.

"I have great respect for you."

He snorted.

"What do you want me to say?"

"I want you to tell me that you love me, that you can't live without me and that you'll never leave me."

She stared at him, astonished. Then she pressed a hand to his forehead. He grasped her wrist and pulled her down upon him.

"Let me up," she said.

"Nope. I want to kiss you. I want to do more than kiss you."

Her eyes widened. The mere mention of kisses brought her pulse racing.

"Jake, what are you saying?"

"What I should have said back there in the desert, when I nearly lost you. I'm in love with you, Emma. Have been for some time. I just was afraid to say it. I don't know what happens now."

The uncertainty and restraint dissolved in a wave of joy. She kissed him hard. One arm went around her as she fell beside him onto the furs. His kisses trailed down her neck.

He loves me.

Her fingers delved into his thick hair as she brought his mouth back to kiss her once more. He slid into the gap between her legs. The pressure of his arousal made her still. He meant to have her. She hesitated only an instant. She loved this man and she trusted him. He would never hurt her.

He grasped her hand and brought her palm against his arousal until she had the measure of him. Her touch made him tremble.

"See what you do to me," he whispered low in her ear.

In that moment she knew the power of a woman's body. When his palms covered her breasts, she gasped at the sharp, exquisite shaft of pleasure shooting through her. She became aware of a rising liquid heat between her legs and the irresistible urge to press herself against him.

"Let me love you, Emma," he whispered as his hands moved under her tattered skirts, releasing the ribbon at her waist.

Clothing fell aside, slipping with a whisper down her thighs. Next he lifted the edge of her buckskin shirt, drawing it away. He stilled to gaze down at her naked figure.

"Lovely as summer in the mountains," he said and kissed the tender skin below her collarbone.

His shirt had been discarded long ago to allow access to his wound. He released the fastening of his breeches.

Now he drew her against him. She thought the warmth of his body and the soft merging of flesh, the sweetest sensation in the world. She stroked his chest, marveling at the mat of hair, coarse and curling beneath her exploring fingers.

His hand descended between them into the nest of hair at the junction of her legs. Her head fell back as a gasp of pleasure escaped her. His gentle petting sent a shower of sensation pouring through her. The urge to move came strong now and she pressed herself against his hand.

"That's my sweet Emma. How I long for you. Come and let me make you mine."

She wanted nothing else in this life than to be his. He rolled between her legs. The stroking continued, as he descended to kiss her neck.

His teeth bit at the lobe of her ear as she noted a pressure between her legs. She realized he had entered her as he slid smoothly forward.

"You're mine now."

Was she? She rocked against him and he slid farther within her passage. This time the movement brought only a building tension. She recalled the pleasure and craved it.

They rocked in opposition, first away, then together, each stroke of his body into hers bringing a tightening preparation, like a river building behind a dam.

Then the river broke free issuing out in all directions with waves of pleasure rolling through her. She cried out, arching backward to accept him, feeling their bodies fuse together in that instant like molten lead. They were one.

He gripped her hips and held her.

"Emma, how I love you." His body slumped onto hers and she accepted him into her arms as she floated on her river, the echoes of the pleasure he brought her rolled like a gentle wave to the beach.

"I never knew it could be like this between a man and a woman," she whispered.

"Only with the right one."

"I always thought that being with a man made life unbearable. But despite the hardships, my time with you has brought great joy."

He smiled. "I feel that way, too."

"Maybe there is a way for men and women to coexist, without crushing each other."

He blinked, his eyelids heavy.

"Maybe so."

He pulled away and she reached out to keep him there with her, in her. But he slipped.

"I'm too heavy," he apologized.

She would bear his weight, gladly. He moved to make her more comfortable. Why then did she feel abandoned? Foolish, she decided. He was right here with her. She stroked his hair.

"I love you," she murmured into his ear.

His eyelids fluttered. Sleep took him. Emma lay her head upon his chest comforted by the slow rhythm of his heartbeat.

That night they slept together flesh to flesh. Emma thought there was no greater comfort in the world than resting in his arms. When he moved, she followed as if they performed some courtship dance.

She slept soundly and did not wake until Sparrow entered the lodge. Emma smiled and blinked at the woman, then realized she lay upon Jake's bare chest wearing not a stitch of clothing.

Sparrow's eyebrows lifted. Were Indian women shocked by such things? She did not think so, but Sparrow made a hasty retreat.

Emma took the opportunity to slide from Jake's arms. He reached for her, but she already stood beside the bed.

"Where are you going?" His voice was hoarse from sleep. "I want to make love to you again."

"Sparrow was here."

Jake smiled as if unconcerned. She slipped on her buckskin shirt, bloomers and the tattered blue skirt. Before she had her moccasins on Sparrow returned with Talks to Wind.

Sparrow brought Jake his meal as usual. He did not seem the least concerned to be found in a compromising position with her and ate with a good appetite.

"Where is his medicine?" she asked.

The two exchanged looks and Emma pointed to the bowl they used to bring him the medicinal tea. They shook their heads.

MacInnes arrived shortly afterward, scowling fiercely. Emma lifted her chin as if she was not ashamed, but her cheeks heated.

"You have slept with him?"

"That's none of your affair."

"Talks to Wind tells me to say that your man is healed. He does not need the medicine. His mind will clear this evening."

"What do you mean? There is nothing wrong with his mind."

MacInnes snorted and ducked out of the lodge. Emma did not understand why a cold sweat broke out upon her forehead.

"Jake, did you hear him?"

Jake extended the empty bowl to her. "That was good."

After his meal, he slept again. She watched over him, waiting for him to wake. To fill the time she worked tanned buckskin into a shirt to replace Jake's ruined one. She could not look at the bloodstains or repair the damage done when the garment was cut away. Sparrow helped her cut the leather and bore the holes for lacing. Rain fell on the cabin roof. MacInnes reappeared, shook off the water and sat beside the fire smoking a pipe. Talks to Wind arrived and began grinding dried roots into powder beside the fire.

Finally Jake stirred. Emma stroked his head.

His eyes opened and his smile reassured. Then he glanced around and started up to his elbows.

"Where the hell am I?"

"What?"

"Where's Nikki?"

"Nikki? We escaped him."

"Then whose cabin is this?"

"I don't know. It belongs to the Indians."

"What Indians?"

MacInnes stepped forward and gave her a hard stare. "I told you the tea clouds the mind." Then he turned to Jake. "I'm Alexander MacInnes from Fort Vancouver. You were injured in a knife fight."

"I remember."

"But not what came after. This woman was discovered in the woods above this village with you. Your wound was putrid and your fever high. This man is Talks to Wind." He motioned behind him at the medicine man.

Emma's stomach knotted, as understanding seeped into her mind. *No, it couldn't be.*

"He cared for your injury. You were unconscious for several days. When the fever broke he gave you a healing medicine. As you see, the wound is better."

Jake glanced at his shoulder and his eyes widened to see the wound closed. "Why don't I remember?"

"The medicine affects the mind—temporarily."

Confusion filled his eyes and he turned to Emma. "How long?"

She could barely draw a breath. He didn't remember, them, last night. All gone.

Jake turned to MacInnes. "How long?"

"A month."

Jake gaped at him. "What's the date?"

"January first, eighteen thirty-one."

He fell back to the bed. "My God."

Emma swallowed the lump in her throat. Her voice squeaked when she finally found it.

"I've been so worried." She gripped his hand. He didn't pull away.

"How did we get out of the camp? How did we do it? The last thing I remember is getting on Duchess. A month. It can't be."

Emma cried for the loss. He did not love her or if he did, he did not remember their night of loving.

Jake rubbed his ear absently as he studied her.

"It's all right, Em. I'm well again."

All she could do was nod stupidly as her heart broke in two. Nothing had changed, except now she knew she loved him with the shattered remains of her beating heart.

Did she regret giving herself to him?

No—only that he did not remember.

He stared at his wound, taking in the puckering red scar that sliced along his collarbone. With one finger he traced the track left by the Russian.

Then his gaze locked on hers. "How did we get out?"

"The fog. It was so thick they couldn't find us. You got on your horse and…"

"You led us to safety."

She nodded.

He took her hand. "Amazing."

"These people—they treated you. The wound festered and your fever was so high. They saved your life."

MacInnes stood behind her. She cast him a look.

"I think it's time for our patient to be up and about."

Jake nodded. Upon sitting, however he swayed dangerously. After some moments he rose and walked. He wanted to leave immediately, but recognized his weakness.

It took three days for Jake to recover enough to ride. Then he thanked his hosts and left them with knife blades, ribbon and beads. Trading with the British made these things more common, but they were gracious in acceptance.

He bartered for dried fish for their journey. Emma helped him pack their belongings. She stood beside MacInnes, a short distance from Jake.

He rested a hand upon her shoulder. "I know you love this man, but he does not seem to feel the same."

Emma swallowed her grief. "There is nothing more common than that."

"True, because I love you."

She felt she must deny his feelings, but realized she could not.

"So you must ask yourself if it is better to journey with a man you love who does not love you or stay with a man who does. Perhaps in time you might love me, too."

"You and I share the same lot. I am sorry for us both." She kissed his cheek and mounted Scout. When she lifted her head she found disapproval in Jake's gaze.

"Let's ride," he said.

He seemed annoyed with her and did not speak again until that evening.

"What exactly went on between you and that Scot?"

"Nothing." She could not keep the sorrow from her voice.

"Didn't look like nothing. He make advances?"

"Yes."

Jake's face turned red. "I knew it."

"He asked me to stay with him."

That stopped him. His mouth gaped and he blinked for a moment.

"Can you remember any of it?" she asked, desperate to know.

"My recovery? No. It's like a dream. You can almost remember before it fades."

She lowered her gaze to the flames.

The irritation faded from his voice. "You wish you stayed?"

She shook her head, unable to speak.

The fire crackled as the silence stretched on. That night they slept on opposite sides of the fire.

Chapter Twenty-Four

They crossed the Sierras and the rolling grasslands beyond. Emma wondered what her mother would say about her daughter's adventures? In her mother's condition it was doubtful she would even understand Emma's predicament. Their last conversation had been so bizarre. Her voice came again, urgent, secretive and hoarse from the shouting.

"For you, for you…" said her mother.

Her mother had pressed the gold earrings and necklace into her hand. Emma had stared down at the glinting metal. That was the last time they had spoken. Shortly afterward, her father had discovered her playing with the treasures and taken them.

Her mother had been a wealthy woman, disowned when she married beneath her. Now in her madness she had no one but her husband.

How similar their situations.

Emma had no one.

She did not know what to do. But she must tell Jake. Even if he thought her a loose woman or her actions some kind of plot designed to trap him, they were not.

Something was wrong with Emma. Jake pondered what had changed. It must be that damn Scot. Since leaving the Pacific

Indians, she'd grown silent as a ghost and had thrown up several times.

They'd crossed out of California, stopping only to recover his chronometer and struggled over a new pass in the Sierra Nevada in early March. Everything went well so he could not explain the gnawing uncertainty that filled his belly.

He also couldn't explain the dreams.

At first he'd thought them just some fantasy, Emma naked beside him, whispering she loved him. Holding her, loving her. But then he remembered the Indian woman, the wife of the medicine man, changing his poultices. Other details that he could not know emerged like bubbles from dark water and he began to wonder if these were not dreams, but lost memories.

The idea filled his veins with ice chips. Could he have loved Emma in his condition? He didn't know, but as more and more images flooded his mind he could not dismiss them any longer.

You need to focus on this damn desert. Remember the last time.

This time he guided them north of their original passage. They'd left a spring three days ago and found more water yesterday. Holes in the surface revealed a stream running beneath the rock. He'd used ropes to lower his pot and fill his skins. The water was sweet, better than what he carried.

No sign of water today and he concluded that they would find none until they reached the Great Salt Lake. Emma threw up again this morning.

He wondered if her mood made her sick. She grew pale. Porridge seemed the only thing she held down. Odd that she could not tolerate the sight of raw meat.

When he asked her about it, she said it would pass in time. Could this be some female disorder?

That thought sent a chill down his spine.

What if she—she was… My God, it happened again? Could he possibly have been stupid enough to get a woman with child?

No. He had not. He glanced at Emma and found her gazing

dully at the horse's mane. She could have orchestrated this, just like the other one. But then why not tell him?

This was Emma, not Helen. She told him she did not want to marry.

"I love you." Her words came to him from somewhere in his mind.

Just like Helen.

That evening he threw the supplies into a pile with more force than necessary. Emma stood watching with cautious eyes.

He made no fire, preferring the light of the orange moon rising full above them, as it cast no heat. He offered her the dried elk and water and she ate in silence.

Jake watched her, glancing at her middle on occasion. If she did carry his child, why didn't she say so?

Why didn't she say?

Emma woke and lay completely still. She knew from experience that once she moved, she would likely be sick.

Eventually the pressure of her bladder forced the decision and she sat up, waiting for the wave of nausea that preceded her losing the contents of her stomach.

It never came. She swallowed tentatively. For six weeks she had carried this child. Perhaps her body now grew accustomed to the task. Rising with caution, she felt no worse. She sighed in relief as she made her way behind the rocks for a little privacy.

When she returned, Jake faced her, hands on hips as if fixing for a fight.

"Not sick today?"

She shook her head; a tingle of apprehension crawled up her neck. She wiped her palms on her leather skirt.

"There something you want to tell me?"

She stared at his rigid expression and resentment simmering in his eyes like boiling water. Not like this, she thought. She'd been waiting for the right time and place. It never came.

Now he demanded answers. She breathed deep gathering her courage as a feeling of defeat pressed down upon her.

"You slept with me. Didn't you?" The accusation was evident in his voice.

"I did."

"Why?"

He dared her to say it, to verify that she wanted to tear off his wings and close him in a jar.

"Because I love you."

Confusion rippled over his face then it settled into granite again.

She pressed on. "That night you told me you loved me, as well."

"I was out of my head!"

"I didn't know that until afterward."

He threw up his hands and turned away, then rounded on her again.

"You with child?"

She nodded.

"God damn it!" He slapped his hat against his leg.

Her head sunk. "I never meant for this to happen."

"I told you, we needed to take precautions. But you still grabbed the first chance to slip into my bed."

"That's not what happened." The defeat vanished, replaced with white-hot anger, like the fog dissolving in the brightness of the sun.

She raised her chin in defiance.

Why did he admire her, even now? He did love her, though he never meant to tell her so. He even thought they might come to some arrangement, perhaps continue on as they were, traveling, exploring the West and each other.

But a child…

He couldn't. They couldn't. A child needed a home, a place, one place. His stomach constricted, slowly turning to stone. The air pressed from his lungs. He couldn't do it. He'd lose Emma and the child. My God, why did he have to choose his freedom or her? Fear swallowed him whole. In desperation he lashed out.

"I'll not marry you."

Her eyes narrowed and he felt hunted.

"Have I asked you to? I am not Helen. My entire purpose in life is not to see you hamstrung. I shared your bed because I love you and I stupidly believed you felt the same. I accept my mistake."

"It's our mistake now."

"Leave me alone." She turned away and he snatched her back.

"That might be a little hard to do out here."

"Mr. Turner, you do not have any rights to me, nor shall I be giving you any, so take your hands off me *now.*"

He did, releasing her with such speed, she stumbled.

"What are you saying?" he growled.

She threw her arms up. "Did it ever occur to you that I might not want a man who feels marriage is a trap? That I might not want to be bound for life to a husband who sees me as some kind of evil seducer who ensnared him at a weak moment. The only thing of which I *am* certain is that I don't want to marry you."

Confusion etched his forehead. "What do you mean?"

She took a step toward him, lifting a finger to stab him in the chest with each word. "I won't marry you. Clear?"

"What about the child?"

"What about it?"

"It's mine."

She lowered her chin preparing to defend her own. "Are you saying you wish to take it from me, because you won't."

"You won't marry me?"

Finally he understood.

"Is that such a shock? You've treated me like a leper since you first suspected I might be with child." She laughed at his scowl. "You didn't think I noticed how you stared at my stomach and searched my face."

"What will you do?" he asked.

"Once we part ways, that will no longer be your concern."

Jake stood speechless. Good, serves him right, the arrogant man. She'd be better off alone than with a husband that hated her.

"I could give you my name, but not stay."

He watched her lips thin as if refusing some bitter pill. At last she swallowed.

"I don't think so." She turned to retrieve her saddle and found it lifted from her hands.

"I'll do that," he said.

What did she mean, she didn't want to marry him?

Duchess made her way up the foothills of the Rockies toward their final test, South Pass. He had no one to consult about the winter's snowfall. No word from any traveler of what he might find there.

From the looks of them, the snowfall had been heavy. He should be studying the mountains, instead of dwelling on Emma.

Since she'd said she would not marry him, it was all he could think about. She was his. Hadn't he saved her from Indians and snatched her out of the desert? Hadn't he taught her to use a compass and figure their position? She'd become a part of him and he couldn't imagine life without her.

Now she talked as if she hated him. Funny way to treat a man you said you loved.

And if she loved him, why did she want to part from him?

He let his mind take him to possibilities. What would it be like to be married to Emma? Certainly she would not castrate him as Helen would have.

She told him that she hadn't planned for this to happen. God help him, he believed her.

Had he told her he loved her?

She said he had, said it was the only reason she'd surrendered to him. Flashes of memory heated his skin and made him ache to hold her again.

Since she'd spurned him, she had not broached the subject

of marriage. That confounded him. He could offer his name and
the safety of his arms.

And that was about all.

Perhaps this was why she wouldn't have him. Did she think
he had nothing? That he was some wandering vagabond without the wherewithal to support a wife and child.

He was still a lieutenant in the army. He had his commission. If he chose to leave the military, he could find work as a
surveyor or guide. Soon wagons would thread through these
mountains like pearls about a woman's neck.

He planned to be part of that.

Where would Emma fit in?

Could he ask her to wander about like a gypsy with a child
strapped to her back? The Indian women did. But she was not
an Indian. Surely she would prefer to stay at home and wait for
his return.

He might be gone for years.

The idea of being separated from her so long made his gut
twist. To think he once thought of her as baggage. Now he could
not imagine his world without her.

What the hell would he do now?

The more Emma thought of it the sadder she became. Jake
seemed perpetually annoyed with her. Just a sample of what
she could expect if she did agree to his ridiculous marriage
proposal.

Seeing her mother in an unhappy marriage made Emma
sure she would never repeat her parents' mistake. But for a time
there, when she lay in Jake's arms, she'd forgotten that and believed it was possible to love a man and be loved in return.

Thoughts of her mother resurfaced. What had she meant
when she pressed the precious gold chain into Emma's hand?
It was the first time Emma ever saw the necklace and she knew
by her mother's actions that she wanted the gift to be a secret.

Had her mother meant for Emma to use the jewelry to escape her father's tyranny? That possibility stuck and she could not shake it. Suddenly the words made sense.

"For you, for you." What else had she said? "You'll need them to escape, to find me. Hide it, don't let him see."

But how could a mad woman be capable of such forethought?

A chill ran up Emma's spine. Was she mad or had she used the madness to escape him?

Emma slumped in the saddle. Feelings of abandonment resurfaced, squeezing her throat and making breathing difficult. Had her mother left her?

Mother had begged to go east to see her family. Always he had denied her, watched her, guarded her.

One certainty rose above the rest. She would not be returning to her father—ever.

Instead, she would search for her mother.

Chapter Twenty-Five

"I don't remember this path," said Emma.

"That's because this isn't Union Pass, it's South Pass."

She drew up on the reins. "South Pass!"

He paused looking confused. "That's right."

"We crossed over on Union Pass."

"That's right, but that's a hundred and twenty miles north of here."

"I can't go over South Pass."

He tugged on the brim of his hat. "Why not?"

"My father's fort is at the base of the mountains. I'll be walking right back into his control."

Jake sighed. "Now, Emma…"

Suspicion gripped her. "You mean to bring me back. I won't go."

Panic took her now and she wheeled Scout around, to head back down the trail.

"Emma. Emma—stop." He grabbed Scout's harness, gripping as her mount tossed his head.

"Damn bad-tempered beast."

"I'm not going back to him."

Scout yanked the leather from Jake's hand. "Who asked you

to? He's on the Bighorn, twenty miles or more from the trail-head. We can skirt him well enough."

"Skirt him?"

"Leave the trail and avoid the river. He won't know you've crossed the divide."

She stared. "Jake, don't lie to me."

"I won't."

Her palms sweated just thinking of coming within her father's reach once more. She lifted her gaze from the trail to study Jake. His serious stare seemed to beg her to trust him.

"All right, then."

He smiled and turned Duchess back toward the mountain.

Halfway up South Pass Jake knew that they were in trouble. The horses pushed through snow brushing their bellies in places and he did not like the feel of the snow.

Uncertainty rode with him as he contemplated turning back. He pulled up.

"What's wrong?" asked Emma.

"Snow is too deep. We haven't topped the pass yet and no telling what we will find on the eastern slope. We should turn around."

"We have to cross eventually."

"Maybe in a month or two."

Emma set her lips together in a gesture he recognized. She was gathering to fight.

"I can't wait two months," she said.

"Well, you'll have to."

She glared at him. "How much longer do you think I can ride? I'm already blossoming. I need to get over these mountains now."

"Snow is unstable. See how the top is crusty and the bottom kinda soft?"

"I don't give a damn about the snow. I'm crossing."

They stared at each other.

"I'm not putting my child at risk," he said.

Her eyes glittered dangerously. "You have no say."

"I will if I marry you."

That shocked the tightness from her face. Astonishment now covered her features. Then her eyes narrowed suspiciously.

"I'll not marry because you feel guilty over this child."

"Why the hell not?"

"This might come as a dreadful shock to you, but I think it is possible to find a man to love who will treat me as a partner, not his jailer. If I can't find that man, I'll stay single."

"I treated you as a partner."

Her expression softened as she nodded. "Right up until you decided I did this on purpose."

"Didn't you?"

She glared a moment then kicked Scout forward, driving Duchess into the snow.

He watched her go. Damn stubborn woman.

Of course he was right. They had only crested the highest point of the trail at sunset. Emma pressed on into the dark, her big strong gelding pushing the snow before him like a shovel. There was no place to stop or rest. The wind howled between the peaks as the horses struggled on.

When one mule fell, Jake had the devil's time bringing her to her feet once more. The night passed cold, wet and miserable as they made slow progress.

At sunup they stopped to feed the horses and eat. Circles ringed Emma's eyes, but her jaw remained set in steely determination.

Finally, they headed down below the cloud cover and into the sunshine on the eastern slopes. The snow shone brilliantly. Emma brought her hat low over her eyes. As the morning progressed, the sun climbed and temperatures rose. He knew better than to remove his coat, but he unfastened the toggles.

As the horses broke the top layer of snow, it fell in sheets, cascading down the trail before them, picking up speed and clearing a path.

He took point again, leading them away from the gap.

"Why are you going across the trail?" she asked.

"I'm getting out of the low point."

Tension knotted his shoulders as he glanced from one snow-covered peak to the next. How thick was the layer above them? A little farther and they'd be clear of the most dangerous spot—the gap.

The first sound reminded him of the surf on the shore of the Pacific. He turned toward the low rumble. Above him, ice broke from the cliffs hitting the smooth surface beneath. The layer collapsed, tumbling downward.

"Ride!" he shouted.

Behind them the avalanche rushed, booming like thunder and gathering speed as a mountain of snow collapsed before it like a breaking wave. Emma kicked Scout and they rushed horizontally away from the approaching menace.

He beat his heels into Duchess's sides and she lunged into the deep snow, breaking a path. He glanced behind and saw Emma struggling with Scout and the mules all tied in a string. Behind them the white death hurtled nearer.

"Cut them loose!" he shouted, but the thunder of falling snow drowned his words.

The ground beneath the last mule collapsed taking the creature off her feet. She pulled down the next and they disappeared into a white wave dragging the packhorse along. The line jerked Scout and he reared up.

Jake wheeled about, dragging hard on Duchess's mouth as Emma vanished in the cascading snow. Jake halted on packed snow as the white river of ice cascaded just before him.

He fought the urge to dive into the current. If Emma died—no, he would not finish it. He'd find her. He'd save her.

Down the slope he raced, Duchess somehow managing to keep her footing as he pressed her to greater speed.

He saw a mule rise like driftwood on a wave and disappear once more. The river slowed and solidified with terrifying speed.

Boulders of ice lay stacked like beer barrels. How could she survive? In that icy moment of dread he understood that he needed her with all the strength of his soul. It didn't matter if she was pregnant or how she became so. He was a stupid, heartless fool.

"God, give me one more chance to make it right with her."

A mule shook herself some fifty yards down the mountain. His gear lay strewn along the slope before him, scattered like wreckage from a ship. Where was Scout?

The big chestnut had vanished, gobbled up by the greedy mountain. He kicked Duchess onto the frozen river. The ice bore his weigh easily and he understood the snow might crush her to death, robbing her of the air she needed to live.

He galloped across the field, around a boulder of ice the size of a cabin and saw Scout, his haunches trapped and his reins buried as he struggled and pawed to escape the icy hold.

Where was she?

She might have fallen from him and been swept away.

"Emma!"

Scout extracted himself from the snow, leaving a crater. Something dropped from his stirrup. Jake jumped from his horse and ran to the hole seeing Emma's leg, disappearing into the crush of snow.

Jake clawed at the ice but made little progress. Using his butchering blade he attacked this predator sending crystals flying. Her skirt appeared and next her hip. Judging where her face might be, he moved and dug again, using his hands.

His nails broke and the ice turned bloody as he fought to reach her. At last he clutched a wisp of hair and then saw the line of her jaw.

Find her mouth, her nose—hurry, hurry.

He dug faster. Ice clung to her lashes and packed her nose. He cleared her mouth.

Her gasp was the sweetest sound he'd ever heard. Relief weakened him and his shoulders shook with dry sobs.

Thank God, thank God.

He worked slowly now, carefully. Scout blew hot breath

onto his shoulder as Jake struggled to unearth his mistress. When he reached her hand, he found her fingers still gripping the reins.

Lifting Emma from the icy grave, he felt her chilled skin and shuddered himself. He had to warm her. He left her only to gather the animals, finding a single mule and the packhorse. He tied them in a line. Then he wrapped Emma in his buffalo robe and carried her to his horse.

He held her in his arms as he rode down the mountain. She did not shiver, but lay ice-cold, blue lipped and still as death. Twice he stopped just to assure himself that she was breathing.

The final descent seemed endless. At last he reached the tree line and wasted no time in building a large fire, sending dark smoke to the sky. The signal might bring friend or foe but he needed the heat to warm his Emma.

As he stripped off her clothes, he found ice packed beneath her dress, in her moccasins and clinging to her hair. He fastened the lionskin cloak about her neck, lay out the buffalo robes and pulled her against him. Cocooned within the shaggy fur, he rubbed her frosty limbs. His clothes kept his heat from reaching her, so he stripped them off then drew her close, once more terrified at the temperature of her skin.

"Emma, it's Jake. Can you hear me?"

She lay limp as a rag doll as he struggled to bring her heat. He sweated beneath the robe, beside the fire wondering if she felt him?

"I love you. Please, Emma, give me a chance to prove it."

She moved. At first he thought he imagined it, but gradually he understood. Her body shivered, quaking against him with tiny tremors.

He sighed, knowing she was warming.

"Wake up, Em. Wake up and look at me."

He brushed damp hair from her pale face and fanned her with his hot breath.

That was when he heard the distinctive click of a cocking

pistol. He glanced up into the face of a bearded man. Jake's gaze flicked to the others behind him, all stood with aimed weapons. He returned his attention to the leader and saw his red face grow brighter as a blue vessel at his temple pulsed. He knew the man.

"Just what, in God's name, are you doing with my daughter?"

Jake struggled up to his elbows. "Lancing, wait."

Her father looked apoplectic. "I ought to shoot you between the eyes."

"She's hurt."

He snorted, reminding Jake of some great wild boar. His beady eyes squinted. Lancing turned to the wiry man on his left. "Pull him off."

Two men dragged Jake up by his elbows. He knew he could shake them off, but he couldn't evade the company of men all taking a bead on his heart.

Her father leaned in, his voice strangled with rage. "I'll hang you for this."

Jake stood naked before Emma's father. He studied his enemy and saw an overfed, self-important dictator.

"Put on your trousers, you damn filthy bastard," said Lancing.

Jake made no move to follow his order and that made her father tremble so his jowls shook.

"Mr. Lancing, I believe you'll want to look in my bag there before you shoot me."

"You little whelp, are you telling me what to do?"

Jake smiled. "Yes, sir."

He slapped Jake across the face with an open palm. Jake absorbed the blow without recoiling. His face stung and his jaw tightened.

"With respect, sir, I'm an officer of the United States Army."

Lancing hesitated and Jake knew that the man understood that killing him would seal Lancing's death warrant. His recovery was quick. The man let his gaze drop. "Out of uniform, aren't you?"

"That bag." Jake pointed. Since leaving Spanish territory, there was no reason to secrete his maps and letters in the stock of his gun, so he'd moved them to his pouch.

Lancing snapped his fingers and pointed in the direction of Jake's gear. "Bring me his damn bag."

In a moment the leather pouch lay open and Lancing had his fleshy hand about Jake's journal.

"In the back. There are three identical letters."

He knew the moment the man saw the seal of the office of the president.

"Is this some kind of joke?" Lancing said, waving the letter as if just discovering more evidence to condemn him.

"Open it."

The man's eyes narrowed at the direct order, but he looked off balance now. He broke the seal and his gaze scanned the page.

Jake knew what lay within.

The bearer of this letter operates under the orders of the President of the United States and shall be afforded any assistance he requires.

Andrew Jackson
President

"Where did you get this, you scallywag?" asked Lancing.

"President Jackson."

The men around him shifted uncomfortably as uncertainty weighed upon them.

"This is some kind of trick. I could have you—"

"Hanged or shot?"

"Don't you use that impertinence with me. I don't know who you are but—"

Jake took a step forward closing in on the man.

"But we met at the Rendezvous. I'm Jacob Turner, lieutenant in the United States Army on special assignment and Emma needs care."

"That assignment include kidnapping my daughter?"

Jake hesitated. "I kept her alive."

Lancing sniffed. "So I see."

"Your daughter nearly died in that avalanche. Now I want her tended and I want my gear collected from the mountain. You going to follow the orders of your president or not?"

Lancing spun away. "Lower your weapons, men. Randolph, pick a detail to gather Lieutenant Turner's belongings. See he has a horse and food and turn him loose."

Jake slipped into his buckskin trousers and skirt. "I'm not going without Emma."

Lancing turned to face him. "That letter doesn't entitle you to my daughter."

"You're not taking her."

"Watch me." He turned to a boy with fuzz upon his cheeks. "Andrews, get my daughter on a horse." He faced Jake. "You need anything else, see Randolph here."

Her father lifted Emma wrapped only in a lion skin to a ruddy-cheeked boy mounted on a gray. Jake took a step toward her and heard a pistol cock.

"One more damn step and I *will* shoot you."

Jake met Lancing's cold stare and held his ground.

Lancing waited, the barrel of the gun aimed at Jake's chest while his men gathered his belongings. Behind him, the others descended into the trees carrying Emma from his sight.

Lancing mounted up. "Goodbye, Turner. I hope the Blackfoot find you sleeping."

Emptiness swallowed Jake.

He'd lost her.

Emma kept her eyes closed as she inhaled. The scent of her father's tobacco came to her and she stiffened. That wasn't possible.

Where was the breeze?

She pinched her lids tight, refusing to look. A dream—no a

nightmare. If she could only sleep again, everything would be all right.

But it wasn't.

The ring of the blacksmith's hammer in the yard outside her window tolled mournful as a church bell. Her eyes opened to take in the unpainted planking above her head. Fort Lancing—she had arrived.

Her mind stretched back to her last memory. Duchess rearing up and Jake shouting words she could not hear past the thunder of falling snow. Scout fell and she rode upon him like a sled as they rushed down the mountain.

Was that why her body ached? A stab of fear pierced her and she reached for her belly, felt the slight swell and collapsed in relief. The baby was all right.

Jake found Jim Bridger on the Green River.

As the most respected trapper in the area, Bridger had considerable influence. He appeared gaunter than Jake remembered and he wondered if the man might have had a tooth pulled to account for the deepening hollows in his cheeks. His smile was still warm and winning and his handshake iron.

"Turner, been some distance since I seen you last."

Jake nodded. "A bit."

He enjoyed the mountain man's propensity for understatement.

"And did you run out of land?"

"Yes, Jim, I did."

"I'd love a gander at your maps."

Jake never before had such trouble restraining himself. He needed to get to Emma. But her father barred him from his trading post. "That might be arranged in exchange."

"Ah." Bridger lifted his chin in understanding. "So this ain't purely a social call."

Bridger motioned to a downed log that served as his office

and Jake sat. Bridger straddled the bark facing his guest and offered his tobacco pouch.

"I would, but I lost my pipe," said Jake.

"Pity. Want me to borrow you one?"

"Thank you, no."

Bridger stuffed the bowl and used a bit of bark to carry the flame from the fire to the pipe, then glanced up, his eyes sharp as a hawk's. "I can see you're busting to say something."

"I had a partner with me."

"Good thing. Difficult trail for one man. What's his name?"

"Emma Lancing."

Bridger choked and then laughed. "You took Emma Lancing?"

"You know her?"

He laughed again. "Her pa's been tearing up the territory searching for that gal. Figured the Indians took her. I heard he had her back, but nothing more."

"I have to speak to her."

"Why?"

That stopped him. It seemed so obvious. "I don't know if she's sick or injured."

"If she is, that's her daddy's business, unless you married her." He lowered his chin and his eyebrows lifted.

"I want to marry her, if she'll have me. Can you get a letter to her?"

"Don't know, but I'll give it a try."

Jake's shoulders slumped with relief. He reached in his bag and handed over his precious maps.

When he came, Emma feigned sleep. Now that the meals disappeared, her father knew she was conscious. He hovered in the door, his harsh breathing scratching at the air.

If only she were a little stronger, then she could face him. She forced herself to stillness as her heart pumped madly in her chest. Her breathing followed, gaining speed like a galloping horse.

"Emma? You awake?"

His voice sent a chill down her spine. Why didn't he leave? His footsteps came next as he approached the bed.

"Open your eyes, girl, I know you're awake."

She did as he ordered and found him looming over her with no hint of concern in his eyes. His fixed gaze reminded her exactly of the vulture that came too close. Only now she did not have her pistol.

"Can you give an account of yourself, girl?" he said.

She shook her head.

He snorted. "Thought not. I knew your mother's blood would be the ruin of you. Did you whore for him?"

Her eyes widened, then she turned away. Now at least she could not see the hatred on his face. His words still pierced her.

"Doc O'Sullivan says you'll be lucky not to get pneumonia. Serve you right. You haven't got the sense of a mule. What the hell happened out there? I lost twenty men and I'll know the reason."

She wasn't strong enough. All the past nightmares of this man rose up. How many times had he reduced her to tears?

Too damn many.

Her eyes opened. The first thing she saw was her lion-skin cape hanging from the bedpost. She focused all her awareness on the glowing eyes, remembering the day she shot the animal and how Jake had told her some of the lion's spirit was hers.

Where was that courage now?

"Look at me when I speak to you." His voice menaced, reminding her of the deep throaty growl of the lion she'd killed.

Her jaw clenched.

She *was* strong enough. Her courage hadn't disappeared in this room. It was still inside her.

Emma cast off the covers and swung her feet to the floor. Then she stood to face her father, narrowing her gaze upon him.

"All right. I'm looking at you."

"Don't you take that tone with me, young lady."

She smiled. "I'm not young, nor am I a lady."

Confusion wrinkled his forehead. He hesitated as if about to venture onto a frozen lake and not quite sure it would bear him.

"You looking for a beating, girl?"

"I wouldn't try that."

"And why not?"

"Because I'll fight you."

He cocked his head, now certain something drastic had changed. "Emma Lucille, you've been ill. You don't know what you're saying."

"I know."

"I don't think so." He retreated.

She drew a breath feeling suddenly taller, stronger and then she heard him throw the bolt. She rushed across the room, tugging at the latch. But the door remained locked.

Chapter Twenty-Six

Bridger returned the letter. "I didn't see her."

Jake's shoulder's slumped. "Any word?"

The big man gave a nod. "No one but her pa and the smithy see her, so I figured while I was at the fort, I'd have him fix my bridle buckle."

Jake smiled.

"He said she was off her head with fever for a while."

He stood at this news, ready to ride to the fort, ready to fight.

"Sit," ordered Bridger.

Jake's knees went to water and he landed hard on the stump.

"Now the fever broke. But she's acting peculiar, screaming and such. Her father locked her in his quarters."

"He's keeping her captive."

"His men say she's mad, like her ma."

Jake's stomach dropped. Could that be true? For a moment he dangled in the grip of doubt, then he shook his head. "That's a lie."

"Then I reckon she wants to come after you and that don't sit right with her pa. Why not offer for her hand?"

"Because he won't speak to me. Emma believes he does not wish her to marry."

"Ever?"

Jake nodded.

"That's unnatural."

"I have to get her out."

"They got a small cannon up there. Guns, too. I don't think you're walking through the front gate."

"I mean to try."

"Funny thing. Those traders ain't much at hunting. Fact is my men supply them with game or they'd starve to death." Bridger smiled. "More than one trail to a place, Jake."

"That there is."

The food shortage began immediately.

Emma faced them both.

The bristly cheeked smithy named O'Sullivan and her father stood like a human wall, barring her exit.

"He needs to examine you," said her father. He used the tone he often adopted when there were outsiders about. His voice sounded authoritative and concerned. None of the venom or contempt would do now. All her life she'd played this game. In public she was dutiful and suffered in private.

She set her chin, considering the retribution she would reap by her defiance. After her last outburst, he'd locked her in this room for a week. Here were her first visitors, O'Sullivan and her jailer.

"He's no doctor. He's the blacksmith," Emma said.

"He treated your fever," said her father. "Now sit down and do as you're told."

She glanced toward the shuttered window and in that instant realized she looked for Jake. Some part of her still pined and hoped he would ride in on Duchess and rescue her.

Why should he? More than likely he was happy to be quit of her. He didn't come. Her father said he'd run him off. She knew it was a lie. If Jake stayed away, it was because he wanted to. Had he given her to this tyrant or had her father killed him? The emptiness echoed like a rock thrown down a well, bouncing along the wet stone walls until the water gobbled it up.

When she returned her gaze to the men, something inside her hardened. At first she did not realize the difference. Her heart beat in even rhythm, full of strength and power, when by rights it should be pounding with the speed of a captured sparrow's. Her knees locked straight and stiff instead of turning to liquid.

She swallowed the last of her doubt and was ready.

"No."

O'Sullivan turned to her father who had barely time to contain his snarling expression into a mask of rigid concern.

"You've been ill," he reminded her.

"With good cause."

"What cause?" asked O'Sullivan, hesitating as if afraid to approach. She almost pitied him, having to face a hostile female.

"I am with child."

Her father gaped and she allowed herself a triumph at his shock.

Then he turned to the smithy and asked, "Can you do anything about this?"

Now Emma gaped. Did he mean to kill her child? She'd not allow it. All her life he'd controlled her. Now she would fight.

The blacksmith had not recovered so quickly. He stammered as he spoke. "D-do? To aid her you mean?"

Her father scowled. "To remove it."

He spoke as if she brought some weed to his garden.

The man balked. "That is not only illegal, it is immoral."

Emma stepped toward the door.

Her father gripped her upper arm, squeezing until she had to force her lips together to keep from crying out.

"Where do you think you are going?"

"To visit my mother."

He shook his head.

"You misunderstand," said Emma leveling her gaze upon him. "I am not asking you. Let go."

"Just who do you think you are?"

"If you mean to keep me you'll have to lock me in again, just like you did to my mother."

Her father's gaze flashed to the smithy and then to his daughter. He clearly did not want a scene. His grip tightened as he turned to his man.

"Out," he ordered.

The smithy looked greatly relieved and took a step toward the door.

Emma met his gaze and held it. "He means to lock me in. If he doesn't release me, he'll break my arm."

The man hesitated.

"Sir, I think you should let go."

"Oh you do, do you? Well, I don't give a damn what you think. She's my daughter and I'll have her disciplined. Now get out."

O'Sullivan could not meet Emma's eyes. He kept his gaze on the floor as he departed.

Emma met her father's look of derision. "Let go."

A smile twisted his mouth. "Insolent bitch, I *should* break your arm."

His grip turned cruel and she fell to one knee in a vain effort to relieve the bone-crushing pressure. She glanced about, but he'd left her no weapon. The fingers of her free hand curled into a fist and she struck him in the belly. A whoosh of air escaped him as he doubled and his fingers slackened.

She stood as he fell. In an instant she held his pistol, barrel raised.

"Have you gone mad?" he gasped.

A flicker of doubt licked her insides. Had she? This was her father and she held him at gunpoint.

He seemed to pounce on her hesitation. "Mad, like your mother and a whore. Now put the gun down, Emma, and we will see to this quietly."

Her hand trembled and he lifted one foot, placing it upon the floor as he prepared to stand. In his eyes she saw the glow of victory within his grasp.

She steadied her hand and aimed the pistol at his heart.

"I've never been more sane in my life. Now sit on that bed."

He did.

She recovered her coat, lion-skin cloak and stepped out of her room for the first time in weeks.

"Emma, don't go." He held his open hands before him pleading as he made his entreaty. "Don't leave me."

A flicker of sorrow ignited within her at his look of utter despair. The throbbing of her arm brought clarity.

"Goodbye, Father." She closed the door and slid home the bolt. An instant later he hit the stout wood with a howling cry. A shiver danced down her spine at the familiarity of the scene. The last time she'd heard such a wail, it was her other parent locked in her room and raving.

In the parlor she took her shotgun and rifle down from above the hearth and packed her buffalo robe, provisions and needed supplies, then headed to the stables.

Two of her father's men looked startled as she galloped through the open gate, but none could stop her.

Lancing came to see Bridger personally. When he saw Jake his color darkened.

"What's *he* doing here?"

"Parlaying, same as me," said Bridger, never losing his easy tone of authority.

"I won't negotiate with him."

"Fair enough." Bridger stood, calling an end to the meeting.

Lancing's hand lifted. "Wait. I have to speak to you about supplies."

Bridger glanced at Jake and winked.

Jake faced this new enemy. "I need to see Emma."

The man ground his teeth together. "You can't."

"That's my condition."

"It's blackmail."

Bridger folded his arms. "How those boys coming at deer

hunting? Seems I seen them head out every morning, but they don't look to be bringing nothing back. They eating all that meat in the hills?"

Lancing glared from Bridger to Jake. Then he spoke in a rush as if trying to expel something foul from his mouth.

"She's gone. I don't know where."

Jake rose bellowing like a wounded bear. "What?"

"Alone?" asked Bridger.

"Took her horse and supplies. Stole them."

"How'd that little gal get by your men?" asked Bridger.

Lancing rounded on him. "None of your goddamn business."

"Oh, like that is it?" said Bridger. "I guess you seen the last of that gal."

Jake faced Lancing.

Her father inflated his lungs in a failed attempt to look intimidating but did not match Jake's height or bulk. "I should shoot you where you stand."

"Same thought occurred to me." Jake hoped he'd reach for his pistol.

Lancing broke eye contact and sat, showing his true colors. A tyrant, a bully and a coward. Jake turned to Bridger. "Thanks, Jim. I'm heading out."

Bridger followed him to his horse, laying a gentle hand on his arm.

"That girl know how to navigate?"

"I taught her." Jake felt confident in Emma's ability.

Bridger's concerned face made him uneasy.

"Then maybe she ain't looking for you. If she was, you would have seen her by now."

Where did you go, Emma?

He'd searched the rivers and trails for weeks. No one had seen her. He had to accept the possibility that she was dead. The skills she'd gleaned might not be enough to help her evade Blackfoot, find shelter and hunt for food.

He'd been everywhere, spoken to all friendly tribes, offered rewards for information to no avail. He feared the worst.

If she lived, she'd now be heavy with his child. He tried to picture her that way. Instead the vision of her alone and unconscious at the feet of a grizzly filled his mind.

Oh, Emma.

After three months, he ran out of places to search. The trip east would take at least six weeks. He could put off his mission no longer. Somehow he had achieved his goal, done the impossible. Instead of elation, he felt dead inside. This final journey became only one more obligation to be done with.

He turned Duchess east.

In St. Louis an idea struck. Baltimore lay between him and Washington. Could she be there? She once had mentioned she'd like to see her mother. But to make such a journey alone— he shook his head admitting the idea was desperate. Emma's mother was in some sanitarium. But he'd go, tell her about her daughter and hope the woman could understand. Perhaps she had word of her Emma.

He knew the possibility was too slim to foster hope, but he grasped it just the same. When there is nothing else, small hope is better than none.

Emma stood before the private residence and checked the address written on the calling card. On arrival in Baltimore she visited both sanitariums and found neither had any record of a patient named Lucille Brady Lancing. They assured her that if she had been a patient, they would know, even if she had died.

Bewildered, Emma went to the only home she knew in Baltimore, that of her mother's sister, Alma Brady Webb. The woman would not see her, but her butler gave Emma this card.

"You will find your mother at this address."

But the address was a private home of modest proportions. How could that be?

If her mother was well, why hadn't she written?

Perhaps she wanted nothing to do with her daughter. The possibilities rolled endless as wind across the prairie. Emma considered that living with the uncertainty might be preferable to facing her mother's rejection. If she hadn't wanted the child, certainly she would not welcome the unwed daughter now in desperate circumstances.

She had been lucky in her journey from the Rockies, coming across a group of missionaries only eleven days into her travels. She had supplied them with fresh meat and they had provided protection on their journey to St. Louis.

Trading the stolen otter furs for passage, she reached Cincinnati. There, she lost her shotgun and rifle to a pawnshop in order to secure a rail ticket to Baltimore.

She had arrived, barely able to climb onto her horse and well past the time when a woman in her condition should ride. She hesitated on the doorstep of the house of the mother she no longer knew.

Where else could she go?

She wiped the dampness from her forehead with the back of her hand and mounted the steps of the simple limestone town house on Bond Street. Her fingers trembled as she reached to pull the bell. She paused watching her hand quake like an old woman's.

Her fingers clenched into a fist and she tried once more, this time pulling the bell.

Footsteps approached. A shadow moved behind the lace curtains and the door swung open.

There stood a girl on the threshold of womanhood. Her pale blond hair resembled her mother's. The girl did not smile, but instead looked Emma up and down and seemed to find her lacking. A frown creased the girl's forehead as dark eyebrows descended over green eyes.

Emma had shed her buckskin in St. Louis, but her tanned face and swollen belly made her feel like a crow before a dove.

"Yes?" said the girl.

"Does Lucille Brady Lancing reside here?"

The girl maintained control of the door as she spoke. "She's my mother."

Emma's insides jumped and her gaze fixed on the girl before her. Mother, did she say?

A familiar voice drifted out from inside the house. "Who is it, Ann?"

The girl lifted an eyebrow.

Emma's dry mouth made speech nearly impossible. She choked on the word. "Emma."

"Someone named Emma," called Ann.

The sound of a dish shattering came an instant before the drumming of running feet. Ann turned toward her mother, now hurtling down the hallway, her arms outstretched to Emma and had time only to swing the door open wide. Emma braced as her mother clutched her, weeping madly, and fear gripped her once more.

"You came, you came after all these years. You got my letter at last, you came."

Emma wrapped her mother in her arms and inhaled the familiar mixture of violets and dusting powder she'd long since forgotten.

Emma patted her mother's back. Had she always been so small? Her head now only reached Emma's shoulder. She glanced at Ann, who stood clutching the doorknob as if it was all that kept her standing. Her mouth hung open like a garden gate and she blinked in disbelief.

Her mother pulled away in order to capture Emma's face in her small hands.

"Let me look at you." Her gaze swept her face and she smiled. She stepped back to study her and Emma felt her ears heat as her mother discovered the swell of her belly and gasped.

She glanced to the street as if expecting someone—a husband perhaps, but seeing no one she tugged Emma inside and closed the door.

"Come, my dear, into the parlor. I am so happy, I think I might faint."

Emma recalled her mother fainting often in her childhood, particularly when her husband's temper grew explosive. Emma forced down the resentment.

Her mother was not mad. Emma had a sister.

Sunshine spilled across the dark wood floors and over the faded Persian rug. Her gaze took in the furniture that looked lush and cushioned, far grander than anything she'd seen in years.

Her mother pressed her into a love seat and perched beside her smiling broadly.

"Ann, fetch some water."

The girl stood gaping a moment longer and then hurried through the door.

"I'm so happy you came at last."

"I don't understand. I thought you were still in the sanitarium."

Her mother's face mirrored confusion. "What sanitarium?"

"Where you went to get well, after your…"

Her mother gripped her hand as some possibility dawned.

"Did he tell you I was mad?"

Emma nodded, remembering the wild howls coming from her mother's rooms, the shattering of the water pitcher and bowl and the terrible scraping as she dragged her bed across the floor. A shudder rolled up her spine and she could not suppress it as it rocked her shoulders.

"The man is a demon." Her mother stroked Emma's hand. "My letters. Did you get them?"

"What letters?"

Her mother cried then, lifting her hands to cover her eyes. "I knew it. He burned them or kept them. My God, I hate him. He is not fit to burn in hell."

Emma glanced to Ann, now returning with two glasses of water, walking with slow measured steps as she negotiated the liquid to the table before them. She looked frightened at her mother's outburst. At last, her mother lifted her head showing bloodshot eyes and skin flushed with emotion.

"I wasn't mad. I told him I wanted a divorce."

Emma gasped. Then an inkling of suspicion crept past the shock.

"Why did you howl like a madwoman?"

"He would not let me see you. He would not let me take you. I could not leave you with that man, but I could not stay. I fought him in court, but he won your custody. An unfit mother." She wept again, the words choked between sobs. "I wrote you every week. I wrote begging him to let you come to me." She waved a fist at the ceiling and shouted. "What did he do with my letters?"

Emma shook her head as uncertainty rolled in her belly.

"He kept them from you. He told me that if I wanted you, I had to come back and be his wife. Oh God, Emma. I'm so sorry. I couldn't do it. He wanted Ann, too. When I learned I would have another child, I knew I had to get away. But he took you from me." Her mother searched Emma's face. "He told you I was mad?"

Emma nodded. Her mother clasped a hand over her heart as if the pain might kill her.

"What you must think of me. How you must hate me. Dear Lord. I can't breathe."

Ann offered the water and her mother drank half in rapid swallows. When Ann reached for the glass, her mother clasped her hand.

"This is Ann, your sister."

Ann's eyes looked huge in her small, heart-shaped face.

Emma smiled.

Her mother continued. "This must be such a shock to you. How did you find me?"

"Aunt Alma gave me your address."

A gasp. "The old witch, I'm amazed she even did that. What did she say, that I live in shame over the divorce? It isn't true. I'm free from that tyrant." Her scowl lifted as she met Emma's gaze. "But you, how have you survived with that ogre?" She wept again.

Emma took the water in her hands and stared at the clear surface. The words spilled out of her like a waterfall. How she had met Jake and how she loved him. How they had traveled together. She kept her promise to Jake, not revealing the purpose of their journey. But she told of how he hated her after he'd learned of the child and how she'd fled her father and made her way alone across the country to visit the mother she thought mad. She did not realize her mother wept or that tears streaked her own cheeks until she stopped, still clutching the water. Then she drained the glass.

Her mother's fingers moved to rest upon Emma's knee and squeezed. She shook her head. "What you have endured. But that is all behind you now. You are back where you belong, in the bosom of your family. Ann and I will love you and your child. Never fear. You're home."

Chapter Twenty-Seven

Fall leaves fluttered down outside Emma's window as she walked with Franny upon her shoulder, pacing back and forth across the room past the lion skin now hanging upon the nursery wall. Gradually her baby quieted and dropped off to sleep.

Tranquility filled her heart.

Her daughter was the piece of Jake that she could cherish. The gift he had given her in love, whether he remembered or not. She lifted little Francisca.

The door cracked open and her mother appeared. She scowled at the lion hide then directed her attention to her daughter and mouthed the word "asleep." Emma turned to show Franny's little face and her mother smiled.

Emma placed Francisca in the bassinet and straightened. Her shoulder still clung to the warmth of her child. She stared down at Franny, hoping she would keep her dark hair. Would her eyes change from blue to green to match her father's?

A stab of regret struck as it always did when she thought of him. Her mother's arm slipped about her waist, strengthening her.

Her mother had done it—a divorced woman and she had survived, no, she thrived, alone. But Emma was not divorced nor widowed, because Jake had never married her.

Was there anything sadder than giving her whole heart to one who cared not at all? Her fingers brushed her daughter's fuzzy head. Perhaps Francisca would have better luck in love than her mother or grandmother.

The two women slipped silently from the room. Once in the hall her mother spoke.

"That lion rug will give her nightmares."

"It will help her be strong."

Her mother shook her head in disapproval, but said no more, turning instead to another familiar subject.

"I have a meeting of the Moral Reform Society. I hope you'll come along today."

"I have to watch Franny."

Her eyebrow quirked. "An excuse. Ann is old enough to mind her for the hour you'll be gone."

"What if she needs feeding?"

Her mother gave her a look that showed she knew her granddaughter's schedule as well as her mother. Emma lowered her gaze to the narrow hall carpet.

"Time to go out and face the world again."

Emma met her mother's confident gaze. Once Emma had longed for such freedom. Now she had it and all it cost was a broken heart. She forced a smile.

"All right then."

"Good. My friends are so excited to meet you. I could barely keep them away."

Not her family. No, her mother's family had washed their hands of their divorcée daughter, with the exception of providing a small allowance, which kept them fed and a roof over their heads. Her mother supplemented that meager living by making and selling hair-care products and scented lotions. Her father's entrepreneurial spirit grew strong in her. Despite her exile from her family, Emma's mother had built a solid core of friends who shared her determination to fight society's views on the rights of women.

Emma admired her. "I'll be happy to meet them, as well."

Her mother took her hand, leading her toward the stairs. "There is life out there and you must live it."

Emma nodded. "For my daughter's sake."

"No, my dear, for your own."

Yes, that was right. She took a step and then another, away from the nursery and toward the outside world.

Jake could not find Emma's mother in any sanitarium or any hospital in Baltimore. What was her maiden name? Brady—of the shipping family. He searched the city records and found her birth certificate, but no record of her death. With a sigh of relief, he ventured to the address listed for her parents and found them still in residence.

The stony-faced butler barred the door. "They will not see you."

Although Jake didn't plan to shoot the messenger, he did rest a hand upon the butt of his pistol and squint. "Why not?"

His actions caused the man to lose control of the door as he retreated. It also seemed to loosen his tongue.

"They have disowned her."

"Why's that?"

"I'm not at liberty to say."

"You best be or I'm going to shove you on your ass and step over you." Jake loomed, letting the man feel his presence in the grand white marble entranceway.

"I'll send for the police," said the servant, his voice conveying more panic than authority. His eyes shifted as if already planning his escape.

"They won't get here before I bust open your nose."

The butler pinched his lips together. Then a look of resignation replaced belligerence. "Miss Lucille divorced her husband and lives with her daughter in the city."

"Emma?"

"I believe the child's name is Ann Beverly Brady."

"What about Emma?"

"I am not aware of her."

"The address."

"I cannot…" The man's protest fell off and he heaved a sigh. "Sixteen South Bond Street, just beyond the flower shops.

"Obliged." Jake tipped his new hat and stepped outside.

The butler slammed the door.

Jake mounted up and headed into the city. He grimaced at the smell of rotting fish near the harbor. Handcarts clattered over cobblestone making his ears ring. How did anyone sleep in this racket?

Black smoke belched from chimneys sending coal dust drifting down over him in a fine mist. Disgusting. He tasted the infernal stuff at the back of his throat. The sooner he could make his way to Washington and be quit of the East, the better.

Everything looked smaller, darker and dirtier than he remembered. Had the cities changed or had he?

He hadn't seen this many people in the last year and now they came at him all at once. The woman on the corner selling bread and cheese did a big business. A clerk, in a dark coat and ink stains on his fingers, dropped several coins in the woman's palm.

Jake's jaw tightened as he realized that could have been his life.

He was so intent on avoiding stepping on the children that darted before Duchess that he nearly missed Bond Street. Down the wide concourse he went, finding number sixteen.

The house looked neat, with lace curtains and a window box filled with leggy-looking flowers yet untouched by frost. He swung off Duchess and tied her to the hitching post, pausing to give her a pat and loosen her girth. His horse sighed.

What would he tell her mother? All the miles and weeks of travel and he still had no answer. He only knew he must see her.

He tugged at the short blue jacket of the uniform he had not worn for two years. The warmth of the day made the wool too heavy. He'd polished his boots and brass and could not account for why he felt so uncomfortable in his dress blues.

Because you want her mother to like you.

He stepped sharply across the porch, his boot heel rapping on the wood planking, then lifted his gloved hand and knocked on the broad green door.

He made out only a shadow as someone approached. Suddenly he felt he should have brought something, but could not think what.

The door swept open revealing a girl who so closely resembled Emma that his tongue ceased to work. He gaped as she considered him. The color of her honey-blond hair matched Emma's though she wore it in an elaborate coronet unlike anything Emma had ever concocted. Her eyes were steel-gray, not the smoky color that made his pulse pound. Even so, as she lifted a dark arching eyebrow, a chill descended his spine.

"Yes?"

He cleared his throat and then remembered to remove his broad hat, folding the brim beneath his upper arm. "Is your mother at home?"

She nodded and motioned for him inside. He stepped into a narrow entrance sandwiched between a staircase and a wall. The young woman shut the door.

"Who is calling?"

She seemed to be holding her breath now and he noted she locked her fingers before her, motionless, as if praying.

"I'm Lieutenant Jacob Turner."

A smile broke across her face and Jake's heart ached.

"You're Emma's sister, aren't you?" he asked.

She grinned. "Wait here."

He paced up and down the hall along the thin carpet. Surely the girl did not know of Emma's situation or she would have shown some grief at the mention of her name.

If he didn't know better, he'd say she expected him.

"Lieutenant Turner?"

He came about to face the older woman who could only be Emma's mother. She was smaller than her daughters, much smaller, with pale blond hair now fading to white. Her eyes shone blue-gray and her smile was unfamiliar.

"Mrs. Lancing?"

"Won't you come in?" She turned and led the way to the parlor motioning to a settee as she perched herself in a chair with spindle legs. "What can I do for you, sir?"

"I've come to speak to you about your daughter, Emma."

Her expression held pleasant calm and his heart sank. She did not know.

"She has been through a great deal on your account."

His breath halted as he stared.

"She has contacted you?"

The woman inclined her head.

Jake was on his feet. "When?"

"Please sit down, Lieutenant."

He reined in the urge to shake the woman and eased into the delicate furniture.

"In my opinion, your behavior with my daughter left much to be desired."

He leaned forward bracing his feet before him to prevent himself from toppling onto the carpet and gripped his knees. His voice came as a mere whisper. "Is she alive?"

She sighed and pressed her lips together. "Emma is upstairs seeing to your daughter."

One hand slipped from his knee and he lurched forward, catching his weight on one extended hand.

Then he sank to the floor and he rested there, waiting for the explosion of emotion to pass. He trembled as he struggled to draw a breath. He folded his hands and lowered his forehead to them.

"Thank God."

"Thanks to Emma, apparently. My former husband did not provide her an escort. I know her story, now I would like an ac-

counting from you. For as I see things, there are many reasons
why I should show you the door and only two why I should not."

He could think of no reason for the woman to make him welcome. He crawled back to his seat.

"Why didn't she come to me?" he asked.

"I believe you know why, unless you do not recall your final
conversation with her. Should I refresh your memory?"

Jake could not forget the day the avalanche took Emma. Before that he'd accused her of intentionally getting with child in
order to trap him. Her pained expression seemed branded in his
memory.

"I remember."

"Well then, you should not be overly shocked that she sought
out her mother, even believing me insane, rather than turning
to a brute who clearly did not love her."

"I do love her."

"Excuse me if I do not believe you."

"I want to see her."

"You'd be shocked to know how little I care what you want,
Lieutenant. Right now my concern is for my daughter. You
broke her heart, you know? I see little reason to allow you opportunity to do so again."

"I'll marry her."

Her mother waved a dismissive hand. "A bad marriage is
worse than none."

"Mrs. Lancing, what would you have me do to earn your
approval?"

"First you can explain this change of heart. According to
Emma, you are resolute in your aversion to the convention of
marriage."

"I was wrong."

"What led you to this revelation?"

"I had a bad experience once. It made me gun-shy. Now I
see my mistake."

"She mentioned a woman, though she was hazy on the details. Yet, I fail to see how that should permit you to paint all women with the same black brush."

"It took me some time to reach that same conclusion."

"Is that where you have been these many months—reaching conclusions?"

"I've been searching for her."

"Commendable, yet this still fails to move me to allow you another opportunity to hurt her."

"I never will. I'll provide her a home, I'll settle down. Anything to have her."

"She is not an object to be had."

"You seem set against me. How can I gain your consent?"

"It is not my consent you must gain, sir, but Emma's."

"May I see her, please?" If he shouted for her, would she come or flee? The realization that she might have nothing to do with him cut him across the middle like a saber.

"I will tell her you called. Where are you staying?" She stood now signaling an end to their meeting. He rose to protest as the door swung open. Emma gripped the knob.

He took a step forward and she stumbled into the wall. In that moment, he knew he had lost her.

Jake spoke but Emma could not hear past her heart thundering in her ears. How could he be here, filling her mother's delicate parlor like a grizzly bear in a flower shop?

She hardly recognized him with his clean-shaved face and long hair neatly clipped. She stared at this stranger dressed in a formal uniform, clean white gloves folded over his black leather belt.

He reached for her. She stared at his familiar hands, strong and broad as paddles and then at his face. The corners of his eyes crinkled as his hands clasped hers.

"I found you," he said.

Had he been trying? In that instant she recognized her father had deceived her again.

"Jake?"

He nodded.

She could think of nothing else to say.

Her mother stepped forward and took hold of her elbow steering her to a chair. Emma folded into it like a collapsing house of cards.

"Emma, look at me."

She could not. Her gaze stayed glued to Jake's strong face. Her mother's voice seemed faraway.

"He can't do anything to you. He can't force you to marry him."

"Marry him?"

Jake knelt before her.

"I want to. Will you marry me, Emma?"

Her mother tugged at her sleeve. "Emma, be careful. Marriage can be a terrible trap."

A trap. Yes, that was what Jake thought. So why did he kneel before her like every suitor she had ever imagined?

She pulled her hand away. "You don't want to marry me. You told me so."

"I was wrong. I love you. I've been miserable without you."

Miserable, yes, she understood that, but not the rest.

"Wrong?"

"I can't live without you. I tried to get to you at the fort. Your father wouldn't let me see you."

She blinked. His words confirmed her suspicion.

She leaned forward. "You tried?"

"Yes, and then you were gone. I searched the Green and Bighorn. I talked to every trapper and Indian west of Fort Lancing. I never thought you'd go east."

She smiled. "You followed me?"

"I hoped your mother might have some word. I thought you dead."

The pain in his features as he revealed his fears, touched her. He suffered, too. All the while she thought her sorrow to be singular, and instead, Jake grieved believing her dead but still he had searched. In the deepest, safest places of her heart she had never stopped hoping he'd come.

Her mother's voice held urgency and she glanced her way.

"Emma, he's an army officer. Even if you do love him, you'll spend your life trapped in some barbaric little fort. I've only just found you. I won't have you return to that wilderness."

Jake faced her. "I'll resign my commission and take her to Jessup's Cut. I can clerk for my father. He's a judge now."

Her mother smiled at this. Emma felt the trap snap on both of them.

"No." She stood to face Jake. "You are not clerking for your father. I won't have it."

Jake's smile broadened. "What *do* you want Emma?"

"I—I want to love you without trapping you. I want a lifetime of waking in your arms. I want to see the Rockies again and our valley."

He nodded. "I can arrange that."

"You can't drag my granddaughter into that wilderness."

Emma watched the smile drop from Jake's lips. He looked uncertain now. The confidence faltered as he remembered their daughter.

Emma faced her mother, understanding the fear in her eyes.

"You are the one who told me to live my life, not just for my daughter, but for myself."

Her mother could not deny it, so she remained silent, speaking only with her eyes. Emma turned away.

"I will not be the wife of a clerk, nor an army bride."

"What then?" he asked.

"My husband is a cartographer and I am his partner."

Hope replaced uncertainty, but some shadow of doubt still shone in his eyes.

"What about our child?"

"I'll carry her on my back until she is old enough to ride."

His smile lit the room. She opened her arms and he enfolded her in his embrace. His voice whispered over her.

"Are you sure?"

She murmured, "I can't breathe in this city. I can't even see the sky."

He swept her off her feet, carrying her in slow, dizzying circles. "I'll show you the Yellowstone. There's no place on earth like it."

At last he set her on the ground.

"Do you think the U.S. will take California?" she asked.

"Just a matter of time."

"Then you could put in for a land grant."

"I'm sure."

"For our valley."

He smiled and she knew he remembered the waterfalls cascading to the ground, the wide meadows and granite escarpments.

"Good hunting that," he said.

She smiled at the understatement.

He lifted his eyebrows as if something troubled him. She hesitated, holding her breath.

"We can ask Jackson when we see him."

She gaped. "What are you talking about?"

He gripped her hand and squeezed. "I have maps to deliver and I can't go see the president without my partner, can I?"

"My daughter will see the president?"

Emma realized Jake had inadvertently gained her mother's support.

Lucille beamed, clasping her hands before her. "You could mention the objectives of the Moral Reform Society."

Emma laughed. "I'd be happy to."

"Does that mean you'll have me?" asked Jake.

"Yes, Jake. I'll have you."

He kissed her then and she relished the demanding pressure of his mouth. When he drew back, Emma was surprised to find herself still standing in the parlor.

Her mother's eyes looked misty. "I suppose I'll have to give you my blessing."

Jake stepped forward to receive her kiss. When he straightened, he stared at her quizzically.

"You said there were two reasons you didn't throw me out, Mrs. Lancing. I'd like to know what they are."

She smiled. "Emma still loves you."

A grin quirked the corner of his mouth. "And the second?"

"You came after her."

Jake wrapped an arm around Emma, his gaze locking to hers. She warmed in the glow of his smile. The peace she felt, standing at his side came with a certainty of the rightness of this match. They were not her parents, nor his. They would blaze their own trail.

"Would you like to see our daughter?" she asked.

Jake's eyes moistened and he swallowed hard. He pressed a hand over his mouth for a moment then nodded. When he spoke his voice cracked with emotion. "Lead the way."

She took his hand and guided him up the stairs to the nursery where Francisca Lancing Turner waited to meet her father.

* * * * *

Harlequin Historicals®
Historical Romantic Adventure!

FROM KNIGHTS IN SHINING ARMOR TO DRAWING-ROOM DRAMA HARLEQUIN HISTORICALS OFFERS THE BEST IN HISTORICAL ROMANCE

ON SALE MARCH 2005

FALCON'S HONOR
by Denise Lynn

Desperate to restore his lost honor, Sir Gareth accepts a mission from the king to escort an heiress to her betrothed. Never did he figure on the lady being so beautiful—and so eager to escape her nuptials! Can the fiery Lady Rhian of Gervaise entrance an honor-bound knight to her cause—and her heart?

THE UNRULY CHAPERON
by Elizabeth Rolls

Wealthy widow Lady Tilda Winter accompanies her cousin to a house party as chaperon and finds herself face-to-face with old love Crispin, the Duke of St. Ormond. Meant to court her young cousin, how can St. Ormond forget the grand passion he once felt for Lady Tilda? Will the chaperon soon need a chaperon of her own?

If you enjoyed what you just read,
then we've got an offer you can't resist!

Take 2 bestselling love stories FREE!
Plus get a FREE surprise gift!

Harlequin Historicals®
Historical Romantic Adventure!

CRAVING STORIES OF LOVE AND ADVENTURE SET IN THE WILD WEST? CHECK OUT THESE THRILLING TALES FROM HARLEQUIN HISTORICALS!

ON SALE APRIL 2005

THE RANGER'S WOMAN
by Carol Finch

On the run from an unwanted wedding, Piper Sullivan runs smack into the arms of Texas Ranger Quinn Callahan. On a mission to track outlaws who killed his best friend, Quinn hasn't got time to spare with the feisty lady. But he can't help but be charmed by Piper's adventurous spirit and uncommon beauty....

ABBIE'S OUTLAW
by Victoria Bylin

All hell is about to break loose when former gunslinger turned preacher John Leaf finds himself face-to-face with old love Abbie Moore. Years ago, John took her innocence and left her pregnant and alone. Now Abbie's back and needs his help. Will a marriage of convenience redeem John's tainted soul and bring love into their lives once more?

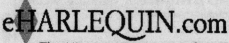

Harlequin Historicals®
Historical Romantic Adventure!

ESCAPE TO A LAND LONG AGO AND FAR AWAY IN THE PAGES OF HARLEQUIN HISTORICALS

ON SALE APRIL 2005

THE VISCOUNT
by Lyn Stone

Lily Bradshaw finds herself in a dire situation after her husband's death and seeks out the only person she knows in London: Viscount Duquesne. Guy agrees to marry Lily to protect her and her young son from harm's way. Will their marriage of convenience turn to one of true happiness and love?

THE BETROTHAL
by Terri Brisbin, Joanne Rock and Miranda Jarrett

Love is in the air this spring, when Harlequin Historicals brings you three tales of romance in the British Isles. *The Claiming of Lady Joanna* features a beautiful runaway bride and the man who is determined to claim her for his wife. In *Highland Handfast*, a Scottish lord agrees to a temporary marriage with an old childhood love, but plans on convincing her to make it permanent! And in *A Marriage in Three Acts*, a noble lord finds himself enchanted by a beautiful actress when her troupe of traveling players arrive at the lord's estate.

HHMED42